iMMersed

Book 2 of the Configured Trilogy

JENETTA PENNER

IMMERSED

Book 2 of the Configured Trilogy

By Jenetta Penner

IMMERSED

ISBN 10 : 1548585300

ISBN 13 : 978-1548585303

Printed in the U.S.A.First printing 2017

1043913

To my readers.

CHAPTER ONE

My twin brother lives. My mother is dead. Gone.

Not Bess, my birth mother; she's still alive. *Missing*, but alive.

Darline, the mother who raised me, the one who—at least at the very end—told me this existence held value, is not coming back.

I breathe in the antiseptic of my room, the acrid scent burns slightly at the back of my throat. Sitting on my bed, I fiddle with the gold heart encircling my neck, dragging the charm from side to side over the chain. Ben gave me the necklace when we were almost four, before he died.

But that's the point—he *didn't* die. He's been alive, here, in New Philadelphia, all this time. I found out as I was escaping from Elore, and I haven't seen him since. Or anyone else, for that matter, in the last three days since we arrived. Only the medic, who comes into my room every two to three hours, pats me on the hand, and says, "You're doing great, sweetie." Then she pokes and prods, scans my body, and adds a "Not long now" when she leaves. What's a "sweetie", anyhow? I don't want to be a sweetie, I want answers. Where's Meyer? Where's my father? Where's Ben?

I flip through a book the medic dropped off yesterday. The raised print on the cover reads *To Kill a Mockingbird*. Tangy mustiness from the yellowed pages wafts to my nose. The topic's something concerning a girl named Scout Finch. That part caught my eye because her last name is a bird, too. Lark ... Finch ... birds. I've never seen a book with paper pages before, and the chance to read one should excite me, but I haven't been able to focus on reading more than the first couple pages, so I toss it to the end of my bed, mostly unread.

I peer down at the unfamiliar clothes I'm wearing. Gone is my dull suit, replaced by a pair of stretchy pants and a teal top, loosely hanging on me kind of like pajamas would. My restless feet beg for a run after being cooped up. I hop up and pace the sterile room, back and forth, around the stark bed and plain metal chair, but it's not the same.

Click, click.

The door whooshes open and I flinch. Maybe this will be the day they let me out. I turn toward the sound, expecting the medic. Instead, a boy—nearly a man—stands in the doorway, holding a tray of food. His uniform bears three red stripes on the sleeve, and he's got a jacket slung over one arm. My eyes snap to the writing printed over the pocket of his uniform.

Porter.

It's not his last name. But it's Ben. It has to be.

The door slides shut behind him. Not knowing what to say, I stare at the familiar spray of freckles daubing his nose. He has the same hazel eyes and the same chocolate-colored hair as me.

"If you read the sequel, be warned. It's not what you'd expect," he says.

"What?"

"The book." He points to it with his free hand. "*To Kill a Mockingbird.* It's a good story. I'm the guard assigned to you. Brought you lunch." He says it almost too casually and slides the tray of covered food onto my bed, placing the jacket next to it.

"What's a 'story'?" I ask.

He tips his head and doesn't reply, but the question's not important.

"Who are you?" I whisper, knowing the answer. My stomach knots after voicing the question.

He clenches his jaw, changing his attention to the charm I still hold between my fingers.

"Officer Ben Porter," he finally answers.

Even though I already knew the answer, my mind dances with new activity.

Where have you been? I thought you died. They told me you died.

But before any of these words can coalesce and spill from my mouth, Ben's arms wrap my shoulders, squeezing me as if he wants to hold on forever. I clasp him back and an electric jolt instantly consumes me, making the space around us go sparkling white. Not the white of my holding room, but of nothing. The color dissolves and memories roll through my consciousness.

Ben snaps back, eyes wide, but doesn't release me completely. He felt it too.

Short, shallow breaths escape my lungs. "What was—?"

"Shh." Ben presses his hand to my mouth. "I've received permission to take you on a limited tour outside the facilities." He looks up to the corner of the room where an audio surveillance device rests. "Told them it would do you good." He raises his voice, apparently to make sure 'they' hear. "What do you think?"

Ben extends his hand and I take it. Still confused, I manage to mumble, "Uh, yeah. I'd love to."

"You must remain under my supervision around the clock. Do you understand?"

I nod, and he glances again at the audio device.

"Oh ... yes, I'm clear." A million questions bubble to the surface, but I have no idea where to start. Continuing to grip my hand, he grabs the jacket, guides me to the exit, and activates the door. It slides back, and he pilots me into the hallway.

A weight lifts from my shoulders as I pass through the doorway. Ben leads me through a facility bustling with medics working together, not speaking in hushed tones, but in real conversations, a smile tossed in here and there. As we pass a room with more medics eating, I hear a laugh.

People happy *on the job?* What a concept. No one I knew in Elore ever laughed like that. Citizens are so focused on duty there; no one laughs at much of anything.

Ben hands me the jacket and I put it on. We push through a door to the outside, my eyes stinging in the bright sun. I throw my hand up to cover them, squinting at my surroundings.

"You still have it," Ben says, leaning closer and glancing at my neck.

I bring my fingers to the charm. "Of course I do. I hid it for years."

"I was so afraid you'd forgotten me."

I stop and clutch his arm. "There wasn't a day I forgot you. You've always been there." So much of me can hardly believe Ben and I are here together. It seems like a dream.

A look of relief washes over Ben's face, and he gestures for us to continue. I release him and we step off the sidewalk onto the green yard, which stretches away from the facility toward a tall perimeter fence. The soft grass yields like carpet beneath my shoes, and I fight the urge to kneel and run my fingers over the dewy blades. The single place in Elore that has grass is the park. I inhale the earthy aromas of the dirt and grass; even in Elore I associated them with the smell of freedom. I'm not sure if Ben is leading or following, but we wind up on a stone bench after about a five-minute walk.

"What happened back there?" I whisper, sitting next to Ben.

He takes in a deep breath. "You felt it in Elore, too? When you grazed my arm in the bunker?"

I nod.

"When I saw you, I knew who you were," he says. "But there was nothing I could do. Then when you passed and we touched ..." He pauses and shakes his head. "The flood of memories ... I still couldn't let on."

"Why?"

"Well, a family reunion wasn't exactly in order." He chuckles. "But, also, Affinity and Philly are not aware of my abilities. To their knowledge, there's no other connection between us."

"Then how are you assigned to be my guard? That would be way too big of a coincidence."

Ben smirks. "And you'd be right about that. I hacked into the system and had myself assigned."

"Regular hacking, right?"

Ben raises his eyebrows. "No, Avlyn."

I pull back from him, frowning. "You can immerse?"

"Is that what you call it? I don't remember, of course, but Dad said one day I was completing pre-primer school exercises and manipulated the program in ways that seemed impossible. He removed me from the system and ran additional tests in secret."

"When was this?"

"A few months before our fourth birthday," he says, sadness in his eyes.

Memories of the experiments performed on us, especially those on him, reverberate through my mind. Everything in me craves to hug him, to make up for the lost years, but this is not the time, not private enough. Instead, the question that's been reeling in my head for days finally bursts out. "How are you alive?"

Ben looks to the grass below, clasping his hands together on his knees. "When Virus 3005B spread through Elore, Dad took it as an opportunity to contact Affinity. They altered the records to say I'd died, and that my body had been immediately cremated to avoid the spread of the disease. The whole thing was perfectly logical. Affinity smuggled me out and Father followed soon after."

It makes sense. No one cares about the dead in Elore, and it would be unlikely that Ben would be missed. And as for Devan's disappearance, in Direction's eyes it was good riddance. The more Level Ones who lost themselves in the Outerbounds, the better.

"Dad always feared someone would search after us. Find me. But they didn't. He even gave me MedTech that slightly altered my DNA, even changed our last name from Winterly to Porter. So, if I was found, there'd be no connection between you and me. I was not to mention you in public. Bess didn't even know. My dad kept it hidden from her to protect me."

"What do you mean?"

"You know, in case she was questioned. He never said it but I think he believed I might try to contact her somehow when I was younger. Bess not being in on it made that more difficult."

"And would you have?"

Ben leans back on his hands. "At this point, I don't know, but ... maybe. I've worked so hard all these years to hide what I can do. The only risk I've taken was contacting you over the last month."

Of course. It all makes sense now.

"*You* caused my visions?"

His eyes illuminate. "Yeah, that was me. The day it started, I woke up from a dream of you and me running through the grass when we were little. I tried to reach out for you, but you vanished. Nothing like that had ever happened to me before. It felt so real."

Excitement wells in my chest as I sort the recent events. "That must have been the day I received the VacTech update a month ago in Elore. Afterward, I swear you were racing toward me in the stairwell of the university. I thought I was going crazy."

Ben's breathing speeds up. "Me too. At first, I thought it couldn't be real either, but I focused and I connected to you with my mind again, and it was successful. This time you were sitting in a chair by your parents. I couldn't understand what was happening, but I knew you were upset. I wanted to help so badly. The vision couldn't have lasted longer than a few seconds, but I knew it was real. But, as the weeks went by, the ability modified. I couldn't see you anymore, but I could sense what you were doing. Your emotions."

"Do you think that connection caused my ability to develop further? It all started at the same time."

"That could be."

I'm unsure what to ask next, and not for a lack of questions. "Did you tell Devan? Maybe you can take me to visit him."

The color drains from Ben's face. "Um, no. Not now. Dad doesn't live near New Philadelphia."

Disappointment washes over me. "Another time, then. But I should see him."

"Okay," he says, fidgeting his hand on his knee. "What about Bess? What *is* she like?"

Bess? Possibly delusional? And convinced the identity of her own birth family somehow puts us at risk and decided to disappear. Seems farfetched, but whatever. I had a letter she hid for me in her ransacked apartment, but I lost it somewhere between running for my life from Direction and arriving here. Bess never was a strong person, so it's likely for the best she left with the upheaval in Elore. Probably another reason Devan didn't inform her he was moving Ben into the Outerbounds.

No, I can't let him know that. Not yet. But the woman always made me feel uncomfortable.

"I don't know," I sigh. "I only visited her annually and it was awkward to say the least." Memories of her trying to hug me come to the forefront of my brain, confining me once again.

"What does she look like?"

"She looks ... like us, brown hair, freckles." I avoid telling him about the letter; he'd probably be disappointed I lost it.

Bess is everything I fought, overly emotional and trying so hard to connect with me during the few times we met with each other. Even giving me the name Joy when I was born. Imagine that in a place that values duty. It was against everything Direction stood for. With all I've gone through and want now, I should feel a bond with her, but I don't.

Without thinking, I touch my hand to Ben's shoulder and a jolt of energy consumes me. Scenes blaze through my mind. Infant Ben screams as a series of horrific experiments are performed to increase our Intelligence Potential. The scene shifts and the two of us play during one of our yearly meetings.

Then, the visions slow and something strange emerges. It's not a memory ... at least not one of mine. A young boy weeps in front of a slumped man with dark brown hair. A wave of sorrow consumes my being, and I squint to see who it is, but part of me already knows.

Devan, our biological father, is dead.

CHAPTER TWO

I rip my hand from Ben's shoulder and the vision degenerates. "Devan's *dead*? Why didn't you tell me?"

Ben rises from the bench and angles his back to me. I stand and move in front of him.

"*Tell* me," I insist. "I deserve to know."

Ben straightens his back, but continues to avoid my eyes. "I figured you had enough to deal with. And it's not as if you knew our dad much," he says in a hushed tone.

Ben's right. I *didn't* know him. To be honest, I'm not even sure I have strong feelings for him. But I can't get the vision of seeing Devan slumped over, dead, out of my head. This is a man, who for most of my life, I believed to be selfish and weak. One who left Bess because he couldn't handle living. In reality, this was a father who fought for his son. Protected him. Maybe *died* for him. I'm beginning to see Devan was a totally different person than I thought him to be.

"Look at me," I say.

Ben breathes out deeply and directs his attention my way,

conflict in his hazel irises. "My dad ... your dad ... Devan became sick and died. End of story."

No, it's not the end of the story. "I don't understand, Ben."

"Listen, Avlyn. It's that simple. For a long time, Dad and I lived in the Outerbounds. Like ... the *real* Outerbounds. It was low tech, and his nanos from Elore malfunctioned. No one was there to fix them."

"You were scared."

"Of course I was scared. I was a little kid living out in the middle of nowhere. But I made it. I'm here, right?" Ben crosses his arms over his torso, separating himself from me. "Just like Dad told me, I hid my ability and I survived. I didn't want to bring this up now, but you know as well as I do that what we can do will be exploited."

"No one is trying to exploit me. Not anymore. Ruiz got us out of Elore to protect us. Now, Manning, yes, but not Ruiz."

"I've seen your file, Avlyn. I went in and retrieved it so I understood what's going on. Think about it. No matter if it was for a good cause or not, she had you go into GenTech to destroy information. You were unprepared, and she put you in a dangerous position to get an outcome she wanted. Manning could have killed you, or even worse. The single reason you're even here is Manning didn't comprehend your ability and thought locating Affinity was a bigger priority. If he would have, he'd have never let you slip through his fingers. Waters and Ruiz *do* know what they have."

"Who's Waters?"

"President Eric Waters," Ben says. "He's the leader of New Philadelphia."

This whole time I hadn't even considered any leaders but

Ruiz. But if she brought me here, she must trust him.

"But if they were looking to use me, why would they even let me out of my room to wander the grounds? Yeah, I'm with you, but you're only one guard."

Ben shakes his head. "I don't know, but I pay attention to the way the world works. I've had to. I make certain to play it safe. The entire reason I'm taking this risk now is for you. There's no way I'd take it otherwise. You know what Direction did to us. It was a side effect, but they made this happen. And if it gets out that the experimentation had anything to do with causing our abilities, they can create a cyber warfare weapon like no one has ever seen, and we won't be able to stop it."

The experiments.

"Do you know exactly *what* they did to us?"

"No clue. It's not exactly as if I could ask anyone. But before Dad died he told me Direction shut them down after it looked like I died from the virus. But none of that matters. I want you to listen to me." Ben's voice grows serious. "Downplay your ability."

"What?"

Ben leans in closer to me. "You heard me. If your ability grows, you have no idea what it might be used for. There will be no way to control it."

"Ben, you're overreacting. Ruiz is an honest person."

"She might be, but you're not just dealing with Ruiz anymore. The more your secret gets out, the greater the danger. It's why I have a plan."

I narrow my brow. "A plan? What are you talking about?"

"You convince them the ability is fading. Since this is all new, they have no concept what they're searching for yet. Over a couple weeks, Waters will start to lose interest and move on. They might even relocate you off-grounds into the city. When they do, we have to leave."

"Leave? I don't want to leave." My father is here, and he's going to require someone to help him adjust. Who knows where Aron is and what he might need. And Meyer ... I can't abandon him. "Where would we go, anyway?"

A huge flock of pale birds soar overhead in a V formation, breaking my attention from Ben.

He clutches my arm. "There are plenty of places to disappear; towns all over the continent with people who don't want to be found. Being in Elore, or New Philadelphia, for that matter, we will never be free. It will always be about controlling our ability."

"I ... I don't know Ben. This is a lot for me to absorb. My ability has given me a *purpose*. It's a way to help people. If I didn't have it, Manning might have released a new virus in the Outerbounds, including New Philadelphia. It could have had the potential to set the world back like Aves did. I get that it can be used for bad, but think of all the benefit it can make," I plead. "I want to do good things like Ruiz is doing. When she was forced out of Direction, she didn't run like Cynthia Fisher did. Ruiz stood up and formed Affinity. Fisher fell off the map and probably died."

Ben's eyes soften. "I'm sorry. I'm being insensitive and don't want to argue with you, but you should be careful. The reason I made it this far is because I stopped trusting anyone."

With his words, my heart sinks into my middle.

"It's time you get back." Ben checks the Flexx-type device on his wrist. "I have some positive news for you."

My ears perk up and the weight in my stomach lifts. "What?"

"I'm supposed to escort you to see Michael ... your father.

Ruiz made arrangements for him and Waters agreed to it as long as he stays under watch."

Michael. I have no idea what he's been going through over the last few days. He's lost everything. His job, existence ... his spouse. The thought smarts. Since Mother's death in the tunnel, I've pushed most thoughts of her away each time they pop up.

"Do you know if they got my mother's body out?"

The words stumble out unbidden. Ben averts his eyes from mine. "No, but there's a memorial service scheduled for Friday."

His statement punches me in the gut. Well, at least I'm allowed that. Mother and I never experienced the relationship I longed for, but I know now that she did love me, enough to give her life for me. The fact she had to be crushed and dying before she felt free to say it. ...

I had no choice but to leave her in that tunnel, beneath the rubble, all alone...

I suck in air.

Get out of my head.

All the tension on Ben's face from earlier disappears, replaced with compassion. He lightly pats me on the back. A wave of comfort fills me.

"I'm sorry for trying to pressure you. I've been thinking about this for a month. All I ask is that you consider what I've said."

"I will."

"Let me take you to your father," Ben says.

Ben acknowledges the guard standing outside the gray door and activates the guest chime. From inside, I can hear footsteps shuffle toward the door. It slides back, revealing Father, his appearance nearly as bad as when I'd "rescued" him from the Representatives building. His green shirt hangs half-untucked and rumpled. The sight of his sunken eyes drops a brick into my stomach.

"Father! Are you ill?"

Without a thought, I approach him for at least some sort of connection—a hug, a pat on the shoulder, any human contact—but instead, the space between us feels awkward. Viscous. Not surprisingly, he makes no advance for me. Embarrassment rushes over my face. Father doesn't understand the value of emotions yet, and no doubt he blames me for Mother's death.

"Avlyn," he mumbles, looking from me. "I wasn't sure you'd come."

Father gestures into the tiny, sparse apartment, not unlike those in Elore. For a beat, I don't move, but eventually push myself to step in past Father. I twist to Ben, expecting him to come, but he doesn't follow.

"I'm assigned to stay on guard, so I'll leave you two alone," he says.

I lock onto his hazel eyes. It's as if I'm staring at myself. "Thanks."

With that, he nods and turns, assuming a guard's position on the opposite side of the officer stationed at Father's door. The door slides shut, leaving Father and I to ourselves in his chilly unit. I rub my hands over my arms and decide to keep my jacket on. Father drags himself to a tan sofa and plops onto the left side. On the side table sits a tray of dried chicken and rice and two glasses of half-drunk liquid.

"How are you doing?" I ask, lightly sitting not far from him. It's a stupid question, but nothing better comes.

Instead of answering, Father unexpectedly leans forward on his knees and lets out a sob.

My back stiffens, and I stifle the urge to bolt. This is all wrong. I'm in an upside-down world. If there'd been a prize for cool detachment back in Elore, my father would have had no competition. This man taught me breathing exercises to get through even a tinge of an unpleasant feeling. He can't be crying, much less heaving and sobbing like a Level One child.

Risking rejection—or seeking it to put the world right again?—I scoot closer, draping my arm over his shuddering shoulders. When he leans in instead of away, it requires all my strength to keep put. It's what I've always desired, but not like this. Mother's face materializes in my mind, bruised and bloody, and her final words remind me there is beauty left in the world and I should share it with others.

So, I breathe, just like he taught me, until, finally, he breathes too.

"They keep trying to administer calming MedTech, but I won't take it," he mumbles.

I move in to look him in the eyes. Father always avoided MedTech, even in Elore. He intended to prove he could handle the stresses of Elore on his own. That he was strong.

"Maybe you need it."

He grips the device tighter in his right hand. "I don't want her memory marred in any way ... even the end." With the statement, he throws his head into his left hand again. "Everything is so confusing."

"Father, I've been confused for years."

He glances up at me and sighs. "I know. I apologize for the role I played."

I study his brown face. This is not a person I know.

"Father, what happened when Direction arrested you and Mother?"

He shakes his head. "It's not information you require. I will say it's when I started to figure out your importance. Your mother knew first, even weeks before. She noticed something different in you, but I didn't want to hear it. Yet, you came for us in the Representative's building, even though you didn't have to, and you healed Mother after she was shot. Somehow you reactivated her nanobots, but Manning had disabled it during our ... interrogation."

"You saw that?"

"I saw her wound, and without her nanos, she lost too much blood. She was not going to make it. But, when you touched her, it healed. At the time, I dismissed it as me being delirious, but that was incorrect."

"Yes," I say. "It was."

And I have a brother who has the same ability, but Father doesn't need to know that. Not now.

"I still don't understand it," I say.

"Well, from the little you've shown me ... it's amazing. And very dangerous. If the wrong people know about it—"

I whip toward him. "Why does everyone keep saying that? My ability was dangerous in Elore, but we're out of there now. They strive for different things here in New Philadelphia. I can use my ability for good. You can have a new life. A *free* life."

Father furrows his brow and gives me a confused expression. "Yes, I suppose you're right." He pulls a Flexx from Elore from his wrist and unfolds it into a thin tablet. Mother's ID image appears on the screen. Father props the device on the side table and gazes at it. As his fingers trail away, they graze Mother's cheek, lingering on her lips.

In his own way, he loved her.

"What will you do?" From the looks of him, I'm afraid he'll banish himself in this unit with Mother's photo and never come out.

"I can't do anything. I haven't seen outside this unit since we arrived. They've kept me locked in here."

"What—?"

The door chime sounds.

"Can you get that?" he asks.

I stand and look at the monitor to check who's there. Meyer. His handsome, angular face is angled to the ground, and he's wearing a navy-blue striped shirt and charcoal-gray pants, hands shoved in their pockets. He shifts his weight nervously from one foot to the other, and his muscular chest rises and falls as if letting out a lengthy, slow breath.

As fast as I can, I activate the door. My instinct is to hug Meyer, but it feels somehow unacceptable in front of Father, so I resist.

"Hi." Nervousness wells in my belly and suddenly I have no place to put my hands since there are no pockets in my loose pants.

"Hello," he replies, locking onto me with his dark eyes.

I break the stare and peek into the hall. Ben's disappeared, but the other guardian for Father remains standing to the side. Panic settles in my stomach.

"Where'd my guard go?"

Meyer gives me an inquisitive expression. "I told him I'd handle it from here. For some reason, he didn't want to leave."

I glance once more toward the exit, but Ben's nowhere to be found.

"I relieved him. I have seniority," Meyer explains.

I relax. It will be fine. Ben and I will see each other again. "Are you here for me or Father?" I ask.

"For you, but Ruiz ordered me to accompany you back here later instead of to the testing facility. If you want to, that is."

I turn to Father, slumped on the couch, gazing at Mother's sterile, unsmiling Direction ID, the one picture he has. Everything else in his world is gone but me.

"Yeah, that would be best." For the first time in my life, Father might actually *need* me. I bring my attention back to Meyer. "What are we doing now?"

"Ruiz has called a meeting. Phase one of the testing is complete, and she's ready for phase two."

My eyebrows lift. "Phase two? When was phase one?"

Meyer shrugs. "That's something you'll have to speak with Ruiz about."

Disappointed he won't say more, I nod and turn to Father. "Um … I have an appointment. But Meyer says I'm allowed to return when I'm done."

Father looks up from staring at the handheld, his eyes flat. "Yes. I've nowhere to go."

Grief grabs and rattles me. This was a man who always seemed so strong. I know he's in shock now, but maybe his strength was a facade his entire life?

I twist toward Meyer and motion for us to go. Meeting with Ruiz will be a perfect chance for me to ask some questions and find out Aron's location.

CHAPTER THREE

Outside, we amble through a courtyard garden, passing a woman eating a green apple on a wooden bench. Instead of a handheld, she grasps one of those books, like the one in my holding room. I squint to read the title, but she has it angled and I can't make it out. Back in Elore, everyone always had someplace to be and, if you didn't, it was best to stay inside your unit, out of sight from prying eyes. They were definitely not out reading books on benches. Here, people make a habit of milling. Above, a tiny brown bird swoops across the clear sky and dives from sight.

"Why are there more birds here?" I ask as I pause to examine a large red flower on a bush.

"They're near Elore, too, but Direction keeps most of them out of the city," Meyer says.

My nose wrinkles as I frown. "Why?"

"To reinforce the belief of sickness in the Outerbounds. Direction has made such a big deal of the Aves virus for so long that if everyone knew the bird population recovered years ago, they might put it together that outside Elore isn't so bad after all. The electro perimeter sends a deterrent into the sky. So no one knows they're there."

I shake my head. I knew they were liars, but if Direction refuses to tell the truth about a topic as small as birds...

Is everything in Elore a lie?

Feeling lost, I encircle Meyer with my arms as if we'd done it a thousand times before, even though we haven't. Without hesitation, his hands flow over my shoulder blades, sending a melting warmth throughout my body. Ben's idea of running away is bad. I don't want to be anywhere but here.

Meyer's fingers gently rake through my hair, and I pull back, gazing at his face. His eyes are tender, and he uses his thumb to dry a stray tear I didn't even know had trickled down my cheek. He leans into the same spot and kisses it. My body tenses, then relaxes at the warm sensation of his lips.

"I'm so sorry about everything," he whispers as he tugs me close to his chest again. "I know this must be difficult for you."

"Thank you." I drag my hands over the thick, dark hair at the nape of his neck. My heart pounds in time with his. Not quite knowing what I'm doing, I rise up on my toes and guide his face toward mine. Not missing a beat, he grasps me tightly around my lower back. My lips brush his and electricity shoots through my middle. His warm, soft lips press into mine. Meyer inches in closer, snaking his hands into my hair until the vibration of his Flexx throws us into reality.

He steps back and rubs at the flush climbing his neck. "Well ... that was unexpected."

I suck in a breath. My entire self shudders, despite the lingering heat running through it. "Yeah. You should check your message."

Meyer retrieves the buzzing handheld from his pocket and swipes the screen. "It's Ruiz. A reminder of your appointment in thirty minutes." He casts his eyes from the Flexx to me and the corners of his tempting mouth quirk into a shy smile.

I raise my eyebrows and reach for his elbow. "So, we have thirty minutes?"

Meyer breaks into a hard laugh, pocketing his handheld, and I move back, a hot sting zipping in my chest.

He glances down at me and lightly catches my arm. "Oh ... no. That kiss was amazing. I simply didn't expect it. Not here, in the open. You've spent your whole existence concealing your emotions ... I didn't think you'd adjust to that part so quickly, and I never *expected* anything."

The last three days roll through my mind: Mother's death, Kyra's betrayal, learning Ben's alive, leaving my life behind ... Meyer's been one of the few constants throughout the experience.

"I don't have the option of resisting change these days. I might as well learn to be in charge of my feelings."

His lips form into a wide smile, sending sparks up my back. "I won't argue. That said ..." He leans in and plants a soft, chaste kiss on my lips. "So much of me wants to say yes, but the rest knows you're adjusting and might not have a clear head. I'm also not sure Ruiz wants us getting involved. In fact, I know she doesn't. As your handler, it's strictly forbidden."

"Are you still my handler?"

Meyer tips his head as if to ask me to be quiet.

The sensation of the kiss lingers, but he's right. The tingling stops and the task at hand commandeers my attention. I cross my arms over my chest and nod toward the path we walked before we paused. Meyer pushes back the cuff of his jacket, revealing his antique watch and confirms the time.

"So, your guard? He's the same one you talked to on our way from Elore."

My stomach flips with the idea of telling Meyer who Ben is to me, but I can't without talking to Ben.

"Yeah, funny how that happened, right? Back in Elore, I thought I knew him."

"But you didn't?"

"Of course not. How could I? Must have been my mind playing a trick on me from the stress."

The crisp wind whips up. Goose bumps form on my arms either from the cold or the lie. Probably both.

Inside the sparse conference room, a bay of windows overlooks the courtyard Meyer brought me across. Seeing the spot in the garden where I kissed him awakens two sets of butterflies in my belly. The first because I kissed him, the second because anyone standing in this room—maybe even Ruiz herself—would have seen the whole event.

"Well, there you are."

The familiar voice from behind makes me jump. I turn from the window and find Adriana Ruiz standing in the open doorway. The woman is in her mid-sixties, but still lean and muscular. Her tight gray curls hug her scalp. The purple bags under her eyes coupled with a pinched mouth reveals the stressful state she must be in, despite her cheerful words.

"Here I am." I shrug and search for an interesting spot on the floor to stare at in an attempt to hide the flush creeping up my cheeks.

She walks to me, hand extended. When I take it and look at her, she grips it hard and brings her second hand up to my arm, giving my hand a vigorous shake.

"I apologize for being unable to visit after we landed." She frees my hand. "I had strict orders. Until you had clearance, no one could see you. Not even me."

"Don't you give the orders?"

Ruiz sighs and tenses. "Not here, Avlyn. I have a decent amount of authority, but New Philadelphia is not my territory."

I stand there, not knowing what to say, as Ben's warning returns. I have to trust Ruiz with my secrets. What choice do I have?

President Waters, however, is a complete unknown.

Ruiz's shoulders relax. "Before you even ask, please know we didn't keep you quarantined out of something malicious," she says, as if she read my thoughts. "Tests needed to be performed right away to, first of all, ensure Manning hadn't tagged or done anything else to track you in any way other than the Flexx you got rid of. Preliminary tests were then administered to supplement what we already know about your ability to immerse. Waters believes you will be invaluable to New Philadelphia."

I reel with questions. "So, am I still a member of Affinity?"

Concern flashes across Ruiz's face and she crosses her arms over her chest. "It's complicated, Avlyn. When Manning attacked the bunker, our choices were limited." She pauses, as if to carefully choose her next words. "To get Philly to come in after us, I had to not only tell them about Manning's intention to release the virus on the Outerbounds, but also about your ability and how it might be useful to him. If I didn't, we'd all be dead.

Including you."

"You mean I don't have any choice? Do I belong to New Philadelphia now?" Fear ripples through me at the thought, weakening my legs. Ruiz throws out a hand and catches me.

"Let's have a seat." She gestures toward the chairs surrounding the conference table in back of us. "There's no need to be afraid. You belong to no one. President Waters will be joining us soon to explain everything."

"The president's coming?" I yelp.

"Yes," says Ruiz. "The findings from round one of testing have been quite eye opening. He wanted to be here to speak with you, too."

Sudden panic burns in my belly and old habits return. My primary goal in life was always to remain invisible, and these days I'm failing miserably at meeting it. I swing my head around to the closed door. I wouldn't get far if I tried to leave.

"Please, sit down. The president said I could begin bringing you up to speed before he arrives."

Ruiz moves toward the table and drags out a chair, nodding for me to sit. I walk to the spot, gingerly sliding my body onto the cold metal. My thin pants do nothing to block the chill. Ruiz takes a place directly across the rectangular table, then produces and unfolds her handheld into a tablet, laying it in the middle of the table. As she does, a hologram of a brain flickers on and hovers over the face of the device.

"The initial tests we've performed indicate you have an extraordinary brain. Or, at least, it has become extraordinary with the aid of what we tracked back to the current VacTech roll out in Elore."

So I was right about everything starting on my Configuration

Day.

The glowing, holographic brain rotates slowly, highlighting an area on the top and moving its way into the center.

"Prior to the Collapse," Ruiz begins, "and the Aves virus nearly wiping humanity away, scientists worked on implanting humans with technology to stimulate new potential. Several of the studies involved implants adapting to neuron activity, and allowed a limited amount of communication when linked to a computer system."

The vision of Ben screaming as an infant whirls through my mind.

"Implanted? Was I implanted?"

Were we *implanted in the experiments?*

"No ... no, my dear," she says in a calm, flat tone. "There's no evidence you were specifically implanted. But, please, allow me to finish."

Questions bubble to the surface, but I hold my tongue, despite the burning desire to blurt them out.

"After Aves, the goals of Elore consisted of population survival and healing. The vast majority of brain tech projects worked on prior to the virus was tabled, filed for a later date. As Direction grew and concentrated on population growth as well as increasing natural Intelligence Potential, they concentrated tech on keeping citizens fixated on that goal. Integrating the average human into tech has too many liabilities—too much chance of distraction. New Philadelphia never had any interest in the technology. They felt it too invasive."

"So what happened to me?" I search her face for any indication of her awareness of the experimentation Ben and I were involved in, but she gives no clues, and I can't ask without exposing Ben.

"We believe it to be a side effect from the recent VacTech upgrade. Affinity was able to procure a sample, but have been unable to isolate the exact component that created the effect for you. The theory is it seems to have activated a gene which allowed your nanos to approximate what science crudely attempted over one hundred years ago."

I lean in. "*Crudely* attempted?"

"Yes. Compared to what you seem to be experiencing, science's previous pursuits at allowing humans to connect to machines at will were clumsy. Only the simplest tasks succeeded. In your case, as far as we can tell, once within a computer system, you have complete control to simply do whatever you want."

Nervousness stirs in my core. Doing whatever I want doesn't sound great from their perspective. "Am I dangerous?"

Ruiz looks from the hologram to me and tips her head. "No, dear, I don't believe you to be dangerous. But immersion could be, and that's what we're here to speak about today." Ruiz's expression shifts to serious. "Realistically, the ability has as much potential for benefit as harm. We must research it further and provide you with some sort of training, but it's all new so we will be learning together."

The door slides away again and in strolls a compact man, maybe fifty years old, with tan, leathery skin. President Waters, I presume.

"Ruiz. Lark." The president nods to us and walks straight to my side. The haughty energy radiating from him causes a shiver to run down my back, but I shake it off and swivel my chair toward him. He extends his hand, and without standing, I reach to grip it. Father always said a firm handshake conveys confidence. Might as well fake it.

"I'm President Waters." He grips my hand and locks onto my eyes. The shiver returns. Despite my ability, this guy's in charge and requires me to know it.

"Avlyn Lark." I hold his stare for as long as I can but eventually relent. "Ruiz said you were joining us."

Waters drops my hand not pausing for me speak. "Have you explained our findings to her yet?"

"Yes," Ruiz says.

"Well, then."

Waters rounds the table and sits alongside Ruiz, taps her handheld, and the image of the brain disappears. He folds his hands on the tabletop, leaning into me. A lump forms in my throat, and I wipe my now-sweaty palms on my pants, but in order to maintain some sense of confidence, I straighten and look him in the eye once more.

"Ms. Lark, have you been comfortable so far since you arrived in New Philadelphia?" Waters asks.

I clear my throat. "Um, I guess. But not being told anything or allowed to see anyone since I landed three days ago has been … disconcerting."

"I expected nothing less, but we needed to complete the diagnostics to ensure you were not infected with a tracking or data collection device from Direction. We felt it unlikely, but could not take chances. Immediately following this meeting, you'll go to the lab for phase two of testing your ability, as well as to be fitted with a permanent eyepiece."

Shock sweeps Ruiz's face. "Why wasn't I informed? The permanent EPs are new tech. Is it worth the risk?"

My eyes flit from Ruiz to President Waters. *Risk?*

"It is. My top science team has been working around the clock evaluating Lark's information since she arrived." Waters swings his attention back to me. "And I will be honest with you now because you will become aware of this as soon as the implant becomes operational. This EP has been specially designed for you and the ability. Not only will it track your connection to a computer system, the tech is also equipped with special firewall technology to keep your skills in check. This will allow you to have additional freedom within the compound and eventually outside of it. We desire for you to have that freedom. You are a new citizen of New Philadelphia, and you should enjoy it."

I inhale deeply, looking to Ruiz, whose face continues to bear an air of concern. "Will it track everything I do?"

"You will be able to disengage the visuals of the device at will, as you did the removable device," Waters explains. "But even disengaged, it will continue to relay your location and vitals for security. However, any time you have it on, it will record. After the implantation, you will be kept here until you've completed training."

I suck in a deep breath. Part of me wants to fight him on this, but the other knows if I don't, Father and Aron will have no one on their side. I must have leverage. "I don't have a say in this, do I?"

"Unfortunately, for your safety, you do not," Waters says.

Ruiz's demeanor relaxes slightly, but her face maintains a hint of concern. "I wish this were easier, but until we fully understand immersion and are convinced you can control it, you will need to be kept under close observation."

So much for freedom.

"Lark," says President Waters, "do you have any additional

questions about the procedure?"

My mind reels. If Waters hadn't blindsided me, I'd have questions prepared. "How do you intend to use my ability?" I somehow choke out, thinking of Ben and my conversation.

Waters pinches his lips together. "We are still trying to determine that."

Ruiz remains silent, eyes trained on the table.

"Will that be all?" Without waiting for my answer, Waters turns and makes for the door.

Ruiz stands, her chair legs screeching over the tile floor. "Outside you will find an escort. President Waters and I have a few additional matters we need to discuss."

Waters stops and shifts toward Ruiz, a crease forming in the middle of his thick eyebrows. Even in my dazed state, the tension between them is obvious.

If Waters won't answer my first question, at least I can get in another one.

"I do have one more question." I don't pause for him to protest. "During the attack in Elore, a boy named Aron tried to arrest us, but then your men took him into custody. What happened to him?"

Aron's a nice guy who asked me to secure a spouse contract, and in return, I threatened him with a gun. It's not as if I had another choice, but I don't want him to think I'm dangerous and would have killed him.

Waters taps his foot impatiently. "Ah, yes. Barton. He's safely in custody."

I wring my hands together. "Is there any way I can talk to him?"

President Waters scoffs. "No. Barton is a prisoner of war.

He's not exactly seeing visitors."

I take a breath and weigh the possible outcomes. If I keep Waters calm about my ability, he might do something else for me. "Listen, I'm doing everything you ask. I don't want to, but I am. I recognize your position. Now, Aron is a friend of mine—one who *risked his life* to come in after me during the attack on the bunker. He may have been on the other side, but his motives were sound."

Ruiz opens her mouth to speak.

"Please." I hold up my hand to stay her before she says anything. "There's no harm in me seeing him to make certain he's well taken care of."

"Mr. President, she's right," Ruiz says. "Avlyn has cooperated and proven herself to be on our side. Simply speaking with Barton—under security, of course—would not pose any risk."

Waters crosses his arms over his chest. "Fine. I will arrange it, but you have to keep it short."

"Yes, sir," I say. It's a meager victory on a day where so much suddenly seems to be spinning out of control, but I'll take it.

The president taps the screen on his handheld. "Send in Ms. Lark's escort." He looks at me. "Thank you. You are dismissed."

Ruiz motions me toward the exit. With that, I nod a goodbye and follow President Waters' orders.

Outside the closed door, I draw in a deliberate breath and wait for my guardian, hopefully Ben, to retrieve me. As I let the air from my lungs, he rounds the corner.

"You good?" he asks, concern blanketing his face.

"Uh, yeah." I shake my head, searching for the appropriate words. "All this," I wave back toward the door behind me, "is simply too much, too soon."

He grasps my arm and pulls me through the hall and out the front exit. "The emotions I sensed from you while you were in there were off the charts. What happened?"

I check around us to ensure no one can hear, but there's no one in sight. "Waters is implanting me with a permanent EP equipped to block my ability," I whisper.

"*What?*" he hisses. "You can't let them do that. They'll track your every move."

"I know. I'm not sure I have a choice."

Ben's face grows stern. "You *always* have a choice."

"Of course I do, but there are people who need me. In order to keep them safe, I may be required to make a sacrifice."

"And that might be us. The more they know about you, the greater the chance they could find out about my ability."

"Your secret is safe with me."

Ben twists from me slightly. "I know that's what you think, but it doesn't make it guaranteed."

The words punch me in the stomach because, in the end, I know he's right. It's a promise I might not be able to keep.

A dozen techs in white coats bustle about the clean, bright lab, but the bustling turns to gawking when they finally notice me. Hot nervousness creeps up my neck as they stare. One of them, an older man with thin, graying hair approaches Ben and me.

"Avlyn, I'm Medic Harris. We've been expecting you." He gestures to a doorway straight ahead, through the middle of the lab.

"I'll be waiting for you outside," Ben tells me.

I flash him a nervous look, but remain silent.

"Actually …" The medic stops to examine the name on Ben's uniform. "Porter, you will no longer be required at this time." He tips his head for Ben to leave.

Ben glances uneasily at me, but quickly returns his attention to Medic Harris. "Yes, sir." He rotates and exits the room, leaving me alone with the medics.

"The tech team will explain the process to your liking." Medic Harris places a hand on my shoulder and nudges me further into the lab. The curious stares of the lab techs stay glued to me as I walk to the opposite side of the room. All I want to do is disappear into the floor.

In the adjacent room, five more white-clad lab techs surround a large, sterile-looking chair, the kind that leans back for its occupant to lie in. The wall to my right shows a floor-to-ceiling screen, displaying a full image of my body on one part, and a gigantic, revolving brain on the other. Mine, too, I assume. Stats, facts, and figures scroll down a column in the middle too fast for my eyes to keep up with them.

Harris blabbers on about the procedure, but no matter how much I want to, I don't hear what he says.

"Ms. Lark?" A new, gentle voice draws my attention from the information display.

"Yes?" I yelp.

"The process is about to begin." An attractive female tech with coppery skin guides me to the seat and explains the procedure of implanting a permanent EP. I focus on what's important to calm the nausea rolling in my stomach. I can handle a permanent EP, and playing along with Waters and Ruiz will give me additional time to evaluate the situation.

Medic Harris taps the arm of the chair and it reclines. From underneath, a silver shield emerges from either side and meets with a click over the top part of my body, dimming the bright lights of the lab.

"We'll immerse you in Virtual Reality, Ms. Lark. Doing so will allow a portion of your brain to interact with the program and absorb it much faster. But first we'll sedate you and perform a series of tests prior to the implantation. The sedative will cause a form of short-term amnesia, so even though you will be alert during the procedure, you won't remember it. Do you have any final questions, Ms. Lark?"

Of course I do.

"No."

"Then I will begin."

The darkness of the shield melts, replaced by a generated schematic of the lab.

Something pinches at my arm, and before the room fades, President Waters steps into my virtual world.

CHAPTER FOUR

I open my eyes to find them hazy. Breathing hard, I blink a few times and the murk clears, slowly replaced with silvery, sparkling wisps floating in the air. I reach out to one, but it repels from my touch. The sparkling vision swirls about me and eventually solidifies into cylindrical shapes.

Incubators. The same type as the testing pods in GenTech's secret lab. Those pods contained Level One citizens who Direction tested a deadly new virus on, one they intended to force on their own citizens—the ones with lower intelligence potential.

Nausea burrows its way through my belly, and I lightly step toward the shapes, afraid of what I might see.

Each holds a human form, void of features; only blank, translucent, sparkling faces. I place my hand on the surface of the pod and words immediately scroll across my vision.

Project Ascendancy

"Identify Project Ascendancy?"

Over the top of the pod, a 3D version of a brain twirls slowly in my vision, appearing much like the hologram of my own brain Ruiz showed me. The identical points are highlighted as on mine.

Neuron Implantation procedure to facilitate a bond between human and technology.

Panic rises up my frame. This is the same procedure Ruiz was telling me about. Why would someone be studying this again?

"Who oversees Project Ascendancy?"

As if cued by the question, the medical pod in front of me disperses and blows away, as if a gust of wind took it.

"No!" I yell, grabbing for the pod. I need to know more, but it's gone, and I'm left standing in a fading, empty lab. My head goes light, and I brace as the whole digital world twists and arches.

My eyelids burst open, and with them, a gasp escapes my mouth. My pounding heart threatens to escape my chest until my eyesight clears, revealing a plain ceiling overlain with information floating over my vision. I release a long breath of relief and fall back onto my pillow.

8:10 AM
Location: New Philadelphia Research Facility

The EP.

Memories pour back. I had an eyepiece implanted, and it seems to be working. Without having had access to one for several days, I'd forgotten how annoying they are. Helpful, but annoying.

My pulse slows upon the realization that what I just saw wasn't real. The door to my room slides clear and a short male medic comes through.

Medic Luis Rodriguez
Age: 35
Sex: Male
Security clearance: B

The words slide across the bottom of my vision in green.

Well, this EP gives me more information than before.

"Good afternoon, Avlyn. I'm Medic—"

"Rodriguez," I mumble.

"Yes, that's right." He cocks his head and smiles warmly. "Ruiz and President Waters will be here shortly to assess your progress. For now, you should rest."

Medic Rodriguez places his hands around the pillow behind my head and fluffs it slightly. From his pocket, he produces a Flexx and scans my eye. "It appears your implant is functioning properly."

"Can I see the results?" I ask, nearly forgetting about my terrible dream.

"Sure." He unfolds the thin material of the Flexx into a tablet, taps the screen, and hands it to me.

My face mirrors back at me. My freckles are still there,

sprayed over my nose. I touch the area surrounding my eye. I can't feel a difference, and there isn't any evidence of the surgery.

"Why don't I see where they did the implant?"

"It's a simple surgery. Your healing nanotechnology was also upgraded. I'm confident they explained that to you. In the few hours since you were released, it has completely healed. Even so, when you came from surgery, swelling and redness was minimal. If you have any additional questions, they can be answered when you begin training. Right now, it's an excellent time for you to relax. How about you watch the MV?"

"MV?"

He peers toward a black media viewer. "MV on." An image of a man appears on the screen.

"Oh, I don't want to watch the news."

Rodriguez chuckles. "Oh yes. In Elore, all you get is news. This is different. You should check it out. I'm sure you'll discover a show you like. To choose, say 'next program' or use the controller to your side."

I turn and find a glass of water and a device sitting on the side table.

"Call me if you need any assistance."

"Thanks."

"No problem." He smiles a second time and walks from the room.

On the media viewer, an attractive middle-aged woman speaks to a younger girl, maybe her daughter? They say something that I guess sounds funny. The scene then switches to another group of people saying equally funny things because a bunch of laughter sounds on the audio, although I don't see any of them.

I grab for the controller, attempting to link with it, but can't.

Waters must have also implanted a device that prevents me from immersing with tech until they allow me to.

Instead, like a regular person, I tap the controller screen. A new program plays about wildlife and the animal population changes since the Collapse. Apparently, when so many people and birds died, it altered the ecosystem. While some animals flourished, others nearly died off. The few minutes I watch of it are interesting, but I flip through several more programs when my heart skips a beat as a stern face I know suddenly comes up.

Manning. His hair, graying at the temples, accentuates his hawkish stare. As always, he's wearing a white lab coat, his eternal uniform. I suck in a breath, flinch, and deactivate the MV. I stare at the blank screen for a moment, but, unable to quiet my curiosity, I switch on the program again.

"With great heaviness, I am here to give you the latest news of the most recent attack by Affinity on Elore." He leans into the podium, a predator patiently awaiting its prey.

Of course, he doesn't mention New Philadelphia, as if Elore houses the remains of the world's survivors and barely anything else exists. He still wants to maintain that the Outerbounds is limited to a rogue band of traitors instead of a population of five million.

"This terrorist group's singular goal is to destroy the way of life we have adopted. The same life which offers the best chances at survival after the Collapse."

I shake my head at his old lies. His words and seeing him have made my hands go clammy. I rub them over the sheets.

Manning continues. "Please know we have the situation well under control, and are doing everything possible to ensure the safety of each Elorian citizen."

I gasp when Representative Ayers joins Manning. At the sight of him, Kyra's terrified face when she told me what he'd done to her comes to the forefront of my mind. Why would Manning be teaming with Ayers? His Level Two privilege runs deep, but if Manning were to defer to anyone else, it would likely be a Level Three representative.

Manning finishes whatever he was saying and nods for Ayers to take his place at the clear podium. Ayers does so emotionlessly.

"Elorians, I am Level Two Representative Ayers, and I am here to present you with a warning. From this day forward, anyone discovered as a member of Affinity will not only be taken into custody and publicly put to death, but so will the members of their immediate family, no matter what level." His nostrils flare and he puffs up his chest. "Direction will no longer tolerate anyone expecting to destroy all we have strived for."

I clamber over the end of my bed and struggle for breath. "Turn off." I gasp and clutch my middle, squeezing at the nausea worming in my belly.

This is my fault, because of my escape. Innocent people will be murdered because of me.

I turn from the screen and make for the exit. There's not enough air in the room. Direction can't be doing this.

I throw my hand up to activate the door and it slides back, but not from my opening it. Medic Rodriguez rushes in. I shove him off before he has the chance to slam his body into mine, but he recovers in a snap and blocks the exit.

"I have to get out of here," I pant, looking over his shoulder into the hall.

"No, no." He steps toward me, hands slightly raised. "You're not authorized to leave without an escort yet. Ruiz will be here soon." He gently places a hand on my shoulder and tips his chin to the MV. "I'm sorry you saw that replay broadcast. We didn't realize you were watching it until too late. I'm sure Ruiz plans to speak with you about it as soon as she arrives. Now please, lie back."

"I don't *want* to lie down!"

Rodriguez pinches his lips together. "I know, but running around out there is not going to do you any benefit."

"Fine," I relent, but I don't move, and neither does he. I realize it's no use, so I back away from him, slink back to the bed, and flop onto it. "This is a huge mess."

"Avlyn, this world has been a mess for a long time. It's nothing new."

Behind him, Ruiz comes in through the doorway. For some reason, a new wave of mistrust wells over me.

Is Ruiz a good person like I thought, or was Ben right in saying her giving me up was a way to save Affinity and her own skin?

The feeling quickly passes.

Adriana Ruiz
Age: 64
Sex: Female
Security clearance: A.2

"Thank you for containing the situation, Medic Rodriguez. I came as soon as I could."

"Yes, ma'am." He gestures goodbye to me and leaves.

"My dear," Ruiz says in a gentle voice, "that's not how we

intended for you to awaken."

"I don't want to do this. Any of it." I flick my gaze to her and quickly return it to my lap. "I'm responsible for Direction killing innocent Citizens. Their deaths are on *my* head."

"Avlyn, this isn't your fault. It's Direction's. Manning is greedy, and he's found other greedy people to surround him. Take Ms. Lewis, for example, and what she was willing to do."

My heart leaps at the mention of my best friend. "No, not Kyra. Manning's manipulating her."

Ruiz steps toward the bed and sits beside me. "Power is a tempting problem. Since your escape, we've accessed Kyra's records. She has ambition. She sees helping Manning as an in. As a Level Two, she probably wouldn't make director, but the Level Representatives have a measure of influence. Kyra may have forged a political path for herself."

"You don't know Kyra. Yes, she was focused, but not *cruel*. You don't know what happened to her." I pause and gulp down a lump in my throat. "What Representative Ayers did to her. She was threatened, I know it, and now Ayers is speaking for Manning. Something's going on."

Ruiz tips her head, confused. "What are you talking about, Avlyn? Kyra almost got you killed. Her choices nearly killed *all* of us."

I shake my head. "I know what went on, but you're not seeing the entire picture."

"Then tell me," Ruiz instructs patiently.

Nervousness crawls up my chest and arms at the thought of telling her Kyra's secret. "A few days before the escape, she came to my unit and told me something had happened."

"What exactly occurred to her?"

"She ... she was raped.

Ruiz's eyes grow wide as saucers. "*Raped?*"

"Yes. By Representative Ayers. He threatened her into keeping quiet, but she came to me anyway. While we were in my apartment, the guardians came and raided Lena's unit. The whole thing scared Kyra so much she ran away. When I tried to speak with her the next day, she ignored my messages." Hot tears threaten the corners of my eyes. "The last time I saw her was when she released me at the Representatives' building."

Ruiz stands and shifts from me, crossing her arms over her chest. When she turns back a pained look dresses her face. "I feel terrible, but I don't know that there's anything we can do at this point."

My fists clench. "So you'll just leave her there for Manning and anyone else to use her? To abuse her?"

"I can't risk pulling her out at this time, Avlyn. There is too much at stake, too many larger issues. Also, she's not a member of Affinity, so what would we be able to do with her? Imprison her?"

"There has to be *something*," I insist.

She places her hand on top of my clenched fist. "If we can do something, we will. Right now, it's not a possibility. Our goal is to protect *you*. You are not merely necessary for your skills, but also as a person. Valuable to our team, to Affinity and New Philly."

Sweat coats my hands and I wipe them on my pants. Ruiz seems sincere, but in the end her words are cheap. I'm sure without my ability I'd be a nobody to them, like Kyra.

"Listen." She places her hand on my arm. "I've lost people to Direction too. Friends, family. Let's get started with training. With you on our side, we may be able to stop losing the ones we love. Including Kyra."

Believing her or not, I twist and fall into her arms. Tears stream my face and soak the fabric on her shoulder. A light, sweet scent I'm unable to identify fills my nose and reminds me of my mother, even though she never smelled that way. If only it were her holding me instead of Ruiz.

Mother's not coming back, but Kyra is still alive, and I must help her somehow. As far as Ruiz and Waters know, I'm the only individual with the ability to immerse. That alone gives me some sense of power.

Ruiz envelops me in a tight hug and doesn't loosen it until I do. I wipe my face and slow my breathing.

"When do I begin training?"

"After tomorrow. We still have a few tests." Ruiz pats my leg. "Rodriguez will bring you a snack. After that, you should sleep. Don't keep yourself up with the news. There'll be plenty of that later."

She rises and exits the room, and I stare at the blank MV. Manning's announcement replays in my head, his cold, gray eyes burrowing through my brain.

CHAPTER FIVE

Kyra's eyes burn with fear and her mouth opens into a silent scream. She stretches for me, but when I seize her hand, she explodes into millions of pieces of shimmery code. The blowback shoves me straight up from my pillow.

Panting, I fumble to ring for Rodriguez and throw back the damp sheet from my body. Within seconds, the door slides free. A male frame stands backlit in the doorway.

Rodriguez

"I can't—sleep," I say between ragged breaths.

"Let me provide you with something." Rodriguez steps into the room and reaches toward me with a handheld scanner. "Give me your hand."

I don't obey and shove my hand beneath the sheet to my side. I've taken that MedTech before, and I didn't like it. "I thought that stuff was bad."

In Elore, my friend Lena warned me about the sleep MedTech, but she's dead now. Killed in an attempt to rescue Meyer's adoptive father Jayson from Elore's detention center. Her memory raises a lump in my throat and I swallow it down.

The moonlight streaming through the window falls over Rodriguez's face. A crooked smile works at his lips. "It can be addictive, but your upgraded nanos are designed to monitor the tech and won't allow dependence. In general, the nanos should keep you functioning optimally on their own, but ..." He scans my head and body with the handheld and it beeps. "Your stress levels are decidedly high, so they need an additional aid. Remember, this isn't Elore. We're not trying to control you."

I want to believe that, but a lifetime of lies tends to ruin you.

Despite my doubt, I place my hand on the screen for the upload. The device beeps.

"There." Rodriguez pockets the device and pats me on the head. "That should stabilize your elevated cortisol and any nightmares."

"Thanks," I mumble, the tension already falling away. "Oh, is my guard still outside?" I haven't seen Ben since before my surgery.

"He is. The guy seems rather devoted to your safety. See you in the morning."

The thought of Ben standing guard outside my door overwhelms me with the warmth of security. Rodriguez exits and I focus on the moon out my window until it fades into a pinprick of light against the nothingness of sleep.

A muffled female voice tunnels its way into my consciousness, rousing me from a dreamless sleep. "Avlyn? Wake up."

A vaguely recognizable face cuts through my groggy state. Coppery skin and ice-blue eyes. Long, dark ringlets tickle my nose, and I wipe the itch.

Sanda Brant and the rest of her information overlays my vision.

"Sanda?" I ask.

"Yeah. We don't have a lot of time."

I bolt upright, looking past her for Meyer or Ben. *Are we in trouble? Do we need to run?* The muscles in my legs tense at the thought, but then she grins, confusing me.

"Relax. You're released into Meyer's custody today for an off-grounds facility tour."

My heart slows, and I scan the room. "Where's Meyer?"

"He's on his way. When he messaged me this morning, I came straight over."

Still unsure, I shake my head. "Why are you even here in New Philadelphia?"

"Well, to see my savior, of course." Sanda smiles and pats me on the side of my upper arm.

Sanda does appear immensely better than the last time I saw her, but I have a feeling that nearly dead people never look great. Direction tortured her and Jayson at the detention center and deactivated their healing nanos. After the escape, Meyer thought I should use my ability to attempt hacking her nanos. Unexpectedly, it worked, and here she is, alive.

"You can't be here just to see me."

"No, but it was a perk. Ruiz sent me to New Philly to

recover. The medics are way better in the city than out in the field. I should know, since I have a little field training."

"How are you?"

She glances down at her body. "Healing up nicely, thanks to you." The sparkle in her eyes dims slightly. "My heart's still having a bit of trouble, though, dealing with my losses. I really miss my dad."

Jayson was Sanda's bio father. He made sure we got Sanda out of the detention center first, and because of it, he and Lena didn't make it out.

"I lost my mother, too," I say.

She catches my gaze and places her hand on my shoulder. "I know."

"Hey, ladies." Meyer's voice interrupts our moment of shared sorrow and Sanda swivels toward him.

My pulse skips at the sight of Meyer, and thoughts of yesterday's kiss erase some of the sadness creeping over me. There will be time for mourning later, if I survive through this. Today, a little distraction will be good for my morale.

"Hi," Sanda and I reply in unison.

Meyer claps his hands together. "Well, let's get going. We only have today. After that ... who knows?"

"I should go take care of a couple things before we leave. I'll see you two downstairs." Sanda waves and exits.

"Did you sleep ok?" Meyer asks as he walks to the bed.

I did when Rodriguez gave me the sleep MedTech.

"I guess."

He smiles, leans in to peck my cheek, and it's as if lightning explodes in my center. His clean, recently showered scent fills my nose, making me want to melt into a puddle.

I snatch his hand. "Can today last forever?"

"I wish." A gleam sparks in his nearly ebony eyes. "Now get ready. I'll be outside with Sanda."

After he leaves, I find a change of clothes in the bathroom and quickly shower. When I come out, toweling my hair dry, Ruiz is standing stiffly in my room, arms across her chest.

"Oh. Uh, hello," I say, slightly startled.

"I wanted to see you this morning before you left," she begins. "I convinced Waters to let you go on a short tour of the city en route to your appointment. Getting your bearings is important, but be aware today will be your final outing for quite some time. At least until we have a better understanding of your abilities. You will be visiting a gentleman today who might be able to give us a better idea of this. Porter, your guard, will also be accompanying you on the excursion."

"Yes ma'am," I say. "May I ask a question?"

Her stance relaxes. "Please do."

"Why are you still dealing with me if I was handed over to New Philly?"

"Because I negotiated it. You require someone on your side who comprehends your background in Elore." She produces a Flexx and pokes at the screen. "I'm disabling your EP for the time being. She taps her handheld and the greenish glow framing my vision disperses. With that, she nods and exits the room.

Outside, Meyer dashes ahead, leaving Sanda and I behind. Ben and another guard with a face full of freckles and hair the color of carrots trail us. His uniform identifies him as Smith, and without the enhancements from my new EP, that's all I know.

Sanda's gold-tipped curls dance in the sunlight as we jog from the medical facility. It's an unassuming, two-story building, grayish and concrete. After living with the elegant buildings of Level Two in Elore, this one has an almost shabby appearance. Nothing too impressive.

I'm glad Ruiz disabled my EP. There's a part of me that wants today to be a surprise, and the device would give me too much information for that to be possible. For one more day, I can pretend I'm a normal person.

Sanda slows our pace, leaving Meyer ahead. "You know he likes you."

Heat slithers up my neck, and I pull at the collar of my loose top to try to conceal it, but I'm pretty sure it's no use. "Meyer? Um, yeah. I think I do."

"Well, he does. After you healed me and he took me to the Affinity camp to find a medic, I asked about you. Despite everything that had happened, when he spoke of you, his eyes still lit up. I've never seen that in him before. Not seeing you for the last couple days has driven him crazy. He's always been super focused on his mission with Affinity and hasn't taken much time for girls, so I can say if he's taking the time for you, you're worth it."

I watch Meyer as he jogs ahead toward a line of storage buildings. His tall frame and strong shoulders move with surprising grace.

"He's worth it, too." I flash Sanda a smile and increase my speed. Ben and Smith enter the unit next to this one, and once I've caught up with Meyer, I ask, "What exactly are we doing?"

Meyer presses his hand to a security pad and a large door rolls up, revealing two red vehicles inside the opening. I guess they're vehicles, at least. They're nothing like the driverless auto taxis in Elore. These have two wheels and a metal body with handles and a place to sit.

Meyer gestures to them. "We're taking a tour of New Philly before we go to Mr. Sloan. Sanda and I thought you'd enjoy seeing your new home, and Ruiz agreed."

"And we're using *these*?"

"They're scooters," Sanda explains. "They're really fun."

She breaks away from the two of us and grabs a bright blue helmet from the rear of the scooter. She puts it on, latches it under her chin, and climbs onto the seat. I scan the rest of the space, and in the far back of the storage unit sit two partially covered transport vehicles.

"What are those?" I ask.

"A couple broken hover pods I've been working on the last couple of days," Meyer says. "Little four seaters. Operating systems are shot. Totally different than the ship that got us from Elore. I'm sure you could fix them in no time."

I turn to check them out. "They're like driverless taxis with no wheels."

Meyer holds my arm and leads me toward the scooter, snatching an extra helmet from a counter on his right. He hands it to me. "That's exactly what they're like, except they fly."

I chuckle. "If I never have to fly again, I'll be happy."

Meyer smirks and gestures to the helmet in my hand. I follow Sanda's example and affix it to my head, then climb in back of Meyer, who's already on the scooter.

"There's a comm in the helmet if you want to speak." His voice echoes inside the headpiece. "You ready?"

Before I get a chance to answer, Sanda zips from the storage bay and Meyer activates our scooter. We're off with a jolt, the wind lashing my face through the opening in my helmet. Behind us, Ben and Smith drive similar scooters.

On the streets of New Philadelphia, we whip around a black, then a red auto vehicle and a large transport carrying multiple people. The blur of the buildings come and go before I even have time to take in as much as I'd like. Overall, it's a mingling of old and new structures, almost like Levels One through Three in Elore combined into one city.

Apparently, New Philadelphia is a bustling metropolis, too. Instead of people focused on handhelds or scurrying to get to their placement, they're milling, eating lunch from a food cart, even going in and out of buildings decorated with goods in their windows. A couple of two-wheeled vehicles with drivers zip by us on the road.

I point to a window front where an artificial, womanly shaped figure models a dress. "What's that?"

Meyer laughs through the helmet comm. "You buy clothes there."

"Buy clothes?" In Elore, you order the necessary supplies online and they're delivered by drone the next day. "Can I buy clothes?"

"Probably, if you can pay for them."

How *do* you pay for goods in New Philadelphia? In Elore credits were deposited into our citizen's account, but who knows if that's how it's done here.

"See the building on your right?" Meyer asks.

A large white structure with columns comes into view. Surrounded by taller buildings, the broad, four-story construction looks out of place. An iron gate surrounds the green lawn.

"That's the president's home."

I remember my tiny, stark, functional apartment in Elore. "Waters lives in that huge place all by himself?"

Meyer laughs. "No, but I guess there are perks to being the president. He does live there with his family."

"It seems like more than they need."

We maneuver our way over the streets, further into New Philly. I stop focusing on the sights Meyer occasionally points out and concentrate on the citizens. I crane my neck to watch a lady with bright strawberry-red hair wearing a tight yellow dress walking a puffy, tan animal down the busy street. When she's out of sight, a man with slicked, purple-streaked hair follows the trajectory of our scooter. His eyes perfectly match the hue of his hair. Some wear vivid clothing, and others dress similar to Meyer or me in their plainer clothes. In Elore, everyone dresses much the same in a uniform style, and hair color is kept natural and refined.

Not here. No one hides or tries to keep attention from themselves. The thought of it makes me feel free, if only for today.

Pulling onto a street marked 'Broadway', we drive up next to a shop with a word over the top of a large, clear window. 'Salon'. In the window, a blonde fiddles with a woman's brown hair. Before we zip past them, the dark hair transforms to nearly white in an instant.

"How'd they do that?" I wonder out loud.

"The hair?" Sanda giggles in my comm.

"Yeah."

"I saw it, too. I've lived in the Outerbounds all my life, and it still amazes me. People like to change themselves up occasionally, if they can afford it."

"How does it work?" I ask.

"It's nanotech. Not permanent. It can be used to change eye color as well."

The guy with the purple eyes and hair comes to memory. He must have visited the "salon" recently.

"We're here." Meyer drives the scooter to the curb and deactivates the vehicle. Sanda parks hers ahead of us and dismounts, removing her helmet and placing it into a compartment on the rear of the scooter.

Ben and the other guardian park their vehicles ahead of Sanda's. Ben throws me a look of mild concern, yet, still, doesn't speak to me.

"Where?" I ask, peeling myself from behind Meyer and swinging my leg to the sidewalk, scanning the buildings. The ones to my side are similar to the clothing shop I asked Meyer about. Again, various merchandise is displayed in the windows.

"Up there." Sanda points at a tall building across the street with no shops on the ground floor, at least none I can see. "Dr. Sloan lives there."

"I'm confused why we came to him." I hand my helmet to Meyer to stow. "Why didn't Waters have him visit me at the lab?"

Sanda gestures for us to go. "Eh ... it was a good excuse to come into the city, but you'll find out when we get there."

"You ladies go ahead." Meyer tucks the helmets away. "I'm starving. There's an amazing food cart with the best burritos in the city. Every time I'm here, I have to grab one." He smiles at me. "I'll get you one, too."

Sanda slaps Meyer on the arm. "Don't forget about me."

"Ouch!" He winces and exaggerates his pain, rolling his eyes. "How could I *ever* forget you?"

"Brothers," Sanda mutters. She slips her arm around my waist and ushers me toward Mr. Sloan's building.

I smile and check for Ben, who remains alert near our side with Smith. Relieved he's continuing with us, I walk with Sanda into the building. She leads us to the elevator and each of us palm the scanner on the inside. The eleventh floor is our destination. Upon our exit, I'm surprised to be met with a simple, tiny foyer and a single door instead of a hall leading to multiple units.

Sanda steps forward and knocks on the door. I raise my eyebrow at Ben, but he's stoic, as a guard should be.

With a zip, the door slides back. Out floats a drone with a slightly human form. No legs, but a torso and head and what looks like two slots where arms extend from the body if needed.

"Why are you here?" the faceless drone asks gruffly.

I inch back from the AI, startled by its rude behavior. Even in Elore, the speaking drones were courteous.

"We have an appointment," Sanda answers.

The drone floats around us, a scan coming from the area where its face would be, the beam raking over us one at a time.

"Come on, Sloan, let us in," Sanda scowls.

"There is supposed to be one additional human for the appointment," the drone says.

"Yes," Sanda says, "Meyer Quinn. He will be joining us soon."

The scanner deactivates. "You may enter. Please adhere to the required procedure."

"Required procedure?" I mumble.

Sanda leans into me. "Don't ask, just follow the instructions."

Once in the unit, another non-human voice from nowhere greets us, this time female and somewhat more polite. "Remove your footwear at the door and begin the disinfecting process by proceeding to the line marked on the floor."

We do as the voice commands, and upon standing on the line, a ray of light comes from the ceiling and surrounds each of our bodies.

"You may proceed," the unseen voice says.

The rude drone hovers ahead and leads us from the entry into a large room. Ben and the other guard don't follow, and instead act as sentinels at the exit. On the opposite side of the room, a bald man has his back to us, working in a mostly dark room at a huge touch screen. To his left is another chair that reclines, like the one in the lab.

"Dr. Sloan," Sanda calls.

The man doesn't answer and continues tapping. A commotion comes from behind us. I turn to see Meyer entering the front door. He's holding a sack and trying to remove his shoes while not placing our food down. Meyer walks to the line and the beam of light surrounds him. After, he joins us.

Finally, the man working at the desk rotates to face us, but avoids looking at the group.

"Now that you have all arrived, we can begin."

I shift my attention toward the others, unsure what's going to happen next. Meyer shrugs and takes a step, the bag crinkling in his hand.

"You can't bring that in here," Dr. Sloan says in a flat voice.

Meyer scowls and tosses the bag across the room. It lands by his shoes.

"And you two can have a seat at the back of the room. I merely allowed you to come because Ruiz said you must be accompanied somehow." He continues to mutter under his breath and taps at the keyboard in front of him, not once looking at us.

"But—" Sanda starts to protest.

"No. Lark alone."

I sigh, shoving off the obvious discomfort this man exudes. The reality, though, is I'm quite used to it. His abrasive personality is worlds beyond that of anyone I've met from the Outerbounds, but he's not unlike most citizens in Elore.

"It's fine," I say, trying to work through his motivation. At his station, I stand next to him, waiting for instructions. Instead of giving them, he continues typing on his virtual keyboard. Finally, he waves a hand in my direction.

"Sit."

I scan the room, then at the reclining chair. "On that?"

"Of course on that."

I look back to Meyer and Sanda. Sanda rolls her eyes and mouths, *just do it.* Ben and Smith still stand at the unit entrance. Slowly, I walk to the chair and lower myself into the seat. As I do, the thing automatically reclines. Dr. Sloan pops up from his chair and grabs two VR headsets, thrusting one of them in my face.

"Put it on," he says.

My eyes widen, but I take it from him and put it on as he places the other over his head.

"I'm disabling the ability damper installed on you yesterday," Sloan explains. "This way the scan will access the data correctly."

Instantly, my vision goes colorless and materializes into a plain, artificial room. A virtual version of Dr. Sloan appears, his body language considerably more relaxed than before.

"Welcome, Lark." Unlike before, he looks me straight in the eye as he speaks. "I've been looking forward to meeting you. I've seen all your data so far and it is *fascinating.*"

"You didn't *seem* like you were looking forward to it," I say, confused by his shift in demeanor.

"I apologize. I dislike the outside world much. It's too ... *stimulating*, to say the least. In here, I can block any sensation I don't desire in order to focus on the ones I do. It makes my job easier when I have to deal with other people."

"Why'd I have to come here then? We could have met in VR from anywhere."

He chuckles. "Oh, I'm certain you're right, but, if you haven't noticed, I'm very particular about things. And I needed you here. Traveling to you was out of the question—the outside is a dirty business I want no part of."

I shrug, but begin to feel somewhat less apprehensive. He's not who I expected him to be. "Ok, then. Let's get started."

"I'll be leaving you alone in here for now to run the tests. The first will include a physical blood sample. Are you okay with that?"

"Do I have a choice?" I ask.

"You always have a choice." He still holds my gaze.

I nod, somehow trusting him. I don't know what it is about him but I know can. "You can take it."

Dr. Sloan vanishes from the virtual room and soon after something sharp pricks my arm.

The sample he needed.

I expect the experience to change, but nothing does. "Dr. Sloan?" I call, not sure if he can hear me. I release from the virtual state and pull off my headset. Sloan is leaning over his keyboard, studying the data on his screen.

"I need a comparison," he mutters, not even realizing I'm no longer under, or at least he doesn't appear to. He spins in his chair and eyes Meyer and Sanda. Meyer stands.

"Not you," Sloan says in a clipped voice. He's totally different out here from the person I met in VR. "You tried to carry your nasty food into my space."

Sanda, eyes wide and apparently a little stunned, slightly opens her mouth. Sloan shakes his head. "You either." He thrusts out his arm, pointing a finger straight at Ben. "You. You are quiet and respectful."

Ben's eyes move to mine. "Um, I'm on duty, sir."

"No matter," Sloan says. "This is your duty now. Come."

Ben inches forward and the AI voice sounds. "Remove your footwear at the door and begin the disinfecting process by proceeding to the line marked on the floor."

Ben follows orders and slowly comes into the room. With every step he takes, my chest tightens. He *can't* use Ben as a comparison. If he looks too closely at our data, he might find too many similarities. Something in me trusts him, but it doesn't matter. I rack my brain to come up with a plan to make it stop.

"Dr. Sloan?" I squeak.

"Why are you out of VR?" He swings around from the screen.

"Um ... I feel sick."

He pushes back in his chair, away from me, eyes wide. "What do you mean sick?"

"I might be having a bad reaction to my implant," I lie. "I don't know. My stomach doesn't feel right at all."

Horrified, Sloan stands and backs further from me. Ben steps in and takes my arm and the data on the screen shifts, scrolling and adding new information. I yank from Ben and clutch at my middle. Ben's so focused on me, I don't think he noticed what happened.

"Leave now. These tests can be done another day. I'm reactivating the block on your ability." Dr. Sloan turns back to the screen, narrowing his eyes and looking confused by the new data. He types on the keyboard and before the screen goes blank I see two familiar words at the top of the page.

Project Ascendancy

CHAPTER SIX

Sloan's AI unit rudely ushers us from his apartment, but I don't care. I can't get out of there soon enough. I must speak with Ben, and I won't be able to do it here.

Project Ascendancy?

That dream I had wasn't a dream at all. It was real. I have no way of knowing what data popped onto the screen after Ben touched me, and I have no way to find out.

Meyer ushers me down to the street and gets me on the scooter. Before he takes his spot, he tosses the very rumpled bag of our food in a container on the street and mumbles about them being cold and no good anymore.

Traveling back, my mind is filled with thoughts of what just happened. But nothing makes sense. Somehow, I find myself at the compound with barely any memory of the trip. Ben and Smith are gone. I can't even remember them saying goodbye.

"You're feeling better, right?" Sanda asks, checking her Flexx for the time.

I nod. "I'll be fine. I think I got nervous or something."

She narrows her eyes at me. "Okay ... I have to take off. I'm headed out first thing in the morning."

"I wish we had more time to get to know each other." I wrap my arms around her shoulders, desperate to tell someone what I saw, but not knowing if I can yet.

"Hopefully soon. But you get to start training tomorrow, and I'm returning to duty with Affinity." She inches back, revealing the sadness in her eyes. There will not be a day like this again anytime soon.

Meyer plants a peck on Sanda's cheek and waves farewell to her then he turns to me. "I'll escort you to your father's unit."

"What happened to Be—I mean, Porter?"

Meyer gives me a quizzical look. "He and Smith were called to another assignment."

Tightness builds in my chest, but demanding to talk with him might raise suspicion, and right now even Meyer can't know about Ben. Anyway, I don't know that any of it means anything. So Project Ascendancy is real. It doesn't immediately make it bad. Maybe learning about my ability sparked new interest in old studies on the topic. And what went on with the data when Ben grabbed my arm at Dr. Sloan's? That could be nothing too.

I'm just jumpy.

We cut through the courtyard. Meyer messages Father, and we are on our way. The buzz of a reply returns seconds later. He glances at it, then holds his Flexx for me to see the screen.

They finally let me out, but go ahead and go into the unit. A package came for Avlyn.

"I wonder what it is." I force a smile and pull Meyer forward to move faster.

Once there, Meyer tails me into the unit. A small package marked *Avlyn Lark* sits on the side table next to the couch. I snatch it up and open the top. Inside is a new handheld. I tap the screen to activate it.

Ms. Lark,

Welcome to New Philadelphia. You are now free to roam the compound without an escort. The handheld device integrates with your EP, and you will receive additional instructions along with your training. Tap the screen twice to bring up your account and follow the directions to set your password. Instructions are to come.

President Waters

For a split second, I wish I could use my ability to tap into the system, find Ben, and contact him, but that's not possible. I poke the link and do as it says. A message vibrates the device.

You have been approved for a monitored visit with the POW Aron Barton for a maximum fifteen minutes. Please click here to schedule a time.

I tap the link and browse the available times. There's one thirty minutes from now. My breath picks up. If I can't see Ben, at least I can see Aron. If it weren't for me, he wouldn't be in this mess at all. Not that being in Elore is much better, but I want to apologize and see what can be done to help him.

I select the appointment.

"I have to go." I shift toward Meyer, who's now standing back to the one small window in Father's unit.

"Where?" he asks. "We just got back."

"My approval to see Aron came in. I need to be there in half an hour."

"Aron?" Meyer swings from the window, eyebrows knitting together, crossing his arms over his chest. "He tried to kill us at the Level One bunker."

"His goal wasn't to kill us ... he was attempting to get me from the building alive."

"But he's one of *them*."

"I don't think so." Squaring myself, I step away from Meyer. I shouldn't tell him this. "Aron was part of my Affinity assignment. To pursue him as a spouse pairing. If Affinity wanted me to be with him, they might have thought him valuable."

Meyer shifts his weight. "Did you arrange a pairing?"

I gulp past the knot forming in my throat. "Well ... Aron did ask for one before ... everything happened. And I said yes. Then, in the bunker, I tried to shoot him when all he was trying to do was rescue me."

Meyer seems to tense more. "Avlyn, I just want you to be safe."

"Aron's a good person." I walk toward him. "Direction is all he's ever known, so his values might be off, but if he were only shown the truth, that may change. He's not so different than I was."

"Do you like him?" Meyer asks, lowering his voice.

"Of course I like him. I wouldn't be trying to see him if I

didn't. But if you're asking if I'm *interested* in him—he's a friend. It's not as if even that much is necessary for someone to request a Spouse Contract. You alone have to be deemed compatible by Direction. Liking the person is optional."

Meyer angles his back to me. "Fine, but I'm going with you."

"I'm sure I could find my way. According to Waters' message, I'm allowed to go out on my own now."

"No doubt you could." He turns and locks eyes with me, not budging.

I shake my head, fold the handheld, and snap it to my wrist. "Let's go then."

On the way to the holding center, Meyer and I don't talk. He continues with his arms crossed and close to his body. At this point, there's a tiny part of me that gets why the Direction Initiative keeps its citizens emotionally distant. Maintaining relationships takes a lot of work, and definitely drags me from what's important. I've never been so distracted in my whole life since meeting Meyer.

A sign on the front of the building reads *Detainment Center*, and we enter through the doors underneath it. A desk sits directly in front of us with two doors on each side. A proper-looking woman with hair pulled into a tight bun sits at the desk.

"I have an appointment to meet with a detainee," I tell her.

The woman peers from her console and looks to a scanner to her side. "Please, place your hand on the pad, and you will be paged on your device when it's time."

Meyer and I do as she says and wait at the corner of the desk, still not speaking. After a few moments, my handheld buzzes with an alert.

Appointment for 15 minutes of visitation with Aron Barton approved for Avlyn Lark.

I return to the woman at the desk, Meyer following me. "The appointment is approved."

"Yes, I see." Her eyes stay trained on her system screen. "Please place your hand on the pad once more."

I do, and Meyer does the same.

"Sir, only Ms. Lark has been approved."

Meyer opens his mouth to respond. I brush his upper arm. "This will be fine. The meeting will be monitored, remember?"

Meyer nods and leans against the wall of the waiting area. I force a smile.

"I'll be back in fifteen minutes."

"I'll be here," Meyer mumbles.

What's the matter with him?

As I walk through the now-open door on the left, a young female guard in a tan jumpsuit meets me. The two red stripes on her arm must indicate her rank, but because my EP is off, I can't identify what they mean. However, the stunner affixed to her belt and the set of her jaw shows me she intends business.

"Follow me," she says. "Your time will start when we arrive."

She pilots me into a long, drab hallway, making two turns; right, then left. The guard stops at an equally drab door marked 107B and palms the security pad to the side of it. It opens into a hall with ten more doors, five to one side, and five to the other. Each door has a small, reinforced window built in.

She indicates the left of the hall. "Barton is in number four. You have fifteen minutes."

"Thank you." I approach the holding cell, stomach clenching. *Fifteen minutes will not be long enough for this.*

I peer through the window. Aron sits in a metal chair, head in his hands. Even his cropped, blond hair appears messy, as if it's been days since it's last been combed.

I place my hand on the security pad.

Avlyn Lark: Approved

The door slides away, and Aron snaps to attention. His blue eyes grow wide and then tear from me, his body returning to its slouch.

"What are you doing here?"

The acid tone to Aron's voice punches me in the middle. I wasn't expecting less, but I'd hoped for it.

The door slides shut and I move closer to him. "I needed to confirm you were okay."

Aron stretches out his arms. "Here I am. Do I *look* okay?"

This time he holds my gaze, and I'm the one breaking away.

"Not really." I hang my head. "But you shouldn't have been in that building in the first place."

"What did you expect, Avlyn?" he snaps back. "I liked you, even asked you to make a Spouse Contract. When they informed me my drone project was to be used to locate you, of course I went in to see if I could get you out alive. You ruined our chance at a contract with all," Aron gestures around himself, palms up, "*this,* but I didn't want to see you dead. I held the tiniest hope it was all a terrible mistake."

"Aron," I whisper, "I like you, too."

Aron's body tenses. "You threatened me with a stunner," he grits out. "Those weapons don't only *stun* at that range."

I step in to him and lower my voice. "Direction had just killed my mother, Aron. Even if they let me live, I had to protect my father and Meyer. I had a chance to escape, and I took it, but I wouldn't have shot you."

Aron sighs and drops his head into his palms again. "It was stupid of me to ever think my life could have the tiniest amount of fulfillment."

"That's exactly why I joined Affinity. I needed answers, and life under the Direction Initiative felt wrong." I almost tell him about Ben, but it's more than he has to know, and if anyone is listening, I don't want them to hear. "You're here now, might as well take advantage of it."

"But these people are trying to destroy Elore."

"If I believed that, I wouldn't be here." I move in nearer and rest my hand on his shoulder. He flinches. "Come on, you trusted me enough to ask for a contract. Trust me now."

Hopefully, with my ability, I have plenty of clout to get Aron released.

"Have they done anything to harm you?" I ask.

Aron shifts in his seat, forcing my hand to fall from his shoulder.

"No, but they haven't told me anything, either. After the bunker, soldiers threw me on a hovership. Immediately on arrival, I was brought here. I've been stuck in this cell for days."

"So, they haven't questioned you?"

Aron shakes his head. "Not yet."

"I'm sorry this happened, but you might be better off here than in Elore, anyway. Manning won't relent easily, so it's going to get ugly."

"Affinity doesn't have a chance. You'll get yourselves killed."

I stare at him. Aron was escorted from the building in Elore and shoved on a hover pod. He probably didn't see much on the flight to New Philadelphia. "You don't know, do you?"

Aron cocks his head. "Know about what?"

"The people in the Outerbounds aren't simply an insignificant band of rebels like Manning would have you believe. New Philadelphia consists of five million, and who knows what's outside that?"

"Five million?" Aron echoes, confused. "That's not possible after Aves."

"It is. Direction has lied to us to maintain control, told us that outside of Elore was a dead zone so no one would venture out."

"So what's the truth?"

"It's *all* half-truths."

Aron closes his eyes and leans back, silent.

"I'm attempting to get you out," I promise. "I start training tomorrow, and I'll speak with Adriana Ruiz. She's the leader of the Affinity movement." President Waters is unlikely to go for it, but I have to try.

Aron's lips form a thin, sad smile, and the dimple in his cheek takes shape. His face really is one I would not have minded looking at for a lifetime, but this time he has no wink for me.

"I didn't do anything wrong. I tried to make things right," Aron says softly.

"No, you didn't … it was the one life you knew."

My handheld buzzes on my wrist.

Appointment with Aron Barton concluded. Please exit the cell.

"I have to go." Before I know it, my arms wrap his neck. He stiffens, not used to people touching him, but then relaxes and lightly places his arms around me. "I'm glad you weren't hurt," I say.

The guard taps at the door and waves for me to come out.

I give Aron an extra squeeze, release him, and head to the door. Through the window I can see as Aron moves from the chair to the bed in the cell's corner, flopping himself on its top. I break down the list of reasons he should be freed in my head. Securing a pairing contract with Aron was my Affinity mission, so he must be useful, and his skills with programming drones are obviously advanced. The micro search drones he made found us almost immediately in the bunker.

The guard leads me through the corridor to the entrance where Meyer waits.

"You get what you need?" he mumbles.

"I did."

But I'd feel much better if I knew what Water's intention for Aron was.

CHAPTER SEVEN

The door to Father's unit slides back.

"Father?" I call as I go inside the living area.

No answer. Little more than a dim auto lamp illuminates the space.

Meyer leans his shoulder against the open doorway. "I'll see you tomorrow," he grunts and turns to go.

"What's going on with you?"

"Nothing. I'll see you in the morning."

I grip hold of his arm. He pauses, but doesn't shift toward me. Despite my lack of practice dealing with emotional people, it's obvious Meyer's not happy. He hasn't smiled since we got the news of my approval to see Aron.

A thought sparks in my brain. *Aron.*

"Meyer, I'm allowed to care about others. Even if they're male."

Meyer twists my way, his dark eyes sad. "You are."

I inch slowly to him, keeping my gaze fixed on his. "Then

stop this."

He inhales deeply and straightens up. "It's not you. I'm upset with myself. I've kept myself closed off to ... *this*, for a long time. Forever. Affinity is my life, and distractions make it too difficult."

"*This?*" I break from his stare and hug my arms over my torso. "Then maybe you shouldn't see me anymore. I'm sure you have plenty else to do, and I do, too."

His eyes soften. "Is that what you want?"

"No, but if you do, there's not much I can do about it. What I want is to get to know you," I say.

"We have no idea how much time we have before everything changes. I might get sent off on an Affinity mission and you will be here."

"Did we ever have much time? Until then, let's not allow things like Aron being my friend or not to stop us. He is my friend, and if we remained the same in Elore, I might have made a Spouse Contract with him. But I'm not *in* Elore anymore."

"I know, and I'm sorry. I've just never felt this way before, and losing you isn't an option."

I lift on my toes and raise my chin. The corners of his lips have turned up ever so slightly, and the heat of his body pulls me toward him like a magnet, but I resist.

Meyer draws me into his chest. My heart beats wildly, nearly matching the erratic pace of his. He cups his hand below my chin, eyes locked on mine.

We're going to kiss again.

"Getting to know you better *would* be nice."

My breath hitches and I twine my arms around his waist. When his lips touch mine, a burst of energy fills my chest and tightens my grip.

Click, click.

The door to the unit slides away and the magnetic energy I felt flips, driving us several feet apart. Heat travels up my back all the way to the top of my neck. Father stands stiffly in the doorway, a hint of curiosity on his face, although not enough to shroud the grief making its home in his eyes.

"Hello, Avlyn," he greets. "Meyer."

Meyer jams his hands into his pockets. "Mr. Lark ... I was just leaving."

"You're welcome to stay to eat." Father enters the unit and holds an unmarked fabric sack. "They allowed me an escorted visit into the city, and I picked up food, since I'm not doing well with food preparation without a printer. I think I got more than Avlyn and I require."

"No. I can't, but thank you. And Avlyn starts training early tomorrow."

Meyer glances at the floor and then to me. I throw him a look that begs him to stay. His lips quirk up and he smiles widely, causing the electricity burst to repeat in my chest, but he shakes his head no, effectively scattering my hope in an instant.

"I need to go." Meyer raises his hand to me. "I'll get you in the morning. Goodbye, Mr. Lark." He turns and exits the still-open door.

"Hungry?" Father asks as his body relaxes, probably relieved he's not required to socialize with Meyer anymore.

"Yes." Now that he says it, I realize there's a gnawing ache in my belly. "What did you get?"

"I apologize for my behavior," Father says as he takes our

plates into the kitchen and dumps them into the sink. "I don't even recognize myself anymore. The medic who examined me last said I was in shock. I hate how my emotions are consuming me."

"You *are* in shock. The life you knew is gone." I move to the couch and flop on it. "It's not possible to hold everything together all the time, Father."

"I always thought I could."

He comes from the kitchen and picks up the image of Mother on the side table, takes a seat next to me, and tells me about when they met. Apparently, she was the one for him immediately, which surprises me because I always thought Father the type to carefully consider his choices. Their pairing calculated as a 95% compatibility match, which was high, but not as high as two of his other possibilities. When they first met in person, Father hid his feelings, but he tells me how her naturally streaked—not that anyone in Elore has an unnatural physical appearance—blonde hair kept falling in her face since she wore it longer at the time. He knew it was illogical, but he couldn't keep from the lovely girl named Darline.

Knowing deep down my father always did care for our family for reasons beyond duty means more to me than he will ever know. It's proof he's human after all.

"Did you request a contract right away?" I ask.

"No. Of course not." He gazes at her image. "You know that's not the way it's done. I didn't know how she felt, and I didn't want to appear overly interested. But she was the only one I considered seriously. None of the other matches came close."

A question rises in my mind, one I've held onto for a long time, but never asked because it wasn't appropriate. Father seems receptive today, so I decide to risk it. "Why didn't you have a biological child?"

Father stiffens at the question, immediately making me feel guilty for asking it, but then he relaxes.

"That's not normally spoken of."

"I know," I say, "but it often crossed my mind, and you weren't satisfied to raise me, so it seemed odd."

Father tips his head and gives me a sad smile. "I apologize. Again. With all that has happened in the last few days, I see how the ideals of Direction are flawed. I was ... misguided." Father stops speaking and a tiny crease forms between his eyebrows. "None of our pregnancies were viable," he whispers.

"What?"

"We tried for three years. But every time, for some reason, they weren't viable. We were not provided with details ... simply that there was a sort of defect in the fetuses. There have been advances in gene repair since twenty years ago. Maybe today they could have corrected the issue."

"When I was placed with you, I wasn't a newborn, was I?"

I'm unsure why I said it. I don't really want to get into the experiments performed on Ben and me.

Father narrows his eyes quizzically. "No. How are you aware of that?"

"It doesn't matter." I have little desire to go into the experimentation Ben and I endured before my being matched with my parents.

He nods and moves on. "Two options were offered: to break the pairing contract and exist as singles, or to be matched to a compatible Level Two infant. In your case, the second came with a substantial increase in credits to take you and not ask questions."

"And that didn't concern you?"

"Why would it? Your mother and I desired to perform our duty and held no interest in a single life. Accepting you as our child solved both issues."

Father rises and pockets the Flexx with the photo of Mother on the screen. "I'm tired," he murmurs, and with that, he walks into his room and shuts the door.

I chuckle at his strange behavior that, in reality for him, is not that strange at all. Baby steps are all I can expect.

I stretch up from the sofa, morning light streaming through the single, small window in the unit. The sofa wasn't too bad as a bed, but after I get settled, my own unit would be nice. I doubt I'll be permitted to live in the city anytime soon, but I can dream.

Maybe I'll turn my hair pink for a few days and get a fluffy animal to walk on the street.

I chuckle at my silliness and push the idea aside. None of that is really likely to happen.

From the looks of the closed door, Father's still asleep in his room. I keep quiet so as not to wake him, but figuring out the food preparation area without making a lot of noise is challenging, to say the least. Apparently, you have to *make* your food here. There's no food printer.

No wonder Father's struggling so much.

I rummage in the cold box containing the leftovers of last night's dinner. Father said it was Chinese noodles. Whatever the name, it's not great cold, but I eat it anyway.

My handheld buzzes on my wrist with a message from Meyer.

Can't make it this morning. Pulled into a meeting.

My stomach sinks, mostly from the disappointing message, but the cold noodles don't seem to be settling well, either.

I dig through the sack of outfits Ruiz sent when I was gone yesterday. It's full of the brightly colored pieces common in New Philly, but entirely foreign to a girl from Elore. I choose a gray top and black pants from the bottom of the bag. The others aren't quite me yet. Maybe tomorrow.

I stuff the sack beside the sofa, message Father where I'm going, and head out, pulling up directions to the training center on my Flexx. Unfortunately, Ben's no longer outside my door, which isn't a big surprise, I guess, since they gave me permission to be without an escort.

But why hasn't he tried to contact me?

The weather is clear; blue skies dotted with silvery, puffy clouds. My heart skips as a large flock of birds swoop and dive across them. The testing center is on the far side of the compound. Along the way, I pass the storage unit housing the scooters we took into the city and the hover pods in need of repair.

Upon entering my destination, a Simulated Intelligence bot floats to my side, oval in shape, and slightly flat on the bottom. The surface of the eighteen-inch-tall bot shines white, almost pearlescent. The two sensors simulate blinking eyes, as if the piece of tech is organic.

"May I assist you?" A digital red line twitches like lips when it speaks.

I stare at the faux lips and stifle a laugh. "Uh. Yes, please. I'm here for my training session?"

"Excellent," it says. "Please place your palm at the specified area on my body."

A digital handprint appears on its "chest," and I lay my palm to it. A slight vibration buzzes up my arm.

"Good morning, Avlyn Lark. Please follow me."

The SI wafts ahead, leading me through a corridor past a few white-coated people and plain sets of double doors. This time my presence doesn't garner the attention of anyone.

Maybe this isn't a big deal. Maybe what happened yesterday at Sloan's didn't trigger any suspicion.

Even so, my stomach whirls as we trek further into the building.

Finally, we end at a set of double doors—gray and windowless, not unlike the rest we passed—and they slide back. Inside, four lab techs bustle about the space. In the corner sits a reclining chair similar to the one I sat in when they implanted my EP. This room also has a wall-sized screen with stats and figures of data the tech must be testing.

At least it's not my stats this time.

"Ms. Lark." President Waters appears from the room to my right, looking hurried and checking the time on his Flexx. The SI floats out the door we came in.

I spin toward him, trying to sound cheerful. "Good morning, President Waters. Is anyone else coming?"

"Only Ruiz." His expression remains serious, and although calm, I suspect he has other places to be. "How about you join me in the conference room and we'll get started."

Without another word, he proceeds past the busy techs. Waters leads me into a room containing a black, rectangular table with eight chairs. I take a seat in the farthest spot from the entrance. A media viewer encompasses the wall opposite me.

While we wait for Ruiz, Waters paces, looking at the Flexx again.

I inhale deeply. "Will you be re-activating my EP today?" Small talk was never my strength, but it will pass the time, and hopefully he'll stop pacing.

He pauses and reaches for the chair directly to his side. "Yes, and a short training session to get you acclimated." Sweat beads on his brow and he wipes it with his hand.

Tingling works its way up my neck from his nervous energy.

What do they know?

The door slides back and in walks Ruiz, who gives me a quick smile. I stand as Waters ushers her to a seat, then taps on his handheld, activating the media viewer on the wall.

"There are a few items of business to take care of before we begin."

I suck in air as Kyra's identification image appears on the screen.

"Ruiz made me aware you continue to believe Kyra is not at fault for setting you up in Elore," Waters says. "She was your friend, and it's difficult for you to see her any other way."

"You don't know what happened to her," I reply.

"I *do* understand, and it's a tragedy, but there is nothing we can do for her at this point."

"Kyra has always been trust—"

The words die in my throat as I realize the ridiculousness of them. Kyra betrayed me. She almost got me *killed*. In Affinity's eyes, her reasons were either to save herself or to get ahead.

Still, she was the one who led me into a trap, almost killing me. The Kyra I thought I knew and the one looking out from the media viewer are not the same person.

"You see something that's not there. Something based on emotions." Waters lowers himself into his chair. "Kyra's actions are likely about political advancement, not emotions."

"You won't even *consider* the possibility that she may have betrayed me against her will?"

I have to believe it was against her will.

"If I may give you advice, Avlyn," Ruiz interjects. "Your awareness of the complexity of this situation remains quite limited. Our goal in this is to help you—and us—grasp your ability before it gets out of control, or falls into the wrong hands, not to involve ourselves in problems we are unable to fix. You're young. Please let those of us with more experience lead this."

"We're both very sorry about what occurred to Kyra." Waters pauses a beat seemingly expecting my interruption, but I don't offer one. "Ms. Lark, whether your friend was once trustworthy or not, she is now part of Director Manning's agenda. You can't let thoughts that she's somehow innocent cloud your vision."

I clench my fists at his order.

She is *innocent.*

Isn't she?

"You must see the larger picture," Waters continues. "From our intel, we are aware Manning's interest in you has grown. He didn't recognize what he had while you were in custody. Now he's discovered his mistake. His interest is why we will be relocating you to a remote base, as this location does not offer the security we need. Elore is at a standstill for the time being with New Philadelphia, but it won't be for long."

"Relocating me? I just got here." I grab onto the edge of the table. "And what about Aron? You took him as a prisoner of war and he's just sitting there. No one has told him what's to happen to him."

"We don't have anything to do with him yet," Ruiz says. "In Elore, he was marked as one to watch. We felt he might be approachable by Affinity, but there were too many unknowns."

"For now, he must wait," Waters adds. "Even so, he's no longer your concern. Tomorrow you will be leaving for training elsewhere."

I open my mouth to argue, but Ruiz cuts me off. "So that means we should get going with the EP activation."

I try to piece together an alternative plan, but nothing comes. I need extra time. There has to be another way to help Father and Aron so, for now, I keep quiet. Anyway, the EP could be useful.

"Yes," I say.

"The techs are ready." Waters shuffles us into the first room and the media viewer flickers on, showing my image, brain, and a mix of facts and figures.

A middle-aged woman dressed in a smock ushers me to the chair and reclines it. "Unlike your implantation, you will be aware of this procedure," she says. "Everything should appear as virtual reality for you in a moment."

Ruiz walks to my side and places a hand on my shoulder. "This will be all right. It's been cleared for me to maintain contact with you while you're away."

"What about Father and Meyer?"

She shakes her head. "I will relay whatever I'm allowed."

A pang stabs through me at the thought of leaving Father here alone. He'll have no one.

"Everyone ready?" Waters asks.

"Yes, sir," says a lab tech from across the room.

The tech to my right raises a handheld and scans my face. "Lie still, please."

I do, but from the corner of my eye, I can see the media viewer go crazy, blipping in and out.

My vision goes white.

CHAPTER EIGHT

The blank virtual reality space transform into a colorless, but structured room. A soft buzzing builds in volume until I can discern a few words, but not enough for me to recognize what's being said. I walk to the wall and place my ear against the surface, but still can't make out anything.

Is this what I'm supposed to be doing?

A flat voice I vaguely recognize drowns out the buzzing background noise. "Avlyn, can you hear me?"

"Uh ... yes?"

"This is President Waters. You'll notice this restricted space has no exits. This allows us to keep your access to information limited for the time being and learn more about immersion. As you progress with your training, we will allow you additional access to the system."

As Waters speaks, the buzzing words become louder, but they are garbled, unrecognizable.

"Are you hearing this?" I ask the empty room.

"Hearing what? You should only be hearing me," says Waters.

"The buzzing—the words." I cover my ears, hoping it will dull the ever-growing noise.

Wham.

The sound forces me to my knees.

"One hundred and ten miles to destination," the buzzing voice says.

The room fades in and out, alternating the white space with the inside of a hovercraft ... or at least that's what I *think* it is. It's similar to the one that transported us from Elore, except this one is lined with soldiers. Men and women stare blankly ahead, weapons in hand. On their uniforms is the DPF symbol. Direction Preservation Force, the Level One army Manning created.

Terror washes over me.

They're coming for us.

I blink twice in the hope that leaving Virtual Reality functions the same as it has in the past. The room disappears and I shoot up from the chair they have me in. The EP fully engages and information about the room and the people in it fills my vision.

"They're coming."

The lab tech places her hand on my clavicle to press me back into the seat. "Whoa, what happened there?"

Sophia Barnes
Age: 45
Sex: Female

Security Clearance: A.3
Heart Rate: Elevated

More words show, but I don't care about any of it. Waters whips around from the media viewer and comes closer to me, followed by Ruiz. The viewer goes dark.

"I'm sorry, sir," a lab tech says. "The system seems to have crashed."

"Who's coming?" Waters demands. "What did you do in there?"

Heart Rate: Elevated

"Manning … Direction …" I shake my head. "They're sending troops into New Philadelphia. One hundred and ten miles out."

Ruiz swipes her device. "Impossible. All the intel indicates Manning is holding. There has been no movement."

"I don't know. I saw it in there. An attack is imminent."

Ruiz snatches me up and pulls me out of the chair. "To be safe, we need to get you to a secure location."

Waters paces while working on his handheld. "Someone get me information!" he shouts. "If what Avlyn says is true, we have approximately twenty minutes to launch a defensive." Waters eyes Ruiz and then looks my way. "Get her out."

"I already have a guard ready for you," Ruiz says.

"Is it Porter?" I ask. "My regular escort?"

Please be Ben, please.

Ruiz doesn't answer. As we step outside the lab, a uniformed male soldier with a stunner on his side salutes Ruiz. My hope sinks. It's the same guy who came with us into the city. The guard with the reddish-orange hair. *Officer Nate Smith* scrolls in my vision.

Ruiz ignores the gesture. "Escort Ms. Lark to emergency bunker two-ten."

"Yes, ma'am," barks the soldier, gripping my upper arm.

"Avlyn, do as he says and you will be fine. Contact me using your comm if necessary," Ruiz instructs before she turns and walks away.

Smith wordlessly guides me down the hall and out the front of the building. My EP goes berserk, green information scrolling the bottom and sides of my vision. My first instinct is to blink and deactivate the data feed, but I don't. Some of it might be useful.

"Where's Porter?" I ask.

Could Waters know about Ben's ability? Is that why he's not here? And what about my father and Meyer. Are they in two-ten?

Smith silently continues to pilot me on the sidewalk. I flinch as a shrieking siren noise fills the air. A few people jog past us. Their IDs appear in my vision and disappear just as quickly. My guard keeps the constant pace and ushers me forward. From the way of the city center, a second siren sounds, a warning scrolls.

Emergency Alert: Those in New Philadelphia proper, please return to your homes or to the nearest safety facility in your district.

The Flexx on my wrist vibrates. I catch that the message is from Ben, but not what it says as Smith yanks me.

Alert: Incoming vessel. 3.1 miles Southwest. 1 minute to arrival time scrolls in green.

One minute? That's less time than Waters said.

Smith steers me to the side of a nearby building. *Detention Center*, reads the sign, the facility Aron's being held in.

"Will they be evacuating the detention center?"

"Get down and wait—"

A massive gray ship zooms over the top of us, drowning out Smith's voice as it heads from the city.

New Philadelphia Aircraft 6875

It's one of ours.

A deafening roar blasts from behind us. Both Smith and I whip around to view a second ship with an Elorian symbol on the hull flying from sight, leaving a building partially destroyed and on fire. The flames swirl into the sky, and people pour from the wrecked exit.

Please continue to bunker 210 blinks in red across the bottom of my vision, followed by more instructions.

Smith yanks me to my feet and into a run toward the bunker, yelling, "Let's go!"

There's a second roar, and an unseen force thrusts me to the pavement, Smith landing on my back. Dazed, I lean against the weight, rolling him off me. I throw my hand to my mouth and pull into myself when I see him.

Officer Nate Smith: Deceased

Blood flows from his head and down his freckled face, puddling onto the sidewalk. A giant, jagged piece of the building lay six feet ahead of us. How it hit Smith and missed me, I'm not sure. In front of me, flames cover the detainment center, just like the other building. A chunk of the front lay in ruins.

Aron's inside.

Panic wells up in me and I check Nate another time. Still deceased, according to the EP. I grab for his stunner as another one of our ships darts overhead, shooting at a ship from Elore.

Please continue to bunker 210

My EP directs me to the bunker, and I jump up and head toward it. A deafening explosion sounds from behind me, and I swing around to the detainment center again. Flames lick at the building and workers scramble from the wreckage, some injured, some not.

I circle back. I *can't* leave Aron in there.

With surprising speed, I hurtle through a gaping hole in the wall into the foyer and pass dust-covered people trying to exit. My lungs fill with soot and sting with the desire for clean air. Despite that, I continue, but to appease them I stretch and hold the collar of my shirt over my mouth.

Do not attempt. Risk of injury or death: 92%

Both my lungs and the EP agree that entering the detainment center is a terrible idea, but I don't care. Ignoring the warning, I press into the obliterated foyer of the building. The metal door leading from the foyer is blown out and lies a few feet from me on the ground, contorted and twisted. I race through the opening, down the corridor. A crying woman rushes past me to freedom as I move away from it. The smoke has cleared in here, and I drop the collar of my shirt from my mouth.

From outside, two more muffled booms sound. I duck and wait for something terrible to happen, but nothing new shows in my EP. The drab door marked 107B remains intact ahead, leading to the cells. Relief washes over me. If Aron's still inside, he's probably safe.

My head spins as I try to work out what to do now. I palm the security pad.

Access Denied

I do it again and concentrate. *Why isn't it working?*

Ugh, that device Waters implanted ... it's blocking me. I could try to hack it manually.

A roar sounds from above, shaking the building, and a few pieces of the ceiling tumble onto me.

There's no time. I change the settings on the stunner to maximum and step back from the door. I fire directly into where I assume the locking mechanism would be. The door slides back and an alarm blares. I throw my hands to my ears to block the piercing shriek and move into the breach, peering into the window of cell four. In the room, Aron paces, eyes wide. I slam my fist to the window.

Aron looks up at me and darts over, and though I can't hear

him, his mouth moves as if he's yelling for me to get him out. I wave for him to back up, but he stands frozen until I hold up the stunner and mouth, *Get back.*

This time he listens, and I shoot at the door latch three times. Finally, it slides away with a whoosh. A second alarm blares, alternating in time with the first. Aron dashes from his cell.

"What's happening?" he yells over the alarm.

"We're under attack by Elore. Stay in back of me."

I grasp Aron's arm and lead him through the partially destroyed hallway. Ready for whoever might find us, I keep my weapon extended in the deserted building. Outside, multiple buildings are damaged and burning, and crafts fly above in a shooting war.

My handheld buzzes on my wrist and a message flashes into my vision. I grab Aron and yank him down beside me along the opening we came from.

You are ordered to continue to bunker 210.

"Ms. Lark," says Waters in my comm, making me flinch.
"Yes?"

"You have a direct order to continue to bunker two-ten. I know your escort went down a few minutes ago. Is your EP malfunctioning? Are you injured?"

My stomach tumbles. "No, sir."

"Then what's the problem? Do you require a new escort?"

"Sir, I have Barton. Can I take him to two-ten with me?" I glance toward Aron, who appears about as terrified as when I threatened him in Elore.

"Ms. Lark, Barton is still considered an enemy. I'm sending a new escort team to retrieve you. They will take Barton into custody."

"He will be safe?"

"Haven't you noticed we're in the middle of a *war*? No, I can't guarantee his safety."

"And Ruiz agrees with this?" I shout.

The comm is silent.

"Waters?"

"Ruiz will do as I say," he says. "We don't have a choice at this point."

I tap the comm below my ear and disengage it. I scan the grounds and see no one coming for us yet. Without hesitation, I slam the stunner into Aron's hands.

"Okay ... try not to kill anyone unnecessarily, but I need to do something."

"What are you doing?"

"We have to get you out of the city, and I can't do it if they're tracking me."

Aron's eyes grow wide, but he nods and grips the weapon.

I sink onto my heels and take in a gulp of air, trying to imagine the chaos isn't there. As I breathe, the surroundings disappear and everything goes white. I'm back in the doorless prison they built to contain me. I press my hand to the smooth wall.

They won't control me, I think over and over. I close my eyes and focus on the sensation of the wall. *This thing needs to be destroyed.* I open my lids to see the wall remaining in place. A stinging sensation starts at the tips of my fingers as I lightly press my hands into it, working its way through my limbs and forcing me to push harder on the slick surface. Cracks spread out in a spider web from under my hands, glowing red. The red grows and fills the surface. Popping noises ring out from the wall and it shatters, falling over my body, pricking against my skin.

When I look up, the wall is gone.

"Disengage the EP tracking function."

My surroundings go black, then gray, and then the space around me returns. The solid walls are replaced with iridescent, partially transparent code. The code churns to form geometric shape patterns.

Tracking Disengaged shows in my vision.

The tension releases and I concentrate on determining my next step.

"Show me a schematic of the compound."

An overhead layout of the New Philly compound displays. Our current position glows green, and I search the names of the buildings closest to us to get a better view of the grounds' layout. I tap a spot on the schematic.

"Destination."

The spot illuminates and directions appear in my vision. I touch my hand to the schematic again.

"Download directions."

The schematic glows brighter, vibrates, and, as if sucked into my hand, the whole thing disappears. I shake my head at the tingling sensation the download process caused.

"Information on Aron Barton. Currently held prisoner."

The code swarms once more to form the shape of Aron's ID image and words scroll up the space in front of me.

Name: Aron Barton
Age: 17
Sex: Male
Current Status: Prisoner of war from the city of Elore. Held in custody.
Status: Risk of continued containment high. Scheduled for possible elimination.

Elimination? My stomach lurches and I drop to my knees. Ben was right. I bring up the message that came in from him earlier. The words read in my vision.

Where are you? I'm being called to duty.

I need him here. This is our one chance. I formulate code in my mind and set it loose.

I'm embedding a temporary tracking program in my Flexx. Only your handheld can access it. Use it to find me. Now. It's time to go. If you can, get Meyer, I message back.

My heart surges at the thought of leaving Meyer behind. But he can take care of himself so it's a risk I'm willing to take. I'll contact him when I get to where I'm going. Not waiting for Ben's answer, I blink twice to resume to the real world.

Aron points the stunner ahead of us, hands shaking. Sweat beads over his pale face. I nab his hand and pull the stunner from it.

"Come on," I say.

"What were you doing?" His voice quivers.

No way will I fill him in on everything I saw, he might panic. I need Aron focused. "Waters informed me on the comm he won't guarantee your safety."

"*Can* you help?" he yelps.

"Do you want to be locked up for who knows how long?"

Aron gives me a perplexed expression and shakes his head no.

"Then follow me."

I tear through the compound, adhering to the directions in my EP, Aron in tow. A troupe of soldiers with the red stripes on their shoulders move past and ignore us, moving onto their duties.

As we run, I tap my comm and page Ruiz.

"Avlyn, you need to return to your assigned bunker," Ruiz's voice rings in my ear.

"No. Not before I have more answers. You know about Aron, don't you?"

"Avlyn, return to the bunker, and we will try to get this sorted out," Ruiz instructs firmly.

"You know I can't do that." I reach to tap off the comm.

The bombings have slowed, and I haven't heard an attack or seen any ships in the air since Aron and I escaped the detainment center. The directions in my EP lead us past the facility I was held in for the first three days here and its adjoining courtyard. We cut through the yard and head north. The storage buildings come into view. I increase our pace until we arrive at the roll-up door, placing my hand on the security pad.

I close my eyes and visualize releasing the door. In my mind, the door vanishes and I open my eyes to the actual one retracting.

"Did they provide you with access?" Aron asks, eyes wide.

"I have it covered. Get in."

We slip inside, and I palm the interior security panel to shut the door again. I check my Flexx. No message yet from Ben.

What if they have him?

"Avlyn, what are you doing?"

I take a deep breath. "I don't know yet. I need a few minutes to think. As of now, I have no idea who to trust—"

"And you trust me?"

"You were trying to do the right thing in Elore. You had no concept what you did would have hurt me. I know you're a good person, but Waters and Ruiz won't listen. We have to get out of here."

Panic washes over his face as he realizes what we're doing. "At this point, I'd rather risk returning and take my chances with imprisonment. Please take me where you're supposed to go and let them arrest me. I tried to save you in Elore, and you freed me from the cell before they bombed it more. We're even."

He turns to palm the security pad, but the door remains closed.

Aron swings around to me. "How's this door function?"

"Aron, you don't get it."

"What am I supposed to get? You'll get me killed!"

"If I take you back there, I can't guarantee they'll just lock you up."

"What do you mean? If they intended to kill me, wouldn't they have done it by now?"

"I'm not sure. But I do know you're … you could be locked up forever." Telling him they have him scheduled for potential elimination might be too much right now.

"Forever? How do you know?"

"It doesn't matter. I know, and Waters is sending me away, so I won't be able to protect you."

Aron's shoulders tense. "What are we going to do, take those?" He motions to the two scooters.

"I hope—" My eyes swivel to the metallic four-seater hover pods in the corner and I race for one of them, ripping off the fabric tarpaulin half-covering it. "This."

It looks worse than the first time I saw it; old and as if it wouldn't make it ten feet. I hate the idea of flying, but we'll both fit inside, and it will get us farther than the scooters.

"That's a piece of junk."

"If I get it running, it will get us out of here faster." I palm the security pad on the right of the door. "Release both sides," I command.

The doors on each side of the pod slide up. I stuff the fabric behind the pilot's seat and slide in. The interior is tight, but it will do. Aron still stands outside the pod, and I duck to see out the open door on his side.

"Get in!" I yell.

He huffs and climbs in. "This pile of junk won't operate. You're crazy."

"Meyer said the operating system was shot. I'll fix it."

"Now?"

"Yes, now. It should only take a second." I ignore the incredulous stare digging into the side of my head and place my hands on the touch-screen control panel. Bright white bursts in my vision, and in an instant my consciousness makes the damaged connections link again. The pod whirs to attention.

I blink and the front panel lights up. Aron jolts in his seat.

"How'd you do that so fast?"

"I'll tell you later. Right now, I need you to listen. You can't go back into custody." I search for something reassuring to tell him. "If you come now, I'll try to negotiate getting you released."

"Get me released? Can you do that?" He squints at me slightly, doubt filling his face.

"You've seen the kinds of things I can do. I'm valuable to them."

"Avlyn, this won't work. Take me back." He reaches to free the door and I slam my hand to the console, ordering the pod's operating system to lock it. Aron twists toward me, eyes wide. Eyeing the closed rolling door, my heart sinks. Still no Ben. No Meyer.

"Listen, you're not getting it."

"Obviously not!" he yells.

"Aron, if you stay ..." I pause, but the words must be said, "they're planning to kill you."

CHAPTER NINE

Aron drops back into his seat, breathing shallowly, not saying a word.

Inhaling deeply, pushing my fear of flying as far into the back of my mind as possible, I place my hands on the panel again. The craft lifts, my stomach dropping at the same time. Directions to fly it display in my vision. A bead of sweat runs down the side of my face. How will I do this?

Don't overthink.

I swipe my hands over the control panel, following the EP's lead, and activate the rolling door of the storage unit. The pod hovers over the scooters. The EP displays the best possible route, interrupted as a new alert scrolls across the bottom of my vision.

Missing Person Alert:
Name: Avlyn Lark
Age: 17

Sex: Female
Description: 5'6". Straight, Dark Brown, Chin-Length Hair. Light
Skin. Hazel Eyes.

They'll be looking for us elsewhere now, too.

Map of New Philadelphia, I think. The image appears and lights the screen of the hover pod.

I rack my brain for the word I need. "Salon? Where is the salon located?"

Five potential locations illuminate on the screen.

67th Avenue ... Orange ... Broadway ...

Broadway. That's the one.

Hovering toward the open doors of the storage unit, I peer out for a visual of our immediate surroundings. The sky is clear of warships, and I dart the pod forward to our new destination. According to my EP, most of the activity has moved south, away from our current location.

"Where are we going?" Aron asks.

"Out of the city. But if I don't make a stop first, we won't get far."

I weave unfamiliar, deserted streets, trusting the EP's directions, until I spot the salon. A back entrance illuminates in my vision, so I lower the pod near it, hidden from the sight of the main street. As we kiss the ground, the vehicle groans.

Aron asks, looking around, "Why are we here?"

"Just get out."

"Avlyn?" Aron's voice is laced with frustration, but I ignore him.

The pod doors slide up and I grab for the tarp behind my seat. As I pull it out, Aron's shoulders droop, but he does as I say. A disembodied voice from a speaker orders people to return to their homes. It's the same evacuation message from my EP message earlier.

Once out, I use the tarp to cover the pod and gesture to Aron toward the back entrance of the salon. A small electronic security device is located on the door, keeping it shut. I place my hand over it and concentrate.

Disarm lock and security devices.

The door unlatches and slides away. I poke my head in through the opening and slowly step into the salon.

"Hello?" I call.

No sounds come from inside. Lucky for us, the owners must have obeyed the emergency alert continually playing outside. I motion for Aron to follow and head straight to the front of the shop to search for the tools I saw used the other day. A viewing screen sits to the left of a table.

Aron runs his hands over the back of a chair positioned in front of a mirror. "What is this place?"

"I'm not sure exactly. Yesterday I went into the city. In here, they were doing all sorts of ... well, ridiculous things. Turning people's hair strange colors and such. It seemed silly at the time, but if we're going to hide on the outside, we can't appear as ourselves."

Aron gazes at a digital image of a man with a green streak on the side of his head. The green-haired man's eyes are a shade brighter than his hair. Beneath the image scrolls the words *Hair and Eye Color Alterations. A few minutes will transform your whole image. Latest CosmoNano Technology.*

"Well, if you make me look like that, we won't stand out at all," he scoffs, nodding to the green-haired man.

"Yeah ... I'm not doing that."

"Do you know how to operate it?"

"Not yet, but I'll figure it out."

"Very reassuring." Aron cracks a nervous smile, forming the dimple on his cheek. "I might end up with green hair after all."

"I'll explain to you later, but stop worrying. No green hair. Give me a few seconds."

Next to the viewer sits a handheld marked *CosmoNano*. I pick it up and touch the information port on the viewing screen.

"Um ... *CosmoNano* instructions?"

Shimmering code flies directly in front of me and forms a female head with shoulder-length hair. At the crown, the neutral strands change to chestnut brown. I reach and touch the hair, sending a tingling sensation up my arms.

"Blonde."

From the crown, the hair color shifts, running the length of the strands, changing from dark to light. I shake my head. It's too light, almost white-blonde, and would stand out too much.

"Darker ... three shades."

The hair darkens as if wet, root to tips. I place my hand on the top of the false virtual head.

"Download instructions."

I blink twice and return to the salon. Aron's staring at me, confused.

"Okay. I've got it."

"What are you talking about?" he asks. "You didn't do anything. You just tapped the viewer."

"I told you I'll explain it later—trust me."

Frustrated, Aron crosses his arms and paces across the room.

"I'll change my hair first, and you can watch." I hold the scanner to my head and activate it. The device vibrates in my hand and emits a soft, yellow light. I watch my reflection as I move the scanner along my brown hair. Aron stares, holding his breath, waiting for something to happen. Probably for my hair to turn green. The new color travels down the hair shaft until my entire head is a caramel-blonde color, similar to the color Aron's is now.

Eyes, I think.

The front of the device flips up, and I scan my eye and blink, opening my lids to sky-blue irises in the mirror. Aron steps back and inhales sharply.

I gesture with the scanner to the chair and few feet away. "Purple, right?"

Aron lets out a half-hearted laugh as he perches on the edge of the chair. I roll my eyes and run the scanner over his hair, changing it to a dark brown, similar to my natural color. When the process completes, I adjust the setting for his eyes and morph them to amber.

Aron releases a breath and hops up from the chair. "Well, this is new." He takes a last peek at himself in the mirror, then heads for the door.

With his newly brunette hair and eyes he reminds me a bit of Meyer.

I deactivate the device and place it back where I found it, following Aron's lead. Once we're through the rear of the salon, I secure the door, reset the security alarm, and run to the hover pod. I glance at my handheld another time for a message from

Ben. Nothing. Emptiness fills me at the thought of leaving Meyer and him behind, but I can't wait any longer. I'll have to try to get in contact with him later.

At the vehicle, Aron helps me throw off the tarp, and I free the doors by touching the security lock and visualizing it. We swing into our seats and the doors shut us in. I stuff the fabric into the back of the pod.

"Ready?" I ask.

"Not really." Aron's lips quirk into a small smile and he motions to the console. "But I have to admit this is pretty exciting. When do I ever act so ... *irrational?*"

"Hold on," I say, placing my hands on the console and willing the craft to start.

Small incoming vehicles detected.

My EP reveals the outline of two fast-moving figures rounding to the back of the building. I swipe at the console screen.

"Someone's coming." It could be Ben, but it may not.

"How do you know?" Aron's voice cracks slightly as he swings his head around to get a look.

I don't answer and scramble to get the pod fully engaged. Something inside calls for me to stop. I resist its urging.

As the pod barely lifts from the ground, scooters ridden by two helmeted men skid to a halt, blocking our exit.

Ben Porter
Meyer Quinn

Ben made it, and he brought Meyer. I let out a huge sigh of relief.

Meyer throws off his helmet, waving for me to stop. The scowl on his face easily indicates his mood with me. *What did Ben tell him?* Ben dismounts the scooter and hustles to my side of the pod. No other live forms show in my EP, but I swivel in my seat to check if they've brought anyone else.

I lower the pod and the underside clunks to the ground. At my right, Aron's face goes pasty. He'll start to change his mind if we stick around too long.

"Wait in here," I tell him. "I'll take care of this."

With a whoosh, the pod door slides up. Meyer reaches in and grabs my arm, pulling me out and to my feet. He eyes my newly blonde hair and shakes his head.

"What are you doing? This stuff is only going to get you and other people killed."

"There's more happening here than you know about," I protest and pull from him, not wanting Aron to panic any more than he already is. "Get in."

"Avlyn, there's always more than we know about."

"That was the identical problem in Elore. Too many secrets and half-truths. This place is no different," I say.

Aron flings open his door and moves from the pod. "Avlyn, we should go. If we don't, they'll re-arrest me and send you away."

Meyer stares at me, frowning, and his voice full of concern. "What does he mean they're sending you away?"

Ben scoffs. "I knew this would happen."

I shoot a glare toward Aron. "Didn't I tell you to stay in the pod?" Aron doesn't move and I resume my attention to Meyer.

"Waters said that before the attack. He's relocating me."

Ben's eyes grow wide. "Where is he sending you?"

I lower my voice, stepping closer to the both of them. "All I know is Aron is scheduled for potential elimination. I *can't* leave him behind. It's not right. Waters won't tell me where I'm headed or what he's using me for. For all I know, he's as bad as Manning."

Meyer shakes his head. "You're making too much of this. Let's go back and talk it out with Ruiz."

"They were intending to let Aron rot in that cell while Elore bombed the detainment center!" I object. "No one else would have released him, so I did. They don't care about him—"

Meyer pulls me in again. "I get that you care about Aron's safety, and I respect you for that, but this is ridiculous." He leans in, whispering in my ear, "It won't work. You have no idea where you're going."

"It will work," I insist. "It *has* to."

Meyer lets go of my arm and draws back. "So tell me, what's your plan, anyway?"

My mind reels. I hadn't really thought that far ahead. The plan becomes pretty thin after getting us out of the city.

"Give me a little time. I'll figure it out on the way."

"Wait," Aron interjects, still standing on the passenger side of the pod. Apparently he has excellent hearing. "You're dragging me along, and you don't even know where we're headed yet?"

"You need my help and you're in no position to be choosy. Now get back inside," I yell. He doesn't move, but I flash him a scowl and he lowers himself in.

I address Meyer. "Come with us or let us go." *Please come.*

"No way," he says firmly. "If you do this, you'll get yourself killed. I'm not letting that happen."

Ben moves forward. "Meyer, get in the pod."

I flick my eyes toward Ben. "I'm sorry I didn't believe you before."

"It's fine." Ben activates the pod's back door. "We just need to get out of this place and all drop off the map."

Meyer stands in stunned silence for a moment. "I thought you were helping me escort her back in?"

Ben shrugs. "I guess I lied." He looks to me. "I knew I'd get him to come easier if he thought he was bringing you back in. Took less explanation."

Meyer blocks my path. His dark eyes filled with bewilderment. "I'm confused. You're just Avlyn's guard. Why would you want to go with her?"

"Ben's my brother," I admit, my mind still reeling at the truth of it.

"Your twin?" Meyer looks back and forth between the two of us. "I thought he was dead?"

"Me, too."

Meyer stares at Ben and you can almost see his thoughts revolving. "Wait. Can you do the same things as Avlyn?"

Ben breaks from Meyer's question and flashes me an expression of concern. "Just get in the vehicle." He climbs into the back seat.

"You have no concept of what you're getting into, Avlyn." Meyer stands firm. "Ruiz will guide us."

"I'd love it if she could, but I'm afraid Waters is in her ear." I grasp Meyer's upper arm. "If I go back, I'm gone, and Aron might spend the rest of his life in prison—*if* he's lucky. Most likely, they'll kill him, and if Waters discovers Ben's ability—which is likely now—his life may be over, too. I can't let that happen."

Meyer sighs and shakes his head. He's been in a similarly impossible position before. "Agreed, but I have to make sure you don't get yourself killed. We need assistance. Once we're safe, promise to consider letting Ruiz help. I can prove to you she's doing the right thing." He twists from me and peers into the back of the pod. "Toss me the tarp."

Relieved, I slowly reach into the rear of the pod for the fabric in back of the pilot seat.

Meyer tosses it over the two scooters, covering them completely. "They'll find them, but we'll be long disappeared before then."

Smiling, I pull open the front door and make for the pilot's seat.

"Do you know the coordinates?" Meyer asks, throwing an arm in front of me.

I stop and glare at him. It's not that I *want* to fly, but piloting the pod myself makes me feel more secure.

"No."

"Then let me fly. Please."

"You're letting him pilot?" Ben asks, studying Meyer suspiciously from the back.

"I trust Meyer with my life." With that, I climb into the spot alongside Ben. Aron has the passenger spot in the front next to Meyer.

"Where are you taking us?" Ben asks.

Meyer turns and smiles. "Oh, I have a place."

CHAPTER TEN

On the flight, Meyer has me hack into New Philadelphia's mainframe and plant a few "red herrings," as he calls them. What fish have to do with coding, I'm not sure, but essentially I imbedded false information so they'd search for us in the opposite direction from that of our destination.

As the pod sweeps over the landscape, I'm amazed by the diversity of plant life and terrain, from scrub brush to tall green trees—*Sugar Pines*, according to my EP—and even some other trees with yellow and orange leaves. Elore's trees were mostly a pine variety, so other than on vids, I've never seen anything like this.

"Maybe you can inform us where we're going?" Aron asks. My eyes are drawn to his newly brown hair. From the back, Meyer and Aron look more alike than different. I reach forward and tap his shoulder, willing the nanos controlling his hair and eye color to return them to normal. As he turns toward me, I do the same to mine. He nods, probably realizing what I did.

Meyer sighs. "Gabrielle, the woman who raised me with Jayson, lives off the grid. Jayson gave me the coordinates in case of an emergency before he died."

Hearing Meyer mention Jayson's name pricks at my stomach. I didn't know he had a wife. "I'd say this is an emergency. Is she with Affinity?"

"She's with herself," he says. "A hacker, like you. Pretty quirky."

"Are you saying I'm quirky?"

Meyer chuckles. "Could be. She's a genius and a jack-of-all-trades. Most resourceful person I've ever met. She also has access to Underground Intel and communications that no one else seems to. If anyone can help us, it's her."

Thinking of Jayson and Gabrielle, I realize how I've left my own father alone in New Philly. I open my mouth to ask Meyer about him, but Ben touches my arm and my vision turns to white and forms the shape of a room. The walls shimmer in anticipation.

"Ben?" I call, still not really knowing what to expect from this new type of communication.

Nothing happens, but the code constructing the walls continues to blink faster. I shut my eyes and concentrate. From behind my closed eyelids, the space illuminates brighter. I press my eyelids together harder and take a deliberate draw of breath. A soft buzzing fills my head and grows louder and louder until I throw my hands to my ears.

"Ben!" I yell.

The buzzing stops, replaced by silence.

"I'm here," Ben's voice sounds from behind me.

I flinch and swing around, eyes wide, to my brother standing in our virtual space.

"What's going to happen to my father and Sanda?" I ask. "With all of us gone like this, there'll be a lot of questions. They might think he was involved, but he just found out about my ability a few days ago. My father doesn't know much."

"Sanda left the city this morning. She might be safe. I'm unsure about your father. They may detain him." Ben sighs. "Let's take this one step at a time. Getting you out of the city is my first goal."

I drop into a squat and comb my fingers through my hair. "This is not how I wanted this to play out. Do you know what caused Elore to attack?"

"Power play, most likely. Philly attacked them, so Manning's probably attempting to show that he's not weak."

I nod. "We can see if we can stream Elorian media when we get to where we're headed. Maybe this Gabrielle can help us sort this out."

He takes my hand and pulls me up. "I need you to know I'll support you by following Meyer there, but you have to promise me we will disappear for good soon. We can go somewhere our abilities don't matter."

I sigh. "It seems so selfish."

"What good are we if we're dead, or if someone's using our ability for the wrong reasons?"

The pod jolts, throwing me into reality as it prepares to land.

"Sorry that was so rough," Meyer says with a laugh. "I haven't flown for a while."

"Told you I should have flown," I mumble under my breath.

Aron sighs. If he wasn't already, now I'm confident he wonders what he's gotten himself into.

Meyer situates the pod below a group of evergreens to make it less conspicuous from above. The four of us climb from the pod onto a landscape browned by the autumn air. Wispy clouds float in the atmosphere high above.

"This way," Meyer calls, swiping his handheld as he starts off, leading our tiny group.

"I don't see anything," Aron says, gazing around at our new surroundings.

I shrug and pass him, trailing behind Meyer through a clearing of flat, scrubby grass that scratches across the fabric of my pants. When I catch up to Meyer, he turns his head toward me.

"Can you tell us exactly what we're doing here?" I ask as we walk. "This needs to be a team effort."

"Look, if we were going to go anywhere, it would be Gabrielle's. It's safe and she'll know what to do, but to be honest, I'm not feeling right about having Aron with us long-term."

I want to argue with him, but it's no use. Meyer might be right. Aron's a wild card, and I could be forcing him into an unnecessary risk by staying with Ben and me. Getting him out of New Philadelphia might have been enough.

"You positive you just don't want him with us?" I ask.

A smirk crosses Meyer's lips. "Now why would you think that?" His face becomes increasingly serious. "I'm trying to be practical."

"Fine. I'll consider it as long as we find a secure place for him."

"We will," Meyer promises.

"We will what?" Aron asks as he and Ben come up in back of us.

I catch Meyer's eyes and quickly divert the conversation.

"Gabrielle's place is up here."

"Right," Meyer agrees, studying the instructions on his handheld. "See the grouping of rocks there to the left? The coordinates say it's the location."

A green glow illuminates lightly from and around the rock formation in my EP. It can't identify it, but it knows something's there.

"But there's nothing there," Ben says.

"I know it looks that way." Meyer dashes to the rock formation, and I follow with Ben and Aron behind. He pauses in front of it and swipes at his Flexx, letting out a chuckle. "Hope she's home."

I smack him lightly on the arm and he flinches.

"What?" he says and returns to working on the handheld, a broad smile overtaking his face.

Ahead of us, the ground shimmers and disappears, revealing a metal hatch. Some sort of camouflaging tech, similar to the kind that covered the panel to the tunnel when we attempted our escape back in Elore, but maybe even more advanced. The hatch slides back, revealing a staircase. My stomach roils, memories rushing forward. This is too similar to the tunnel where Mother died.

"We're here," Meyer announces.

"And you're sure she's trustworthy?" Ben asks.

"These days, I'm unsure *anyone* is completely honest," Meyer admits, "but yeah. I trust her."

"Then let's go." Aron sprints ahead and disappears down the stairs.

The staircase ends at a wide corridor, illuminated by a line of lights running along the ceiling. The glow warms some of my tension away as the four of us make our way through the hall.

Meyer's handheld buzzes. He stops and quickly swipes on it to respond. To the left, on the wall, a small panel slides back, revealing a security pad.

"She knows we're here, but is taking precautions. I know there is a little town a few miles from here and occasionally they send traders up," Meyer explains, placing his palm on the pad. A light at the top transitions from red to green.

"Approved. Welcome, Meyer Quinn," says a disembodied female voice.

Next to the pad, a door reveals itself in the wall and skates back. A plump, brown- skinned woman dressed in a loose tan shirt and navy pants stands in the opening, arms spread wide.

"Meyer, it's been too long," she says in a gravelly, low-pitched voice. She looks to be about forty-five.

He moves to embrace her. "A year."

She lets him loose and clears her throat. "So, who are these people, and why are you here?"

"It's complicated. May we come in?"

Gabrielle eyes us and turns to gesture us in. "Be my guest."

She leads us down a dim hallway to a room filled with several media viewers. My EP fills with information, overwhelming both my vision and thoughts, so I blink twice to deactivate it for now. On a table to my left rests a disassembled micro drone, parts strewn out over the surface. Aron walks to the table and retrieves one of the pieces.

"Little project I'm working on," Gabrielle says. "I kind of dabble in lots of things."

Aron returns the tech to the surface.

Meyer stuffs his hands in his pockets and smirks. "So, we're kind of in trouble."

"Hon, I wouldn't expect much less," Gabrielle says. "You were always in trouble. But how'd you go dragging these other nice people into the whole mess?"

"Why do you assume *I'm* the one who caused it?" Meyer asks, eyeing me.

Despite my hesitation, we tell Gabrielle the entire story. *Everything*: how Ben can sense my emotions and was even able to contact me in my mind; that we can immerse into a computer system to hack it. Now Meyer and Aron know the whole of it, too.

A shiver travels through my entire body at the thought. The more people who know about us, the more vulnerable we are. I catch Ben's tight expression and am fairly certain he feels the same way.

"And who's this guy?" Gabrielle nods to Aron.

"Aron is a friend of mine from Elore, but not a member of Affinity," I explain. "Philly captured him on our escape."

"It's not like I'm going to hold not being a part of Affinity against him." Gabrielle chuckles. "Since I left them years ago myself."

"Aron's a genius with drone tech," I offer.

Aron, continuing to stand alongside the disassembled drone, shifts his weight and smirks enough to form the dimple on his cheek.

"'Genius' is a bit much," he protests modestly, looking at me. "I saw how you handled the drones I built."

Heat crawls up my neck. I did shoot the tech with ease, but

I'm a different case than most.

"I'll have to put you to work while you're here." Gabrielle walks to Aron and slaps him on the back. His eyes widen and he moves to the side. His reaction to Gabrielle must be how I was the first time I met Jayson.

"We need a place to stay for a few days and make a plan," Meyer continues. "This was the best place I could think of. Maybe you can figure out somewhere for us to go to lay low long-term?"

Upon hearing Meyer's words, guilt hurls through me. By joining us, he's giving up everything.

"I'll give it my best shot. I have several places you might be able to go long-term, but I need to do some digging." Gabrielle steps over to Meyer. "This place is somewhat remote, and it should buy you some time. You have three days. And store your pod in my underground hangar."

Meyer looks to me and I nod. "Three days should be enough," he agrees.

Gabrielle addresses Ben and me. "Now, let's dig a little deeper to understand this ability the two of you seem to have."

CHAPTER ELEVEN

In the hall outside my room, Meyer tosses me something. I catch it and examine the clear, rectangular plastic package holding a beige bar. "What's this?"

"Breakfast. It's cherry."

"Hmm." I tear the package with my teeth and stuff the wrapper in my pocket, trying to banish thoughts of a plate of pancakes from of my head. Meyer had all sorts of talk about non-printed food, but I've barely been able to enjoy any since I've been out of Elore.

"Gabrielle came in and spoke to me this morning," Meyer says between bites of his own bar. "From her sources and from poking around in the Underground net, she thinks she found some location prospects, but we need to make sure they're safe. Later on, when we have time, we'll try to patch you two in and get additional intel, but first she wants to study some of your data. Apparently, she stayed up late last night and coded a program."

"Sounds good." How Ben will feel about it I'm unsure, but he doesn't protest after I tell him learning more about how our abilities work together is a sound theory.

In the lab, Gabrielle hooks Ben and me up to wires stringing from us to the computer system. I shift on the cold metal seat, trying to block out the fact we'll probably be here all afternoon, but I'm excited to try immersing into a system with Ben.

I touch the wires attached to my head. "Ben and I don't need these to get into the system."

"I know. Hold still." Gabrielle attaches another wire with a sticky substance. "They'll help me monitor you, and I don't have that fancy tech from the city. This does the same job, but it's a little sloppier."

Gabrielle ducks under the wire and heads from the room, leaving Ben and me alone. He gives me a half smile. "You sure we can't run away right now?"

I lift several of the wires hanging between the two of us. "How could we with this stuff all over us?"

"All right." Gabrielle rounds into the doorway with Meyer and Aron in tow. "Everything is ready to go. Meyer, you handle the vitals. Aron, you're with me, guiding the scenario."

She walks around Ben and me, avoiding the wires. "To start, the sequence I'm running you through is self-contained. Avlyn, it's very similar to the VR training exercises you should have received with Affinity. Ben, I'm certain you experienced military training with VR in Philly. You mentioned you controlled the environment with your thoughts, so I want you to work on that first. When you're ready to begin my sequence, cue me to begin. After today, I'll make additional modifications depending on the findings." Gabrielle pats me on the shoulder and has a seat next to Aron in front of one of the viewing screens.

"Will you be able to see the sim?" I ask.

"The program taps into your EP and should relay what you see. Get your bearings in there, and when you're ready for me to start, let me know."

I reach for Ben's hand.

"You two ready?"

Before I have the chance to answer, Ben and I immerse and Gabrielle's lab filled with viewing screens disappears.

The space surrounding us sparkles, and when I stare intently at its makeup, the construct of tiny code becomes clear. The pattern begins to vibrate and whooshes around us as if picked up by a high wind. I grip Ben's hand tighter to make sure the storm of code doesn't take *us* away, too.

"Ready?" Ben asks. "How about you go first?"

"What should we do?"

"How about take me to your favorite place? It will help us get to know each other better and set up the program."

I haven't been anywhere but Elore, and that's not my favorite place, but Meyer did show me a beach scene during training in VR. I have no idea if Ben has ever gone to a real or fake beach before, but let's find out.

"Close your eyes."

After he does, I close my own and embrace the memories of the ocean waves lapping up on the shore, the dampness of the sand beneath my now-bare feet, the pink and orange of the sunset falling over the horizon.

My eyes open to the exact picture in my head. "Don't look yet," I say. "Where are we?"

Ben tips his head slightly, as if listening. "There's water ... a lot of it." He shuffles his feet over the sand. "There's dirt under our feet."

"Go ahead and look."

He looks and gasps, dropping my hand. "It's *beautiful*," he breathes. "What is this place?"

"The beach. I went here with Meyer a couple times on breaks from training. It's so unique from anything I've known. I found it calming."

"I see why." He takes in a breath of the salty air. "I'd love to stay, but Gabrielle is asking us to work. My turn."

"Okay." I shut my eyes and Ben takes my hand again.

I relax and let my mind blank as he guides us to our next location. The white swirls in my head with a buzzing intensity. The sound reverberates through my temples and then stops.

"We're here."

Ben's creation is stunning; similar to the landscape we passed over in the pod on the way to Gabrielle's. Tall trees stretch as far as I can see, covered in orange and yellow foliage. I focus to engage the EP to identify them.

Aspen trees

Ben's landscape is complete with a tall, snow-capped mountain. A bird soars and squawks above us, then swoops from view.

"This is a beautiful place, too," I say.

A sad wistfulness washes over Ben's face. "It's a lot like where Dad and I settled after we escaped Elore. We kind of existed as hermits."

"Why?"

"He was doing his best to protect me. At four, I wasn't old enough to grasp how I needed to hide my ability. In the few years before he died, he spent all his time training me."

The urge to ask Ben more about how Devan died wells inside me. It's not as if I knew the man much, but he was my bio father, too. I deserve to know.

"How did Devan die?"

Ben throws a pained expression my way and shakes his head.

I take the hint and back off. "Devan did a lot to protect you."

"Well, he can't do that anymore." Ben crosses his arms. "Gabrielle, we're ready," he shouts, his voice echoing through the forest.

The scene dissolves and replaces with a very unrealistic one, dark and angular with a streak of light shooting out in front of us. My heart pounds at the thought of not knowing what might happen next.

"Get ready," I say. I have a feeling this will be interesting.

Gabrielle's voice comes from nowhere. "Can you hear me?"

"Yes," Ben and I say in unison.

"Some interesting data came in from your manipulations. This exercise is standard VR. I kept it simple so you wouldn't be distracted from the task. Meyer, Aron, and I are tracking your reactions and how you manipulate your situations. It's set up as a series of levels. Let's see how far we get today."

"Okay," I say.

Ben plants his feet and glances at his empty hands. "Do we have any weapons?"

"That's for you to decide." Gabrielle laughs. "But it would be a good concept."

Ben shrugs at me and I copy the gesture.

"You'll figure it out. Just adhere to the path ahead of you," Gabrielle's voice instructs.

We pause for a beat for any additional instructions, but none come.

"Doesn't tell us much," I murmur.

"Pretty sure that's the point. She wants us to think on our feet. It's what we'll need to do in real life."

My legs itch to go, despite the nervous, sinking feeling in my core. Standing here won't get rid of either of them.

"Race you," I whisper, and without warning I bolt down the darkened path outlined by the thin illumination.

"That's cheating!" Ben yells behind me.

"There aren't any rules in here!" I call in return.

The urge for a weapon floods me as I zip along the path. I fixate on the idea of a stunner in my hand and cold metal fills my palm. I grip the weapon and continue. From ahead, a glint of light sparks in the darkness. The glint multiplies and then repeats a second time. A soft whirring fills my ears. I slow to a halt and Ben comes up beside me, a stunner in hand, too.

"I have a feeling that's the first level," he says.

"Rush it or hold?"

"Rush it."

With a broad smile, he leaves me in the dust, darting off toward the still-multiplying lights. I sprint to catch him despite the buzzing swarm approaching us. *110 micro drones*, according to my EP. Targets overlay several of them in my vision.

"You ready?" Ben yells, slowing to a stop.

"More than you." I smirk, raise the stunner, and fire, following the pattern my EP instructs. The drones meant for me illuminate in red in my EP, the ones for Ben in green. I depress the trigger on my stunner and the beam slams into my targets. They explode, shimmering against the black "sky" before evaporating. Immediately after, another speeds forward to replace it and my EP locks on. I press the trigger and shoot, shoot, shoot. One after another, the devices bursts out of existence.

56 drones

This is easy. Simple target practice.

"They're moving faster, coming for us," Ben shouts over the nearly deafening buzz.

The identical fact shows in my EP. We continue blasting.

24 drones

One of the drones zips our way. The targeting system marks it for me. I swallow as I mentally attempt to steady my now-shaking hands. Several of the devices break formation and speed our way. I push the trigger, and the first explodes into a ball of light, then disperses. Three more approach—two for me, one for Ben. I depress the trigger again and obliterate the next one. The remaining two charge with incredible speed. Ben aims for his and misses. My drone flies to my side before I can lift the stunner.

An electric pulse rips through my back, knocking me flat on my stomach, weapon still firmly clasped in hand. Despite the pain, I roll onto my hip and lock on the relentless device swooping toward me. Before I press the trigger, the tech explodes in the air.

"Ben!" I scream as the green one dives to catch him.

I raise my stunner and shoot at it and then the red one, but I miss both. The two drones take the same course directly for Ben, emitting a white, electric pulse into his body. Ben is slammed onto his back. I scramble to him while shooting at the two devices. The rest of the swarm rushes us. I throw myself over Ben and aim.

21 drones. Odds of defeat: 36%.

I stuff my fear and raise my weapon. The scenario vanishes.

"You let yourselves get distracted," Gabrielle's scratchy voice echoes.

Ben groans underneath me. I roll off to let him sit up. "He was trying to help me."

"I realize, but in the real world, it would have gotten you both killed," Gabrielle says. "You have to be able to think fast enough to deal with your immediate issues and then aid the other person."

Ben clutches at his side. "Is it necessary to experience this much pain in here?"

"It is," Gabrielle says. "If it were easy, you wouldn't take it so seriously."

"What should I have done? Let that thing get Avlyn?"

"You should have trusted she'd be able to handle it herself. Learn to listen to your instincts; and if she truly needs the assistance or not," Gabrielle says. "Instead, you left yourself open to attack, which did neither of you any good. But I did get some solid data."

I pull myself to my feet and reach to help Ben up.

"Play it again," I growl.

CHAPTER TWELVE

The vibration on my wrist shocks me from a hard sleep.

Training results ready. Tap here.

I ignore it for now, rolling out of bed and making my way to the shower. I let the hot water steam the lingering exhaustion from my bones. Once I'm fully alive and passably dressed, I return to my room, flop back onto the bed, and study the training data. Breakfast can wait. Nothing but food bars anyway.

There's a rap at the door.

"Come in."

The door slides back and Meyer steps in, looking freshly bathed too, dark hair still damp. My heart skips when I see him.

"Morning," he says. "What are you doing?"

"Reviewing the training results." I lean my back against the wall behind my cot. "How's it going?"

"Good." Meyer sits on the edge of the bed. "As much as I hate to admit it, Aron did an excellent job getting Gabrielle's micro drones functioning. She put him to work on the project a couple of hours into your testing yesterday. He made upgrades to help us with training outside today."

The door slides away and one of the mentioned drones flies into the room. The device circles Meyer. His jaw tightens as he swivels his head to follow it, then it stops and hovers in front of me.

"Ready for a big day?" emits a digital-sounding voice. "We begin in thirty minutes."

Meyer rolls his eyes and shakes his head.

I smirk at him and address the drone. "Yes, thank you. I'll be down soon."

The drone whirs around Meyer's head again. This time he swats at it, but misses. I'm quite certain on purpose, although, gauging by the expression on his face, he'd rather have hit it. He knows he'd be in trouble if he did, though. From me.

Meyer eyes me as the drone exits the room and I burst into a snicker.

"He's just trying to impress you," Meyer says.

"He already does. Aron's a genius," I reply with a smirk.

Meyer eyes me, playfully lifting one eyebrow.

"But it doesn't mean I'm planning to make a contract with him, or whatever you call it out here."

"Out here, they generally call it marriage. But most people don't get married ... paired right away ... so, dating. Taking the time to find out if you like someone is dating."

"Are we dating?"

"Maybe. Do you want to be?" Meyer asks.

"Taking the time to get to know you better sounds amazing. So, if that's called 'dating', then yes." I set the handheld beside me on the cot and swing my legs to the floor, scooting in next to his warm body.

"Dating is not always exclusive," he says, not looking me.

"Are you hoping to date someone else around here?"

Meyer turns his head toward me, lips pinched together. I lock onto his stare and struggle to hold the laugh building inside me.

His lips curve to form the slightest smile, and I break into a wide grin.

"No," he chuckles, shrugging his shoulders.

"And I'm not, either."

I slip my arm around his waist and he wraps his around me. I rest my head into his chest, inhaling the same scent of the clean bar of soap I used this morning.

He pulls away slightly and leans his face to mine. My breath hitches as his lips softly touch mine. I move my arm from his waist and up to his neck, leading him in closer. In Elore, I never thought much about kissing. I knew it existed, but not like this. Now, I pretty much feel as if I'd enjoy doing this all day.

Meyer's hands press on my back, and the heat bleeds through my shirt, stretching the length of my spine, strangely sending a chill with it.

The feeling quickly passes when I remember about today's testing and realize that dating Meyer could likely be short-lived. I'd assume living on the run will probably get considerably more dangerous. Gently, I inch from his embrace and fix on his dark eyes.

"Thank you for this," I say.

"For the kiss?"

"No. Well, yes." A smile overtakes my lips again. "But for everything. Thank you for *believing* me. I know you didn't only come because Ben forced you. As of now, you've given up everything for me."

"I understand what this means to you. You came with me when I tried to rescue Jayson. I'll be there to help you and Ben."

"But you're risking so much."

"Life is a risk. I might as well take it with someone I care about."

I wrap my arms around him and squeeze. The door skates open and the micro drone from before zips in and circles us. Meyer takes a deep breath, holds it, and exhales. He releases me and waves away the drone.

"We're coming," I say.

"Be glad I don't have my stunner," Meyer mumbles under his breath.

I smack him on the arm and he pretends to wince. "Aron's simply performing his job."

"No, he likes you." Meyer chuckles, gesturing to the door.

In the kitchen, Ben and Aron meet us with more food bars. The micro drone from my room zips past us and hovers alongside Aron.

"No time for a leisurely meal." Ben tosses me a bar. "Gabrielle wants to get going."

"What took you so long?" Aron asks. "We're going to be late."

Instead of answering, I rip the package and stuff the overly sweet, chewy bar down in three bites, following Ben and Aron into the testing room. Meyer sticks close to my side, munching on his breakfast, smirking the whole way.

Gabrielle stands in the lab, working at a table of twenty-four micro drones. The one tailing Aron floats off and lands on the table beside the rest. A glowing blue light on the top fades and goes dark. I activate my EP and an overload of information floods over my vision.

"All right, kids. Now that everyone's here, let's talk about the plan for today. I'd like to take a break from VR and send you all through some practice training up top."

"Up top?" I echo. "Won't that increase our odds of being spotted?"

"I've been out here for years without trouble, but, even so, I'm cautious. Set up a scrambling system on my property ages ago. Anyway, it will be a short operation. There's not adequate room underground for it, and you have no clue what you'll be up against once you all get further into the Outerbounds." She looks at Aron. "And *some* of you lack real-life defense skills."

Meyer leans his back to the lab wall. "I don't need practice. I have other stuff to do."

Gabrielle scowls. "Now you listen to me. You came out here for *my* help. I am aware you have extensive training, so that just means you are excellent leader material. Suck it up and start acting like one."

Meyer opens his mouth to speak, then immediately closes it, probably having realized what a poor decision it would have been to argue.

"What good is one training session?" Ben asks.

"It's better than nothing." Gabrielle nods to Aron and he

walks toward the table of drones. He takes a handheld from his wrist and unfolds it into a tablet, swiping a finger across the screen. The blue lights on the top of each drone blink three times, then holds solid. Each lifts from the surface and hovers a few inches above it.

"The drones will serve as the enemy," she continues. "Two reasons. First, to ready you all, and second, to test out Aron's handiwork. I also have camo suits for each of you." She points to four folded, tan articles of clothing on a desk next to one of the viewers. "They have a chameleon tech to either blend in with your surroundings, or program them to be whatever color you require. The function will help you avoid detection by human eyes. Great in the field."

Meyer grabs the top garment and holds it to his shoulders. The legs of the suit end at his calves. We all burst into laughter, which feels good and makes everything seem as if it's going to be okay.

"It's a little small," Meyer says.

Gabrielle chuckles. "That's Avlyn's. The others are larger, and the fabric should adjust to your bodies. I figured they would be helpful for your journey, and an additional set of clothes is always nice to have on hand."

At the surface, the frosty morning air bites at my skin. Something tells me winter is not too far off. Thankfully, the camo suit plus the khaki jacket Gabrielle lent me from her stash keep my body warm. When I asked her why she had so much extra stuff, she shrugged and said, "You never know what you might need to trade out here." I wanted to ask her if she saw many traders, but she rushed away after Aron and his micro drone army, getting ready for a full-fledged attack on us.

The view of the sun's rays washing over the hills surrounding the valley is a refreshing change to life underground, or even in the city. I breathe in the sweet scent of the dry grasses, hold it in for a beat too long, and let it out again.

The drones hang in the frigid sky above Aron and Gabrielle as they operate a handheld controller. She has Meyer on some errand double-checking the perimeter security. Ben exits the shelter from the same place we entered near the rock formation with a smile on his face. His suit has transformed to a golden wheat color, matching the hue of the scrub grass, and he has the identical modified stunner holstered to his side as I have on mine.

"You seem happy," I comment.

"I am. We must be prepared and this puts us one step closer to getting off the map."

My stomach drops at the thought.

"We're ready," Gabrielle calls as I see Meyer jogging back to us.

"Talk later?" I pinch my lips together and wait for him to nod, then walk over to Aron, Gabrielle, and Meyer.

"It goes like this," she explains. "We'll begin with a target-based sequence similar to the one you two ran in VR." She addresses Ben and me. "No EP information for Avlyn past the first round."

"No EP?" I echo incredulously.

"The others don't have them, and Meyer tells me you didn't have one during your escape from Elore, yet you took out Aron's original micro drones easily."

"I knew her skills were improving from practice in VR, but

when they transferred to real life ..." Meyer says.

"I couldn't believe how she shot them down." Aron sighs as one of his drones buzzes lower and floats inches above his shoulder. "But these perform better. I've used the data we've been collecting to make modifications, so I'm interested to see what happens."

"And anyway," Gabrielle adds, "there might come a time when your EP stops functioning. Deactivate the data feed you see, but keep the tracking. We can download it inside later."

Ben kicks impatiently at the dirt. "Let's move."

"Sounds good." Gabrielle raises her handheld. "I'm uploading the program to your EP, Avlyn."

Data floods my vision, alerting me that the secured perimeter runs in a mile-and-a-quarter circle surrounding the bunker. The test will take place anywhere within it.

"We're linked. You have a five-minute head start. You'll be notified by Flexx when each new level begins after you pass the last. Your EP will shut off automatically. At this point, I recommend sticking together to build on your skills as a team." She looks at each of us. "Any questions?"

I expect Aron to have a few, but no. He only waves his hand toward the drone next to him and it zips away to join its group.

"Oh," she says, "and just as in the sim, if you are hit by a drone, you *will* experience pain."

Ben peers my way and raises his eyebrows.

"How much pain?" I ask warily, remembering the sim.

"You'll have to find out." Gabrielle holds up the handheld and a countdown shows in my vision.

5 ... 4 ...

I grab for my stunner, as does everyone else.

3 ... 2 ... 1 ...

"Go!" Gabrielle yells.

The four of us rocket from our positions and I follow the instructions my EP gives. Ben is right on my tail. Since he can sense my emotions and intentions, it's as if he knows exactly what I'm going to do next.

The area consists of mostly grass and scraggly bushes with clusters of rocks here and there. We dart toward a grouping of bushes marked in the EP and force our way in between them to hide. As we do, our suits transform to a mottled green, perfectly blending with the greenery poking its way into my back.

"Three drones in range," Ben says as he draws his stunner.

The ghosted drones illuminate in my vision, two of them marked for me. My heart pounds as I raise my stunner and discharge at the blinking red drone. I destroy the first one with a single shot. The light on the top shows green, but the second veers and continues pulsing red. Someone from behind me hits the target. I swing around to see who it is, finding Aron lowering a stunner of his own.

"Good shot," I say, surprised.

He lifts a shoulder in a shrug. "I've been practicing virtually."

Meyer moves up beside me and I lean into him. "Maybe Aron's not as untrained as you thought."

"Maybe," he answers.

The EP instructs me to move despite the third drone still in pursuit at sixty feet. We scramble from the bush and I pause to relieve us of our attacker. The pulse leaves the stunner and the light changes to green.

Bullseye!

Level 1 Complete

Immediately, my EP shuts down. "Here we go," I whisper under my breath as Meyer motions to the group to move. We shift and sprint in the direction of a boulder, our suits morphing from green to speckled tan once more. Two more drones lit red on the top fly over us, moving faster than the last. Ben hurls himself down and I follow his lead.

I raise my stunner and peer past the side of the boulder, aiming.

"They're mine," Ben says, scooting forward. He aims and shoots, but this set moves faster, in increasingly evasive patterns. He misses both. The drones zip toward our position and my shoulders tighten. Out of the corner of my eye I see Meyer surge ahead and raise his weapon to the incoming drone. As the scene reduces to slow motion in my head, I turn and observe his face move from tense to relaxed. Then, as if time bursts onward, he depresses the trigger, releasing a pulse. One of the drones changes to green. The second drone zips our way.

I throw my stunner up and fire, but the AI evades. A pulse sound emits and a glowing light hits me straight in the chest. My back slams onto the ground and my stunner flies from my hand, thumping as it lands in back of me.

"Avlyn!" Ben yells.

A sharp pain speeds from my chest into my limbs, a groan escapes my lips as the drone circles back. A pulse sound emits again, followed by the sound of exploding metal.

"My drone!" Aron yells.

Ben leans over me, weapon in hand. "Are you okay?"

My body jolts at the sight of a drone floating behind him, the light displaying green on the top. It's out of weapon mode.

"Whoa ..." Ben says. "Aron must have made some significant upgrades to the weapons system on those things. Lucky for us they were set to stun."

I gasp as he helps me sit. As I do, an unmarked, four-seater hover pod zooms through the sky, beginning its descent as it heads in the direction of Gabrielle's bunker.

"Who's that?" I choke out, my stomach sinking.

CHAPTER THIRTEEN

Ben grabs my hand and pulls me to my feet. My chest still stings, and when the drone lightly swoops in, as if one of its friends didn't just try to kill me, I wave it off.

"Sorry," Aron says. "The upgrades performed better than I thought."

"You think?" I ask, rubbing the hair standing up on the back of my neck.

Aron looks at Ben. "But you weren't supposed to *destroy* it."

"I didn't mean to," Ben says sheepishly. "When it shot Avlyn, I think I automatically reverted my stunner to its kill setting. I was trying to protect her."

Meyer jogs toward us. "You okay?"

"Yeah." I tap on my comm to talk to Gabrielle. "A pod flew over us your way."

Gabrielle's voice sounds a moment later. "Probably nothing. Likely a trader. Tracked it on the screen. Doesn't appear armed, and you were within the cloaked perimeter, so their on-ship detection shouldn't notice the activity, but you should head back anyway. I need to make adjustments before you move on to the next level."

Great ... it's going to get more *difficult.*

"We should get back," I say.

"The pod?" Meyer asks.

"No, Gabrielle's not worried about that." I gather the smashed pieces of the destroyed drone and turn in the direction of the bunker. The last working drone that's suddenly friendly—or at least as friendly as a non-living piece of tech can be—takes its place above Aron's shoulder again, making zipping and buzzing sounds as if it has something to say.

Aron walks to my side. "She mention what the ship was?"

"Trader, probably."

Gabrielle's voice comes onto the comm. "Avlyn?"

"Yeah?"

"You four need to get back here. Immediately."

"Is something wrong?" I ask, motioning for everyone to pick up the pace.

"Nothing. Just get here. There's been a change of plans today." Gabrielle's voice clicks off again.

"Let's go." I reactivate my EP as we dash for the bunker.

The rock formation soon comes into view. Gabrielle stands outside the entrance. A figure walks toward her from the underground hangar and embraces her.

Sanda Brant overlays the body in my vision, but this girl has black, short-cropped curls. Gone is the mop of gold-tipped hair.

As we run, I tap below my ear to activate the comm. "What's Sanda doing here?"

No answer.

We increase the pace, panting when we reach the bunker.

"Wha … what's happening?" Ben asks between breaths.

Sanda breaks from Gabrielle and turns to me, her blue eyes filled with sadness and relief. "I'm so glad you're all safe. You don't know how worried I was until I received Mom's message, so when Ruiz sent me this way—"

Stunned, I look at Gabrielle. "You told her we came to you?"

"She never actually *told* me you guys were here," Sanda contests. "I gathered it from the message."

Gabrielle tips her head toward me. "I had no idea Sanda was coming, but it's fine. Since I moved here, I set up a secure line so I could stay in contact with her."

The words settle heavily in my stomach. Even so, this whole business doesn't calm my fears. Gabrielle should have filled us in. Asked our permission.

"Avlyn?" Meyer must have noticed the stress showing on my face. "It will be all right. Sanda hasn't even seen Gabrielle since Jays—"

"But what if she was followed? Or the message was intercepted?" I ask. "Then Waters or Manning might come here."

Ben steps to my side. "We should have been told." I look at him and his eyes meet mine in a show of solidarity.

"We?" Sanda asks.

"Yes, *we*," Ben replies. "And who are you again?"

"Sanda is Gabrielle's daughter and my sister," Meyer says.

Ben addresses Meyer. "And Avlyn is *my* sister, and I want to keep her safe."

"No, Avlyn is right. I made a mistake," Gabrielle says, breaking the tension. "I've just been on my own so long and have a particular way of doing things. I didn't consider asking permission. It won't happen a second time."

I nod to accept the apology, but still feel like the words aren't sufficient. Our *lives* are at stake.

"So, how long are you here for?" I ask, starting to feel terrible for wanting to keep their family away from each other after losing Jayson.

"My assignment doesn't start for a couple days." Sanda's lips curve up into a tentative smile. "And I have interesting news. Ruiz found Cynthia Fisher. That's who I'm headed to meet."

Meyer's eyes widen. "I thought she was dead? Or at least way off the grid?"

"Who's Fisher?" Aron asks, out of breath.

"She used to be a Director when the council functioned as a team," Meyer explains. "She and Ruiz were forced to step down at the same time, and Fisher disappeared. Most thought she died."

"Fisher came to live with my family," Gabrielle says.

Meyer looks her way with a small frown. "What? When?"

"After Manning pushed her out of Direction. I must have been ten or so. She made it out of Elore and my father and mother took her in. She was pregnant and couldn't remain in the city."

"I'm confused," Aron says.

"I was too. But I was too young to really know what was happening, but something was off. Thinking about it now, I don't think the father was her spouse. She stayed with us until the baby was born; a girl. Days later, she and the child were gone. I have no idea what happened to either of them, but I've been hearing rumors of Cynthia resurfacing recently."

"And the child?" I ask.

"Nothing." Gabrielle chuckles. "But it's not exactly as if she's a kid anymore."

"Why didn't you tell us this?" Sanda asks.

Gabrielle shrugs. "We were sworn to secrecy. But I figure if she's out in the open now, it doesn't matter."

"What do you think Ruiz wants with Cynthia?" I ask Sanda.

"I don't know for sure, probably to join the fight. I should find out soon, since that's my destination after I leave here. I'm here for a couple days."

Nervousness grows in my stomach. "So Ruiz didn't tell you anything?" I move forward toward Sanda. "What if your pod was tracked by her?"

Meyer steps in between us, arms crossed. "Avlyn, are you serious?"

I turn my back on Meyer and stare off over the tan and green landscape of the scrub brush surrounding Gabrielle's bunker.

"It's fine, Meyer," Sanda says. A delicate hand touches my shoulder and I spin. "I know you're upset, and it's obvious you don't even know if you trust Ruiz anymore. If I were in the same place, I'd be wary too, but I've known her my *entire* life. Meyer trusts her, and so did my father."

"Waters may be influencing her," I argue.

"You need to give her more credit," Sanda says. "And about my pod, Mom programmed a little scrambling app I upload every time I come here, so no one knows about this place."

Meyer slips his hand around my waist. "I know you're scared, but it's going to be all right."

I lower my eyes and sigh. I'm mostly confused and don't know what to think anymore. "You're right."

"Let's go inside and discuss this further," Gabrielle suggests, reaching for her daughter.

140

I relax into Meyer's embrace and follow the group below ground.

"I brought more news too." Sanda connects her handheld to Gabrielle's computer system in the lab and taps on the small screen. My stomach clenches as an Elorian vid showing the attack on New Philadelphia plays. Elorian warships cause mass damage to the city.

Father. Is he safe? Still alive?

"Was the damage that bad?" Aron asks.

Sanda shakes her head. "Waters had them driven off quickly with minimal casualties and damage."

"But by showing this, Manning is admitting to Elore that Philly exists," I say. This is totally against everything Direction stands for.

"It's not like he had a choice," Meyer says. "When Waters rescued us, they left multiple buildings destroyed. Either he had to say Affinity had amassed an army, or that there was more to the Outerbounds."

Additional New Philadelphia buildings explode into rubble on the screen. Manning's voice sounds as a voice over. "As you can see from our victory, we are well equipped to ensure the safety of all Elore, and we will continue to prevail over future threats."

"And what does that mean?" I ask, disconcerted.

"We don't know yet." Sanda disconnects her Flexx and pockets it. "He could be planning anything."

For the rest of the day, Gabrielle, Ben, and I analyze the

testing data from the morning, but my heart isn't in it and I head to bed early. Although I'm mentally exhausted, I do little else than stare at the ceiling, lit by a tiny, dim, blue-tinged auto light in the corner of my room. My mind races with thoughts of Father and what my leaving might have done to him. At this point, I don't even know if he's alive after the attack on New Philadelphia. What if Water's decided he's an enemy and put him in isolation? Father supported Manning until just recently. President Waters may not trust him.

Guilt rolls through me. No matter what I do, I seem to lose the people I love.

I roll onto my side and throw the pillow halfway over my head, but it does nothing to slow my racing thoughts.

Defeated, I drop my feet to the floor and into waiting slippers, then stand. After a moment of unsuccessfully trying to convince myself to return to bed, I grab the jacket flung on the one chair in my quarters and find myself in the hall, making my way toward the kitchen. I arrive at the exit and place my hand onto the door's security pad.

Open.

The door slides back. A brisk fall wind meets me, along with a moon so big it nearly takes up the sky. Without hesitating, I pull on the jacket and make quick progress to the underground hangar. Three pods wait, ours, Gabrielle's, and Sanda's. I dash for Sanda's and release the hatch, climbing inside. I scan the controls and place both my hands on the console.

Immediately, my vision goes white, and I rack my brain to think what to ask for. I'm searching for any tracking tech programmed into the pod when I remember the concealment app Sanda said her mother programmed. I visualize the coding it would take if I designed such a program and, certain enough, the symbols swirl in, sparkling and surrounding my body. A warm sensation engulfs me and I reach for the coding. The energy surrounds my hands, absorbs into me, and then it's gone. It's secure.

I rest my hand over my heart while the pounding slows. The pod has not been tracked. How I know this, I'm not sure. It's as if the pod is organic and we've become one. It speaks my language and I understand it. The system's the one thing I can trust. Being a part of it is the safest I've felt in weeks.

The sensation makes me desire to stay, but I must to get back into the bunker. I free myself from the pod's system. A strange loneliness washes me, but instead of dwelling on it, I push it aside and make my way out of the hangar and across the yard, teeth chattering, clutching myself to ward off the cold.

"What are you doing?"

The voice makes me jump and I swing around toward it. Meyer is dressed in pants and a hooded jacket, much like the night I first saw him on the streets of Elore, except when I face him this time, he seems a little confused.

I hug myself tighter. "I ... I needed some air."

Meyer pushes up his sleeve and checks his antique watch. "At this time of night? And in the hangar? The air seems rather stuffy in there to me."

"It was, and that's why I'm headed back." I rotate to face the bunker, but Meyer grabs me by the shoulder.

"What were you doing?" he asks again.

"Nothing." I don't look at Meyer. The bright glow of the moon would give my lie away.

"You were testing to see if Sanda's pod has a tracker on it."

My stomach roils. "Yes."

"And was there?"

"No."

"Avlyn, eventually you have to start trusting that we know what we're doing."

I turn toward him. His eyebrows are furrowed, but not angry anymore. Only sad.

"I spent my life trusting in a broken system, and the worst part is, I *knew* it was broken the whole time. I'm sorry, but I have a bad feeling about Ruiz, too, and I want to listen to that part of myself instead of just ignoring it again."

Meyer's face softens and he reaches a hand out to me. I take it, and he gathers me into his warm, strong body.

"You're shivering."

"What do you think? It's freezing out here."

He rubs my arms. "I'm sorry. I wasn't considering this whole thing from your point of view. It must be frightening to go through."

"You have no idea. First, taking the risk and joining Affinity, then discovering I have this ability. It's dangerous in the wrong hands, and I don't know who the right hands belong to."

He finds my fingers and interlaces his into them.

"I trusted Ruiz, but Waters is controlling her."

"Ruiz saved you in Elore," he reminds me. "If she wouldn't have, you probably would have been dead, or worse, in Manning's possession. Who knows what he would do with you."

The thought sends a shiver down my spine. Kyra is still in Elore. Who knows what they've done to her.

"But Meyer, after my EP implant surgery, I saw something."

His eyes narrow. "What?"

"Experiments. A project named 'Ascendancy'. It was a lot like the lab in Elore, so I thought it was there. There were medical pods with humans inside them. As far as I can tell, they were attempting to recreate my ability. At first, I thought it was a dream, but when we were at Dr. Sloan's, I saw a reference to it on the screen. So, on the way out of New Philadelphia, I commed Ruiz and asked her."

"And what did she say?"

"She knew about it."

"She confirmed that?" Meyer asks.

"Yes."

Meyer shakes his head as if trying to sort out the information. "Just because she knew about it doesn't mean she's involved. Did she say *who's* in charge of it?"

"I didn't give her time. I needed to get Aron and myself out of there."

"Then it might not be Philly. You realize they're not the ones doing the attacking, right? Direction is. Right now, we're lacking the whole picture. Before we make a judgment, we have to have that."

I run through my conversation with Ruiz once more in my head, but it's cloudy. I was so worried about getting Aron and myself out that I could have cut her off. I don't know anymore.

I look up and present Meyer a paltry smile. "Yes. Get me the whole picture."

He leans in and places a gentle kiss on my forehead. Even that tiny, sweet gesture sends a spark up my body, making me crave more.

Meyer pulls away but continues holding my hand. "We're working to keep you safe."

"Ben and Aron, too?"

He grins. "Them, too."

"*Both*?" I insist.

"Yes, both."

"Let's go inside, please," I say through nearly chattering teeth. "These pajamas and slippers aren't cutting it anymore."

Meyer gestures to the opening. "Lead the way."

CHAPTER FOURTEEN

I lean back in my chair, fanning myself to ward away the stuffy air of the lab. Last night's conversation with Meyer keeps rolling through my thoughts.

Everything will be okay. Sanda's arrival yesterday just caught me off guard.

On the opposite side of the room, Ben slumps in his chair, eyelids drooping as if he's about to fall asleep. I chuckle. He tilts his head up and looks straight at me, now smiling. "*Bor-ing,*" he whispers under his breath.

"I heard that." Gabrielle laughs, maintaining her work at the system. "Why don't you remove the connectors and come review?"

"We didn't do anything yet," I say.

"I know, but you need to see this first."

Ben and I remove the wires and walk to join Gabrielle. Both our brain activities show on the screen, different sections lit into a colorful rainbow effect.

Gabrielle rises and gestures to her chair. "Have a seat."

I plop into the chair and Ben comes up beside me.

"So far, this is the data we've collected from the tech immersion tests we did, and the ones from yesterday up top." She points to a large section of red on Ben's scan. "From this, it appears Ben's ability is nearly stabilized. On the other hand," she points to my scan and a much smaller red spot, "yours is much more underdeveloped."

I reach to the screen and trace the section. The word *underdeveloped* makes me cringe. It brings back old memories of not being good enough.

"But your ability is progressing so quickly, it could easily surpass his," she says.

Still touching my brain image, I look toward Ben, who suddenly seems to be lost in thought, and pat him on the arm. On contact, a tingling sensation travels my hand and the room goes white. An image of Ben as a young boy fills my mind. No, not just Ben, but Devan again slumped on the ground and Ben's childish body draped over him, sobbing.

"I didn't mean to—please wake up!" the child version of Ben cries.

I yank my hand back, and with a gasp, the vision is instantly gone. An expression of terror blankets Ben's face and he steps back, stunned.

"What was that?" Gabrielle yelps.

"You saw it?" I ask breathlessly.

"I saw the screen go crazy."

My hand continues touching the screen, and the brain scan has modified. The red area in my scan has grown and intensified in color, nearly twice as bright at Ben's scan.

"What did you see, Avlyn?" Ben demands.

"What? Um ... I don't know. You and Devan. I saw the same scene before, too, after we first met, but it was different this time." I stretch for Ben. "What became of him?"

Ben collapses on his knees onto the floor, his head in his hands. "You'll hate me if I tell you."

"Hate you? You're my brother." I spring from the seat and find myself on the floor beside Ben. "I could never hate you."

Ben sobs, in much the way he did in the vision, and I wrap my arms around his shoulders. The space goes colorless again.

A few feet from me is the young boy lying over his father. The Ben I know now is gone.

"Don't go ... don't. I didn't do it on purpose! I was trying to help. ..."

Devan's lifeless figure lies on the ground. I lightly pad over to the younger version of Ben, kneeling and gently placing my hand on his shoulder. He jerks toward me. Child Ben's hazel eyes plead for me to help, but it's too late.

"What happened?" I ask.

"He was sick ... I tried to heal him." Tears stream Ben's boyish face. He can't be older than nine.

"What do you mean?"

"His nanos stopped functioning, and we couldn't get to a medic. I tried to restart them."

The memory of healing Sanda's nanos sends a shudder up my spine. I might have killed her and myself when I did that. Somehow it worked then, but apparently not for Ben.

"I killed him," Ben whispers.

I envelop his petite body into mine and envision a safe place, a place that is not here. The white space converts to endless blue sky and sand, waves lapping the shore. Meyer's safe place.

"Your intentions were good," I say. "You couldn't have known."

Ben's rapid breathing slows and the sobs subside. In front of my eyes, Ben's nine-year-old self morphs into the Ben I know now.

"You couldn't have known," I whisper.

Ben pulls from me. "I know, but he was my father. *Our* father. I should have saved him."

"You were a kid and had no understanding what you were doing."

Ben shakes his head and wipes away the tears on his face.

Concern for him engulfs me. I need answers about his past. "Where did you go after Devan died? Did you live alone?"

"We lived in a small town. The residents took care of me for a while, but when I turned sixteen, I traveled to New Philly and enlisted in the Guardsman training program. I figured I could help people, protect them. Maybe I knew it would lead me back to you."

"And it did." I graze the heart necklace Ben gave to me so many years ago.

The corners of Ben's lips sink into a slight, sad smile. "Let's get back."

The beach scene dissolves and we're back in the lab with Gabrielle staring at us.

"You know, the two of you are starting to affect the systems without touching them or being wired up." She gestures toward the screen and the colors in the images have shifted again. Ben's slightly, but mine continues to brighten. The red area grew a significant amount. "Your brain is quickly adapting to these new experiences, Avlyn."

"Why isn't mine changing much?" Ben asks.

"I'm not certain," Gabrielle replies. "You've both been forced to use it a lot in an extremely short period of time. Ben's brain might be responding differently."

"I think I know," I say. A wave of fear from Ben hits me, but I press on. "Ben is afraid of his ability. In the past, he's held back in using it. If he didn't, people would get hurt." My eyes meet his. "Devan would want you to use your gift for good."

Ben sighs.

"You're trying to control it now and your brain is fighting it," I say.

"She's right," Ben admits grudgingly. "I've worked on developing it in secret over the years, but every time I'd advance it to the next level, I'd back off. When I used it to contact Avlyn, I almost forgot I was afraid, but even then I withdrew."

"So, possibly if you let go, the ability will naturally progress." Gabrielle rotates to her viewing screen to type in some data. "How about if I keep Ben in here for a few hours and complete some additional tests to see what we can come up with. You can take some time off to rest, Avlyn."

My heart leaps at the opportunity, but I also want to stay here with Ben.

"I can wait in here and watch."

Gabrielle shakes her head. "It will be easier to focus with just Ben and me."

Sanda walks into the lab, breaking our conversation. "Mom?"

"Sanda," Gabrielle scolds, "I asked you to stay away while we're testing."

"Sorry." Her lips form into a sweet smile. I think it's difficult to keep mad at Sanda for very long. Funny how she and Meyer aren't bio siblings, but they still share this trait.

"What do you want?" Gabrielle asks.

"You're out of a ton of supplies. Aron needs additional parts to continue his work, and the kitchen is pretty much bare except food bars. Plenty of those."

Gabrielle scoffs. "No doubt. I wasn't expecting all you hungry kids."

"We need to make a trip into town," Sanda says.

My ears perk up at this. Meyer mentioned a town nearby when we first arrived. That would be another experience I've never had. Living in Elore for seventeen years, I thought barely anything existed in the Outerbounds, yet I came to find out there are people everywhere, scattered here and there. How do these people in Gabrielle's town live? What do they do?

"I'll go." It's a perfect opportunity for me to see more of the world if Gabrielle doesn't want me in here with Ben anyway.

"That would be fun." Sanda looks to Gabrielle.

Ben nudges my shoulder. "No, you don't."

"It doesn't matter," Gabrielle says. "You're not going anyway."

"Why not?" Sanda pouts. "I've been there a bunch of times. It's not as if it's a hub of activity."

"That's why I say *no*. The townspeople like their lives simple. What we've got here ..." she motions in Ben and my direction, "is not simple. Avlyn could be recognized or at least identified later."

I focus on my hair and watch as the tips of it surrounding my face turn to a much lighter shade of brown.

Gabrielle stares at me, stunned. "How did you do that?"

"Something called *CosmoNano* tech," I explain, ordering the

152

tech to return my hair to normal.

"Humph," she grunts. "I've heard of it. Haven't seen it in action, but I still don't want you out there."

"Come on, Mom, it will be *fine*," Sanda insists. "No one will recognize Avlyn. Most of the people there barely get the news. We'll keep to ourselves, get the supplies, and get out."

I look toward Gabrielle for her approval.

"Yes," she says at length.

"I'll get the boys," Sanda calls over her shoulder as she zips away.

Too much energy, that girl.

"But you must lay low," Gabrielle warns me. "You don't understand those people at all."

"What do you mean?"

"She means they're non-techie," Ben says.

Gabrielle nods. "The townspeople, as many of the small communities, fix on simple living. A lot of them feel as if technology played a role in society's downfall; too much reliance on artificial intelligence and lack of real personal interaction. Living in an antiquated way suits them. They're fine with me living on the outskirts and using them for trading, but they like things the way they have them set up."

Gabrielle's description of these people fascinates me even more. The townspeople are essentially the opposite of how I've lived my entire life. I thought New Philly was different than Elore, but this? What would they think about *me?*

"I get it," I say. "Hang back and observe."

Gabrielle eyes me for a few seconds too long. "Yes."

"I'll see you later." I smile at Ben and make for the door to go and get ready for the trip.

I make it halfway through the hall—into Aron's slender frame.

"I heard you're joining us?" Aron says, sounding chipper. Probably excited to get the drone parts he needs to replace the broken one from yesterday.

"I am. You ready to see more of the Outerbounds?"

"Very. I've barely met or seen anything since I've been out of Elore. Unless you count the inside of a holding cell and this bunker." He motions his hands in the air. "But what I've seen is amazing, and I'd love to see more. It makes me believe I can be more than I ever thought possible. Choose what I want to be, who I want to be with."

A lump forms in my throat, and suddenly I'm unsure whether to be happy for him, or slightly offended. Aron *did* choose me, once, but it doesn't matter now, and I shove the thought away.

Excitement flutters in my stomach and I flash him a smile. "We should quit wasting time, then."

"You should go change first," he says, stopping and pointing toward my quarters. Aron's dressed in khaki pants, a button-down shirt, and a brown jacket. Not at all like the typical uniform-style clothes we wore in Elore. These clothes suit him though. He seems relaxed, more at ease with himself.

He catches me looking him over and smiles. The dimple on his cheek makes an appearance, causing me to smile also.

"Sanda should have clothes to allow you to blend in with the locals. Not that it will disguise the fact we're not from around here, but at least they might not know we're from the city. Can you do the thing where you change my hair color?"

"The thing?"

Aron tips his head. "The ... what did you call it?"

"Immerse," I say, and touch Aron's hair. As I do, the strands shift from golden to brown. "There you go."

As if compelled, he reaches out and strokes my face. "You know how amazing you—" Aron pauses and drops his hand, looking slightly embarrassed. "How amazing the *ability* is, right?"

My heart skitters and I glance away, a little taken off guard by the fact that I enjoyed the touch.

Aron steps back and turns to exit. "Um, see you soon."

CHAPTER FIFTEEN

In my room, I find a pair of blue pants and a green sweater in a small chest of drawers and slip them on. Before I leave, I check myself in a small mirror on the wall. As I smooth my bob with a brush, root to tip, the strands change from blonde until the color adjusts to my liking. I concentrate on my eyes and decide on green today to match my sweater.

My Flexx vibrates on my wrist with a message from Meyer.

Where are you?

I'm almost ready, I message back.

Great. Make sure to leave your Flexx behind. We need to blend in.

I shrug, and as I exit the room, I pull the device from my wrist and toss it onto the bed. *Might as well sleep my EP, too.* I blink and the green overlay on my vision I barely notice anymore vanishes.

Sanda, Meyer, and Aron are waiting for me up top. When Sanda spots me, a wide smile overtakes her face. "Your hair?"

Nervously, I touch at it, unsure if it looks right.

"No," she says as she walks to my side and wraps her arm around my waist. "It's beautiful. But quite a difference. It's nanotech right?"

I nod.

"Wish I would have thought of the nanotech option before I cut mine." Sanda raises her hand to her dark, short curls. "At least this is super easy to take care of now."

"Why did you cut it?" I ask.

"Same as you. Everyone in Elore has seen me on the news. A wild mane of curly hair isn't exactly the style there. If I ever have to go back in the city, I'd stand out too much, like the last time. I could have pulled it back, but decided short was easier."

I shudder at the thought of Sanda's face on the media viewer after she graffitied the building in Elore, and how Manning used her to help make citizens believe Affinity is a terrorist group.

"Aren't you afraid to go back?" I ask.

"Of course, wouldn't you be?" she replies with the raise of an eyebrow.

"Can we go?" Meyer asks impatiently, a bag slung over his shoulder.

Sanda whacks him in the arm, her serious expression vanishing. "Come on, I've never had a sister! And a lotta good you are with hair talk."

A mildly annoyed expression crosses Meyer's face, and I catch Aron working hard to stifle a laugh.

Without saying a word, Meyer produces his handheld and maps our route. "It's a couple of miles, should take us an hour or so."

"You got the list?" Sanda asks Meyer.

Meyer pats his pant pocket. "Right here."

The four of us set off. Meyer scouts ahead and Aron trails us, enjoying the mountain view, I guess. I quicken my pace to catch up with Meyer, who seems to be walking slightly too fast.

"You in a hurry?"

He slows slightly for me. "Not really. Just want to get this trading over."

"What did Gabrielle send to trade?"

Meyer smiles and pats the bag. "Weirdly enough, food bars."

"Food bars? They aren't even good."

"I know." He shrugs. "But several of the residents in town love them. They probably hoard them as an emergency stockpile. Or could be they get tired of farm fresh produce. Gabrielle says they always go for a fair price." Meyer reaches into the bag and produces a bar. "Hungry? There's plenty."

I shake my head. "Thanks, but no. I need to talk with Sanda."

Meyer nods and picks up the pace again to remain a few steps ahead of us.

"What's the name of the town?" I ask as I let Sanda catch up with me.

"Thornton, named after the guy who founded it maybe twenty-five years ago."

As we walk down a ridge, I spot the town in the distance. It's not large, but kind of spread out. The majority of the buildings are here and there with vast empty spaces around them. Why they would do that, I'm not sure. In the center sits a cluster of buildings, the city center, I think.

"So why did they settle all the way out here?" I ask Sanda.

"For the same kinds of reasons my mom lives here. To be able to do what they want without too much interference. Mom doesn't like the watchful eyes of any government, and I guess the townspeople really enjoy living off the grid."

"Gabrielle said that, too. What exactly does living off the grid mean?"

"No tech. Or very little, at least. Nearly all of it is unused and only for trading purposes. They store most of it and usually let you go through it if you want to. Some of it's useful, some not. Who knows if they'll have what Aron requires."

"What do they do for communications?"

"For the most part, they don't. The townspeople exist in their own world. Traders come and occasionally they travel up to Mom's for information, but mostly they don't need it. Each time I've gone to town, they seem happy."

"I guess life would be a lot simpler," I say.

Sanda chuckles. "No doubt."

Aron comes up beside us and smiles.

"So what's the story on you?" Sanda blurts out.

I clear my throat. "Aron's from Elore. He's … my friend."

She gives me a suspecting look. "There's more to the story, isn't there?"

Heat prickles over the back of my neck.

"Avlyn was my pairing," Aron says in a rather matter-of-fact way. "We intended to make a contract."

I glance at him. His expression is nearly flat, unreadable. From our exchange earlier when he touched my face, I gather he's hiding some emotion. He and I have years of experience with that, so it's not all that difficult for us.

"No kidding?" Sanda asks. "Awkward."

"It's fine," I quickly say. "Aron and I are friends now. He's a good person."

Aron's lips quirk into a tiny smile. "That barely mattered in Elore."

"Being a good person always matters," I say.

He nods absently.

"And dimples don't hurt either," Sanda adds.

Aron raises his hand to his face and grazes the spot where his dimple sits. A much larger smile overtakes his face than before, and the color of his cheeks turns to a perfect shade of pink, a stark contrast to his artificially darkened hair.

A loud *crack* sounds in front of us. Pulse pounding in my ears, I scan the area, my mind instantly activating the EP. My vision lights with information, but not where the sound came from. Sanda ushers the three of us behind a grouping of boulders. Meyer pulls a concealed weapon from his side and settles beside a tree. *Why didn't I think to bring a gun?*

"What's going on?" I call to Meyer.

As I say it, my vision lights up again, and new words scroll across the bottom of it.

Gunfire: 234 feet, 322 degrees Northwest

"We're under fire. I can't get a lock on the shooter," Meyer says, keeping his voice low.

As I search the area marked in my vision, the EP zooms in—*it's never done that before*—and I spot the gunman. He's alone, and his weapon is ancient.

Double Barrel Shotgun

It's an older guy with a graying beard, shifting slightly as he squats in back of a mound of dirt, weapon gripped tightly in his hand, but not readied.

"There's one guy," I tell the others, nudging Meyer. "How about you try to talk to him?"

"Well, I don't want to shoot him if I don't have to," Meyer says.

I angle toward Aron and Sanda. "You two are okay, right?"

They both nod.

"Meyer, he had the opportunity to hit us easily, but the shot missed completely. Could have been a warning," I reason.

"I'll try to talk with him. You three stay there." He gestures to us to keep low, hunkering himself carefully behind his tree. "Hey, what are you shooting at?"

The man does not respond.

"Try again," I call in a hushed voice. "I'm not sure he's actually dangerous."

"My friends and I just want to talk," Meyer says. "We're traveling to town to trade. Up visiting Gabrielle on the hill and she needs some supplies."

Nothing comes from the man for what seems like too long.

"You kids armed?" he finally yells, slowly raising his weapon.

"Yes," Meyer admits stepping out from the tree. "But only for protection out here. You never know what types of animals you might cross paths with. Some of those big cats get hungry."

An old vid of domestic cats from primer school flashes in my mind and I wonder what Meyer is talking about. How big do cats get?

The man chuckles. "You got that right," he says, walking nearer to Meyer, who's gripping the weapon at his side. "How about you put that gun down and kick it away until I get to know you better?"

"You could do the same," Meyer says as he drops his stunner to the dirt and boots it a few feet from us.

"No, I don't think so." The bearded man stops, still holding his gun, but now it's readied once more and pointed at Meyer. "Now, have your friends come out where I can see them."

I rise slowly and motion for Sanda and Aron to do the same, but don't show myself yet.

The man motions his gun in our direction. "Who are they?"

"They are my friends," Meyer says levelly. "I told you, we're visiting Gabrielle and needed to go for some fresh air. She was running low on supplies, and we volunteered to head into town and make trades." Meyer turns toward us. "Come on out. Let this man see you better."

My heart pounds, but I do as Meyer says and slowly travel to meet him. Aron and Sanda follow. From his posture I have a feeling this man doesn't want to hurt us, but bad things happen quickly.

"What do you have to trade?" He bobs his head slightly in an attempt to see if Meyer has anything interesting.

Gently, Meyer reaches for the sack slung over his shoulder.

"Food bars, mostly."

The guy cocks his head and partially lowers the gun. "Really?"

Meyer smiles. "Yeah, want one?"

The man's face lights up and he lowers his weapon completely. Even though I know this is not over, relief washes through me. At least we're getting somewhere.

Meyer slowly lowers the bag from his shoulder and holds it out to the man.

What if this guy steals all our bars? He's the one with the gun.

The bearded man steps forward and snatches the bag from Meyer, then quickly riffles through the sack, producing a bar and holding the snack high into the air as if it were a tremendous prize. Meyer looks at me, dumbfounded, and behind me Aron snickers quietly.

"I woke up dreaming about a cherry-flavored food bar this morning," the man says. "I said to my wife I was going to have one and she thought I was off my rocker. But here it is, and you brought it." He inches closer to Meyer and hands the sack of bars back.

I breathe a sigh of relief, knowing this guy won't steal our trades, or kill us over them.

He rips open the wrapper and tears off the end of the bar with his teeth. "I'm Boyd. Alen Boyd," he says while chewing. "You said you're friends of Gabrielle's?"

"I'm her daughter," Sanda pipes up.

I hope that will appease the guy so we don't have to spin some story to keep straight.

Boyd squints at Sanda. "Oh yeah, I see the resemblance. I've been there a couple times." Instead of asking anything more, he goes on chewing the bar.

"Would you be willing to escort us into town? Meyer asks.

"Oh sure." He pulls back the cuff of his coat, revealing an antique watch similar to the one Meyer wears. "My patrol's nearly up. I can head back. You can get your gun, too."

Meyer snatches his stunner up from the ground and holsters it onto the back of his pants under his jacket.

Boyd finishes his bar and guides our group down the hill and into the city center. All the buildings in Thornton are short, one or two stories each, and made of gnarled gray wooden slats. Several have silver panels affixed to the roofs.

"What are those?" I whisper to Meyer.

"Solar panels. Apparently some of these people use them for electricity."

The road splitting the middle of Thornton is made of dirt, and a few women meander in front of the buildings, some of which appear to be modest shops and other sorts of businesses whose purposes I'm unsure of. Two women, one carrying a covered basket, pass our group. They both stare, and the first one leans over and whispers to her friend.

"I'll take you to Sheriff Jenkins," Boyd says. "He'll get your information and calculate a fair price for your trade."

The five of us pass several stores, including one marked *Bakery*, displaying an array of deliciously toasted pastries and bread on trays. Why would Boyd ever dream about food bars when he has *this* available? From the interior, the shopkeeper waves at me, and I do the same, adding a smile.

Meyer throws me a look urging me to speed up, and I increase my pace, hustling to his side. Boyd directs our group to an open door. Outside stands a white-and-brown speckled horse tied to some kind of post. Or, at least, I *think* it's a horse. It's been forever since I've watched anything on horses, but the thing is huge and stands there watching us with soft eyes.

I pick up the pace and grab Meyer before he follows the others inside the door, pointing to the animal.

"What's that?"

"A horse. People ride them here." He turns to go in, but I pull him to stop again.

"*Ride* them? For what?" I glimpse back at the horse as it paws its foot—is it a foot?—on the dirt.

"For pleasure, transportation ..." He grins and motions with his head toward the entrance. "We should go in."

Inside, a musty smell hits me, giving me the strong urge to head back to the bakery, but Meyer's hand settles on the small of my back, holding me here. Boyd walks straight to a counter and slams his hand down onto a small, dome-like object that emits a high-pitched sound when he touches it.

"Be right there," a husky voice calls from a doorway beyond the counter. A tall man with reddish hair, probably in his mid-thirties, appears. "Who do we have here?" the man asks.

"Traders, Sheriff Jenkins, from Gabrielle's place. This is her daughter," Boyd points to Sanda, "and a few of her friends."

"Well, Gabrielle's a quiet neighbor," the sheriff says. "Mostly stays to herself and brings excellent trades. What d'ya got?"

Meyer takes off the bag and hands it to the sheriff. While they make their trade, I scan the interior of the room. An old, tan computer system in the corner looks extremely out of place in this town. When Gabrielle said these people live simply, she wasn't kidding. The panels I saw on the rooftops couldn't produce much electricity.

"Don't bother with that old thing," the sheriff says. "It's only there for emergency communications, but we haven't had an emergency in a really long time. Our luck, it probably doesn't operate." He chuckles. "Should rip it apart for scrap."

Not thinking, I brush my hand over the top of the system. In an instant the screen flickers to life.

CHAPTER SIXTEEN

I freeze as words and a symbol of a sun appears on the once-blank screen, my hand unmoved from the top of the system. I quickly pull it away to run it through my blonde hair, grateful I changed the color so these people can't easily identify me.

New Philadelphia Rural Project flashes over the screen, the sun sitting directly above the words.

"Um," I say, my eyes darting to Meyer, whose eyes have grown wide. Did either the sheriff or Boyd see me start the system, or do they still have no clue?

"Wow, weird," Sanda says, walking straight to the sheriff. "My mom did say there were random electrical surges on the grid. You guys are hooked up, but don't use it, right?"

The sheriff gives her a curious look, but Sanda's lie sounds plausible enough to take the heat off me for a moment.

"She did, did she?" He steps from the back of the counter and taps on the old keyboard. "We wouldn't have heard."

Quickly, I back up and let him do whatever it is he's planning to do.

"What a mess." The sheriff shakes his head. "Now they'll follow up with a report. We only use this system in the case of dire emergency, and Philly is going to wonder what it was." He walks to a box on the wall and opens a metal door on the front. Inside, a circular object displays moving dials. "Seems like the main electrical grid has come online, too. How in the world did that happen?" He sighs. "Makes the entire situation worse."

"How come?" Sanda asks.

"Because when we go live, they want to know why. It's a real pain. The whole thing is a network. Means if the main grid is up here, it's up for all the other towns, too." He taps at the keyboard, still not closing the program after several tries. "I'm gonna have to get someone else in here. Alen?"

Our guide, who has been curiously watching the commotion, pops to attention.

"You know if Andrews is around?" the sheriff asks.

"She should be," Boyd says, nodding toward the door. "You want me to go fetch her?"

The sheriff pinches his lips together. The system refuses to shut down from the keyboard. "It would be best. This will cause me a bunch of extra work, and I'd rather get it dealt with ASAP."

"Yes, sir," Boyd says and bolts out the door without so much as a goodbye.

The sheriff moves from the operating system to station himself back behind the desk. "You have a list of the supplies you're looking for?" he asks.

Meyer digs in his pocket and presents the folded piece of paper Gabrielle must have given him. The sheriff opens it and studies the contents.

"This should be fine. I'll have the goods arranged for you, but you're gonna need to hold tight for a bit. It will take some time to get this sorted out." He gestures to the computer system. "Residents will be down here wondering why the grid's active and what I'm doing about it."

"What should we do in the meantime?" Aron asks.

The sheriff plunks his hands on the counter and looks at Aron. "Why don't you kids head to Katherine's. Should be some locals there, and you can get a bite to eat while you wait. Tell her I sent you and will pay her back for anything within reason."

The sheriff ushers us out the door and points out the way to Katherine's, whatever that is. I search for the horse, but it's missing.

"Avlyn," Meyer says in a hushed voice.

"What?" I mutter as I tighten my jacket around me to stay the chill of a gust of wind.

"You know very well *what*."

Sanda quickly moves to my side as a few townspeople scurry past us and into one of the shops, but not before they stop and watch our group. "Hopefully I covered it well enough, so lay off, Meyer. She didn't mean to."

"You did do an excellent job, Sanda," Aron says from behind us. "Quick thinking,"

Meyer shoots Aron a glare.

Aron throws up both his hands into the air in surrender. "What? She did. Don't you think so?"

Meyer turns to me, shaking his head. "What Sanda did was fine. I just want Avlyn safe." Meyer wraps an arm around my waist. "Let's get to Katherine's. Then we'll be done with this place."

"Will you tell Gabrielle what happened?" I whisper to Meyer.

He eyes me, as if in thought. "No. I think Sanda's lie worked, and it will just make Gabrielle nervous."

Katherine's Café is an old wooden building with solar panels on the roof. My guess is each house and business provides their own electricity if they need it, and this keeps them self-sufficient without assistance from New Philly. Inside, it has the same musty odor as the sheriff's office, but intermingled with old and new savory food smells I can't identify. But maybe they have some of the bread I saw earlier. My stomach rumbles at the thought of it. I haven't eaten since early this morning.

Five round wooden tables fill the room, each with matching chairs surrounding it and a vase and red flower in the center. I stroke the petals of the flower on the closest table. Slightly rough and decidedly not real. Fabric.

Why would anyone decorate with an artificial flower?

An empty drinking glass sits before each chair. In the corner, two men, probably in their late forties, sit discussing something seemingly earthshaking, if their slight scowls and whispers are any indication. A sweet-looking, stout woman wearing a knee-length dress with a tiny blue flower pattern comes out from two swinging doors, wiping her hands on a towel.

"Well, who might you be?" the woman asks in a singsong voice as she nabs a handled container from an unused table.

"The sheriff sent us," Meyer explains. "He told us to eat while we wait for a trade."

"Hmm. You must have had a good lot."

Which I still think is incredibly odd. How are food bars a valuable trade again?

The woman gestures us toward a table for four and pours

water from the container into each glass. I claim the first seat, and when Aron moves to sit beside me, Meyer clears his throat, but Aron sits in the chair anyway. Meyer sits across from me instead. Part of me wants to roll my eyes at him and his silly jealousy, but Aron was almost my spouse, so, in a way, I get it.

"What can I get you?" Katherine asks.

Sanda looks up. "Do you have a menu?"

"Not really." She laughs, producing several paper-wrapped forks and knives from the pocket on the front of her dress, placing them in front of each of us. "But fresh rabbits came in this morning. I'm confident we can whip something up with them if you like."

When she says the word "rabbits" the memory of Ben's stuffed one I found in his hiding place in Bess's apartment comes to the forefront of my mind.

"The baker brought over a few loaves, too," Katherine continues, and my attention returns to the present. "I'll get you a basket of slices."

The thought of the bread perks me up a bit, and I imagine biting into the crispy crust and what must be a chewy inside.

"That would be great, thank you." Meyer nods at me and smiles. "Can you bring some extra pieces for her?"

"No problem," Katherine says, spinning on her heels and walking the way of the double doors.

"Thanks," I say to Meyer.

"I saw you ogling the stuff in the bakery window."

One of the men, of medium height and build with leathery skin, rises from his seat in the corner and strides over to our table. The other guy, taller, with brown slicked-back hair, goes out the front door.

"You kids have something to do with the grid activation?"

My heart jumps at his words. *Does he know?*

"No, no." Aron shakes his head. "We're in Thornton to trade, and it happened to come online while we were at the sheriff's. It was really odd."

The man eyes us, causing my pulse to beat faster, and then he reaches for a chair at the table behind ours and pulls it between Sanda and Aron, causing Aron to scoot his chair nearer to me.

The man sits and rests his elbows on the table, speaking in a low voice. "That system hasn't turned on for years, and we don't get a lot of visitors in Thornton. Thought maybe you powered it up."

I lower my eyes to the table, but sneak a look at Sanda to gauge her reaction. The air grows thick in the room until the man bursts into a jolly laugh.

"You are a serious bunch." He chuckles. "It's been forever since the entire town has had electricity. News travels quickly and people are talking about it."

"I don't understand," Aron says. "Wouldn't it be better to have it all the time?"

The man leans back in his chair, placing his hands at the back of his head. "The folks here avoid anything to do with the grid. Better to be self-sufficient. We'd rather be left alone out here to live our lives. Get online, and too much information gets passed back and forth. Then a person with an agenda decides they don't like us, and bam! It's Aves all over."

I have no clue what this guy is talking about. "Aves was a natural pandemic," I say, shaking my head.

The man chuckles. "You living under a rock, girl?"

I throw Meyer a look, but he appears as confused as I do.

"Sorry, sir, we don't get out much," Meyer says. "What are you talking about?"

"You hear a lot from passersby, but I've collected data for years. When the weather's warm, I travel around; interview folks, find old documents. For the winter, I return here, and in my free time I piece all the facts together."

Sanda drifts forward toward the man. "And what do the pieces tell you?"

"That Aves was planned."

"Planned?" I ask, my mind tumbling. "By who?"

"The big guns, the politicians in charge. Had a goal to shape the world the way *they* saw fit. The worthy survived, unworthy died. The point is, more than one group, with unique ideas, created their viruses, unbeknownst to each other. After their release, the viruses merged, mutated, and, from the looks of it, the whole problem spread like wildfire before it was nipped. But that all got buried. Everyone was moving on with surviving. A few leaders emerged with what they thought were the most plausible ideas, and cities were formed."

Meyer leans his elbows on the table. "New Philadelphia and Elore."

"Exactly. See, you kids know," the man says.

"But events are causing change, again," Aron interjects.

The man scratches his head. "They sure are. For a long time they stayed out of each other's way, but Manning and Waters seem primed for a rematch. That's why I feel safer out here, out from under either of their watchful eyes."

Manning's intention to launch a new virus in the Outerbounds makes total sense now. What he's doing is nothing new. The rift has been going on for more than a hundred years, if not longer. There's no way this will end before Manning finishes what he set out to do.

Maybe I was mistaken about Waters. Maybe he really *was* trying to protect New Philadelphia—and me. Manning was always the one attacking while the only thing Waters did was rescue us. The thought of it makes me feel foolish.

"Why are you bugging these nice kids, Vincent?" Katherine scolds as she carries a tray of food, holding it to the side of us. The savory aroma of the rabbit dish meets my nose, making my mouth water, and she places a plate in front of me. The meat is covered in gravy alongside cut potatoes and carrots.

"Oh, they looked as if they'd enjoy an interesting story," he says.

"Stories, hmm?" She lowers a second plate to Meyer, steam rising from the dish. "Don't you believe a word this crazy old coot says. People out here like the quiet life. It suits us. That's it."

"Might be the reason *you* came to Thornton, but not everyone has the same agenda, Katie."

As she places the last plate of food, she smacks him on the shoulder. "Stop scaring these kids with your agenda. They're just here to trade."

With a wave of her hand she shoos him away and he slowly rises.

"Have a good lunch," he says, and with that, he leaves.

"Y'all need anything else?" Katherine asks as she sets a basket covered with a checked cloth onto the middle of the table.

"No," Sanda says in a bubbly voice. "This looks delicious, thank you."

Katherine nods. "Well, you let me know if you do."

As she exits, I lean into the group, whispering, "What was

that? Does he suspect something?"

Sanda shakes her head. "I've seen it before. Residents out here clamor for new blood, new people to listen to their stories. Who knows how much of it was true."

"But it could be true," I press, keeping my voice lowered. "Take Manning for example. It's exactly what he's doing now, with his 'pruning' inside Elore. And he planned to use a virus on the Outerbounds. He told me."

Concern takes over Aron's face, as if the knowledge of Manning's real agenda is sinking in further. Of course, he had no idea of this before. The reality that we can't go back there must weigh heavy since he didn't leave by choice.

"I still believe in Ruiz," Meyer says, finishing his first bite of his rabbit. "Some people want to do the right thing."

"But everyone *thinks* they're doing the right thing. Even Manning," I say.

Meyer plunks his fork down and reaches into the folded cloth in the basket, pulling out a slice of bread. "Have a piece of bread, Avlyn, and let's discuss this later in a private setting."

I grab the bread and tear off a bite. Moist and chewy, it really is delicious. Probably one of the best foods I've ever eaten, but that could be due to not eating more than a bite of a food bar this morning.

"What's in bread?" I ask Sanda, remembering Meyer said she enjoyed preparing food.

"Water, flour, yeast, salt, a few more ingredients," she says. "I've only made it a couple of times."

I haven't actually *seen* flour or yeast or salt. Gabrielle had containers labeled as such in her eating area, but I didn't know their use.

"You'll have to show me some time."

"You got it." Sanda grins and lifts a bite of food to her mouth.

I glance at my meal. *Rabbit, huh?* I try not to think of what happened to get it here on my plate as I stab a small piece of meat with my fork. I pop the morsel into my mouth and taste a savory concoction of flavors I've never experienced. The meat is similar to chicken or pork, which I have eaten, but the printed kind, not meat caught this morning. It's a little chewy, and the carrots and potatoes add a bit of sweetness to the dish. Bits of green plants speckle the sauce. All in all, it's tasty, but with what was just told to us, no one seems to enjoy it much.

We finish our meal mostly in silence. Katherine reappears from the rear of the café.

"The sheriff just came in through the back," she announces. "The supplies you asked for are ready to go. You can pick them up out front."

Meyer nods. "Thanks for the meal."

"You're very welcome. It's my pleasure to share."

"Time to go, people," Meyer says, ushering me to the front door. Outside, he bends to search the two over-loaded packs sitting on the porch of the café. When he appears satisfied, he pulls one of them onto his shoulder.

"Grab a pack, Aron," Meyer instructs.

The two of them lug the stuffed packs, and I walk with Sanda, ready to return to Gabrielle's and see Ben again. As the four of us make our way out to the main road, a few men and women have gathered to study us as we leave. Among them, a young, shaggy-haired boy raises his hand and waves in our direction. I copy the gesture.

Vincent steps from a building near us. "You four be careful on the way out," he calls over. "Never know who or what you might discover on the trail."

The hair on my arms stands on end at his warning. The time I trusted *any* journey I took to be safe is long past.

CHAPTER SEVENTEEN

The crisp air nips at my face and ears, and I snuggle deeper into my jacket, wishing it had a hood. The group has fallen silent. Meyer remains ahead, on guard, and usually chipper Sanda appears lost in her thoughts while she kicks at the dirt on the path.

This time my EP is active so I can detect any humans other than us on the trail. Fortunately, from the lack of illuminated green words in my vision, it's all clear. At this point, I need to learn to keep it on, despite the distraction, but the thing makes me feel less human, and there are so many moments when that's all I want to be.

I jump as Aron speaks up behind me. "So, what's the plan?"

"Plan? What plan?" I ask.

"Well, you've been completing so much testing with Gabrielle and Ben, and she has me on drone production overtime. Meyer's off doing whatever it is he does." He laughs nervously. "Gabrielle *has* found a place for us to go, right?"

My back stiffens. Running away sounded like the right choice a few days ago, but I'm not sure if I can do that anymore.

"I don't know, Aron."

"Come on. You have to know something. Nobody tells me anything."

"It's complicated."

He tips his head and pinches his lips together. "Well, complicated is nothing new for you." Aron chuckles, letting his frustration fade. The dimple on his cheek forms, making him appear sweet and boyish. A flutter twitches in my stomach.

"You're right." I return the smile and think of a way to turn the conversation. "What was your life like in Elore?"

It's not as if Aron and I ever talked much about that, even before arranging a pairing agreement. Only during that one disastrous meeting in the café. In Elore, everything appears to be perfect. Speaking of what isn't only serves to reveal you as an outsider and brings attention to your differences. When all you want to do—*have* to do—is fit in.

The brief smile vanishes from Aron's lips and his eyebrows furrow. Nervously, he brushes a strand of hair from his forehead. Compared to the cropped style he wore in Elore, his hair has gotten shaggy since we left.

"I hated it," he says. "Not surprisingly, my parents never understood me."

I know the feeling.

"As dutiful citizens are, they were—are—very serious. The fact their bio son had a sense of humor was incredibly shameful."

"That's how a lot of Elorians would respond," I say. "My parents had a lot of difficulty accepting me."

"Yeah, but how many times can you hear *'Why weren't you*

deemed a Level One intelligence? Then we could have sent you away and tried for a new child?' before you start to believe it? That and the occasional beating."

I twist toward him. "They *beat* you?"

Aron lowers his voice. "Sometimes, but doing it too much and too often would have left marks on the outside. Words were their favorite weapon, since no one knew about those scars but me. I think they secretly hoped their words would make my personality disappear. There were days I wished it would, too."

Warmth and sadness washes over me, and I reach out and briefly tap his arm. "I'm sorry, Aron."

"When you agreed to the pairing contract with me, I saw it as a tiny bit of hope in my dark world. Something positive, a kind person to look forward to spending my life with."

Guilt eddies in my stomach. The evidence of it must show on my face.

"Don't feel bad," Aron says. "We're not in Elore anymore."

"You know ..." My lips pull into a shy smile. "If we *had* made a contract, we would have been content."

"Content." Aron chuckles. "That is the word I used." He seems to consider his thoughts as we continue walking. "No, not content. Happy. We would have been happy. I used the word 'content' in my proposal because it was the right thing to do. But happy was the word I meant."

I touch him on the arm again, this time changing his hair back to blond. I think for mine to revert too. I smile at Aron and pick up the pace to catch up with Meyer. "We should talk," I say to him.

"Yeah, we should."

"Okay, you first," I offer, hoping maybe he has some sort of solution for what's going on in Elore.

Meyer produces a thin smile and looks back to Aron, who's now hiking alongside Sanda. "I've been a jerk about Aron. This stupid jealousy keeps getting in the way and hijacking my brain." He has a sheepish air about him and, to be completely honest, his ability to admit he's wrong is kind of attractive.

"You know, I'm perfectly capable of making my own choices about what I do and the people I associate with."

"Yes," he says. "I'm highly aware you are your own person. I'm sorry."

I puff up slightly. "Apology accepted."

"Now what do you have to tell *me*?" he asks.

I deflate as the thoughts of Elore flood back. "Running away is the wrong choice. Ben wants us to hide what we can do, and I relate, but if we can somehow end Manning's control in Elore, we should. The problem is who to trust eludes me." I hug myself tight as we continue to walk. Overhead, a few lone birds soar in the cloudless blue sky. "Vincent back there might have been somewhat off, but what he said makes more sense than it doesn't. If there was some sort of unspoken understanding between Elore and New Philly, it reached its expiration when Manning tried to release the virus on the Outerbounds and attacked New Philly. Waters is bound to strike back, and soon."

"That's why we need to bring Affinity back into the mix."

Meyer's words cause my heart to drop into my stomach. "No way. Ruiz gave me up."

Meyer pauses and grabs my shoulders. "Ruiz got you out. You *know* that. She did what she had to."

I hug myself tighter and step back, putting some space between Meyer and I, but he closes the gap.

"The woman is a voice of reason and not consumed in a power struggle. You know we can't go this alone. We *need* support."

I hate to admit it, but he's right.

"I won't go forward with that unless I discuss it with Ben. It's his life, too."

"Take time to process it. And yes, talk to Ben when we get back. I'll fill in Gabrielle and see if she has any ideas."

Hiding *is* the wrong thing to do, but is it smart?

So how is it that a girl who wanted to remain in the shadows somehow keeps thrusting herself into the light?

CHAPTER EIGHTEEN

"Where's Ben?" I ask, rounding the door to Gabrielle's lab.

She spins to face me on her chair. "In his room, I think."

"Thanks." My eyes flit to one of the viewers with the volume inactive. Manning is on the screen. I speed into the lab and activate the volume. Gabrielle comes up beside me. "A Direction vid is on," I say, wringing my hands as I watch.

Manning moves back from the podium, glances quickly to his side off screen, then back toward his captive audience. "I'm pleased to announce the newest program we have in place. The Alliance of New Adults. For those between the ages of seventeen and twenty-one, you will find a new section in your Citizen's account in which you may access specific vids and answers to questions concerning the program. We value this segment of Elore's society highly, and wish to convey the fact through the special program."

What's Manning doing? First, he admitted the existence of New Philly and now this? Forming groups has always been in opposition to the pillars of Direction. Their goal is to keep everyone as isolated as possible.

"With this in mind, it's my pleasure to announce the spokesperson of the Alliance of New Adults, or AONA."

My mouth hangs agape when Manning steps to the right of the podium to allow a tan-skinned, blonde-haired girl with steely-blue eyes to take center stage.

"Kyra," I whisper.

My best friend.

My betrayer.

"You know her?" Gabrielle asks. I don't answer.

Her once-lengthy blonde hair is now cut shoulder length, combed straight with a blunt edge on the bottom. A sharp pain saws at my chest.

"Greetings, Elore." Kyra squares herself toward the podium, drops her shoulders, and raises her chin. "My name is Kyra Lewis, and it is my privilege to represent the Alliance of New Adults. Over the coming weeks, I will be creating new vids with the assistance of Director Manning to explain the program."

As she speaks, a realization comes over me. Kyra *has* changed since she confessed to me about her ... assault. I flip through all the times I saw her in the last few weeks. The memory of her telling me what Representative Ayers did to her consumes me. He raped her, *threatened* her, and I did nothing.

My insides ache as if they crumple into a ball and I rack my brain for what else I could have done. She wouldn't let me help, but I should have done more. I *should* have done more. No doubt they're maintaining these threats over her head; using her and making her comply with their will.

I stare at Kyra on the screen, no longer hearing her voice.

Even her face has changed, too. Hardened. Angry. This person is not the same girl I once knew. My best friend was focused but not ruthless, if anything, she was *scared* the last time I saw her. This Kyra's stare is determined.

What have they done to her?

Whatever it was, I can't let them keep doing it.

Kyra leans in and narrows her eyes. "But my first duty is to announce the manhunt for a citizen turned traitor."

My hands go clammy as she speaks. Tears burn behind my eyes.

Don't do it, Kyra.

To the left of Kyra's lovely, stone-cold face, appears the image from my Citizen ID. I gasp for a breath, but it suddenly feels as if a thousand bricks have fallen on my chest.

"Avlyn Joy Lark has become a traitor to the people of Elore and the Direction Initiative. She is responsible for attempting to destroy the last VacTech update research, which puts Elore in danger of a potential viral threat. Lark is also responsible for the deaths of multiple protection guardians, and the destruction of valuable property at the GenTech facility."

Still struggling for breath, I throw my hand to Kyra's face. I only did those things because Manning intended to destroy the majority of the Level One population because they were not intelligent enough. It had to be stopped.

"If Lark is spotted in Elore, she should be reported at once. Anyone who reports her presence in the city, resulting in detainment, will be awarded an upgrade to privileges of the next Intelligence Level status for both you and your immediate family." Kyra scowls and tucks back a lock of golden hair which has fallen forward. "But I warn you not to engage. She should be considered armed and danger—"

Gabrielle deactivates the screen.

"No!" I yell, rounding on her.

She grabs me by the arms. "You can watch it later if need be, but it's obviously upsetting you."

Hot tears pour from my eyes. Is she being forced to betray me, or is she doing this on her own. I'm not certain anymore. "Why did she do that?"

Gabrielle relaxes her grip and guides me into an embrace. "I don't know, Love."

I pull from her, shaking my head. "I need to see Ben."

I dash from the lab and find Ben in his room, sitting with his head in his hands on the floor. Spread around him is a mess of clothes, supplies, and clear, crumpled food bar wrappers. Stale air accosts my nose, most likely due to too many males packed into one cramped room and the lack of any fresh air in an underground living space. In the corner sleeping area, one of the three bed mats is free of trash; probably Aron's.

"Ben?" I ask.

Ben jumps and sucks in a breath. "Oh, you're back," he sighs, but then tenses as he sees my face. "What's wrong?"

Wordlessly I walk over and slide my back down the rough wall to sit next to him. "Everything."

He shifts his body toward me, guilt washing over his face "I'm so sorry. I was completely wrapped up in my thoughts. I usually choose to be open to your presence and emotions. Sometimes it gets a little overwhelming, so I blocked it."

I tell Ben about the news from Thornton and Kyra's vid.

"Those are the exact reasons we should get away as soon as we can."

Kyra's vid keeps replaying in my head and nausea wells in my stomach. "I think we're wasting our ability by hiding—"

"No, no, no," Ben cuts me off. "You told me staying at Gabrielle's was to get us off the map, and that was it. After that, we'd leave. Disappear. I agreed to let her study our ability ... but even that makes me feel jumpy."

"I can't sit out anymore, Ben. I thought I could, but there are so many lives at stake, and *we* can help them. You and me."

"Who cares about them?" he hisses.

"What happened to you?" I tug the heart charm from under my shirt, showing it to him. "When we were four, you were the risk taker. You gave me this."

"I was a kid. I missed you, so I stole something from Bess and gave it to you. It didn't represent what you think. You believe I'm somebody I'm not."

His words punch me in the gut. The memories built from this necklace brought me to where I am now, brought me back to Ben.

"You don't mean that," I whisper.

Ben looks to the side. "Yes, I do." Black, cloudy emotions radiate from Ben, and I know he's lying.

"No, you don't. You won't fool me. All those years, your memory was with me and pulled me through. The love you had inside you even as a small child was evident. I could sense it."

Slowly he twists his head back my way and lets out a long sigh.

"And I'm doing this with or without you," I say.

"I already know you are. I can sense it. I just hoped you might change your mind."

"Ben, I'm unwilling to let people die because I decided to be selfish."

Ben stares across the room.

"Now, are you with me?" I ask.

He turns his attention my way, lips pinched. "My goal has always been to protect you, and if I can't do it by preventing you, I have to join you. You're right. Manning needs to be stopped. I simply didn't want *us* to be the ones to do it."

I smile and reach for him, but he pulls from me slightly.

"But I'm not going back to New Philly, and I'm not ready to tell Affinity where we are."

The heaviness weighing me lifts slightly, but I'm as wary as Ben of trusting Waters.

"Fine," I agree. "Let's go talk to Gabrielle. Maybe she can help us find another way."

"Eat up." Sanda ladles a meat stew into a bowl and hands it to me. It's full of creamy potatoes and carrots, as well as greenish bits of another kind of plant. A different type than the one speckling the meal at Katherine's Café. I pick out a piece and taste it. Piney.

I spoon the stew into my mouth. The savory flavors dance on my tongue. Meyer was right when he said Sanda was a fantastic cook.

I lean over to Meyer and point to the vegetables. "Where'd we get these?"

"Part of the trade."

"And the meat?"

I'm instantly sorry I asked as my thoughts roll back to the fresh rabbit we ate at the café.

"While we were out today, Gabrielle had time to check her animal traps." Meyer scoops up a chunk of meat with his spoon and eyes it. "I didn't want to ask her what it was."

My eyes go wide and a goofy grin crosses his lips.

"Just eat it." He laughs. "Unless I should grab you a food bar."

I shake my head. "Fine, just don't talk about it again."

The meal really is delicious, a tribute to how tasty non-printed food really can be. As a bonus, we sop up our meal with generous chunks of grainy bread from the bakery. Meyer and Ben serve themselves hearty second bowls before I have even half of my food eaten.

"You kids enjoy tonight. The rest of the supplies will go into storage. Back to food bars tomorrow," Gabrielle says in between bites.

I groan. *No more food bars.* I lift my hunk of crusty bread and examine the fluffy texture inside, tiny holes speckled with traces of, what I now know from Sanda, wheat grains. I squish the spongy bread between my fingers and stuff it into my mouth, letting the yeasty flavor fill my senses. The perfectly sliced bread printed in Elore was never as tasty as this, but it's head and shoulders above the cloying fruit-flavored bars we've eaten since we arrived. I try to oust the thought of them with another bite of savory stew.

"Plus, we should get this show on the road," Gabrielle adds, interrupting my thoughts.

Aron plunks his spoon down beside his bowl. "What work still needs to be done?"

"First, I have to reach my contacts. But, and as much as I hate to say it, at this point I think you should contact Ruiz. I'm

189

not sure how much longer it will remain safe for you to be here. You need more than I can offer you."

I stand wordless as the pit in my stomach grows. I know it's the best choice. We can't go this alone, and Affinity is our only option.

"Before that, Aron must complete my drones with the new parts," Gabrielle says. "I double checked them, and they look great. You made an excellent trade today."

"Where *did* you get so many food bars, Mom?" Sanda asks, effectively lightening my mood.

"Oh, I deal in information, and pretty much everybody needs some. Generally, I ask for food bars in return because I know the high trade value in the towns. I trade whatever I require for them. That, and there's *always* plenty to eat for hungry guests. Not that I have many." She raises her eyebrows in the direction of Ben and Meyer, too busy scarfing a third serving to notice.

Sanda and I burst into a giggle, and even Aron cracks a wide smile. The two boys look up, both sporting baffled expressions.

"What?" Meyer asks, shrugging. "I'm hungry."

"We see that." I chuckle as he resumes his attention to his bowl.

"Nothing wrong with enjoying a good meal, right, Meyer?" Ben adds while shoveling in another bite.

"Mm-hmm," Meyer agrees, his mouth full.

"Well, I'll accept that as a compliment," Sanda says. "And an indication you guys are equally as excited to do the dishes."

Meyer waves in Sanda's direction without glancing up from his food and grunts an affirmative. Sanda shakes her head and returns to her bowl, as do I. It really might be the best food I've ever eaten, but food bars have ruined for me forever. So everything tastes better than those.

"After dinner," Gabrielle says, "I have a few additional tests to perform on the twins. Avlyn, I could use your assistance with theories for infiltrating Elore's mainframes. If Manning is planning anything else, hacking in there is going to be our best bet, and I want to make sure we do it right. So far Direction has been the major aggressor, not Philly."

"No problem." It makes me feel better that Ben agrees something needs to be done about the rift between Elore and New Philadelphia. Plans aren't solid yet, but once we get into the system, we'll get a better idea of what's left to be done.

Gabrielle rises and places her napkin into the bowl in front of her. "There are projects for each of you to start on tonight after dinner," she says, then leaves the room.

I look around at the remaining group. Each show signs of weariness from the job we have ahead. Heaviness hangs in the air, but at this moment, we're simply a group of kids enjoying a wonderful meal together. My brother is here, a dream I never thought would come true. Sanda laughs heartily and slaps Meyer on the back, apparently from a joke I didn't hear. Aron seems slightly uncomfortable from the volume of the others, he's a little stiff, but all in all he's made himself at home in the outside world.

My shoulders slump at the impossible wish that we had the ability to freeze this place in time to create our own tiny haven and let the world fall away.

Meyer reaches for the remaining piece of bread in the middle of the table, but I'm faster. I snatch the slice and have a bite into my mouth before he even has time to react. He chuckles and scrapes the remainder of his stew from the bottom of the bowl using the side of his spoon. I savor the stolen bread, making certain to chew deliberately slowly, holding onto this moment a minute longer.

CHAPTER NINETEEN

I tap Ben's shoulder and he exits the Elore practice mainframe Gabrielle set up for us. It's not a perfect replica, but a valid starting point. Finding weaknesses is our goal right now.

"You done?" he asks.

"It's late and I'm tired." I rub at the tight muscles over my shoulder.

Ben frowns, pushing some brown strands of hair from his forehead. "How are we going to do this, Avlyn? There's so much to sort through here, and this program isn't real. Direction might be hiding the information about it's attack strategies anywhere."

"I'm trying not to wrap myself up in that," I lie.

"Yes, you are." Ben removes the wiring attached to his temples and places it next to the system in front of him. "I can tell what you're feeling."

I scowl at him. It's amazing to have another human so in tune with your thoughts and emotions most of the time, but also terribly annoying. However, the annoyance quickly dissolves when an idea comes to me.

"We're searching in too many places. What if we could take everything out in Elore at once?"

Ben tips his head in interest.

"What if we took them off the grid?"

He pauses to think. "There has to be some type of back-up system. There's no way Direction would make it that simple."

"You're right, and I'm sure the data is encrypted, but I think it's better than what we're doing."

"Yeah, it cuts our haystacks from ten-*thousand* down to a few."

I have no concept of what he's talking about, but I'm too tired to ask.

Ben laughs. He must sense my confusion. "It's worth a shot." He covers his mouth as he yawns and checks the time. "But I need a couple hours of shut-eye. Meet me at five?"

Five in the morning doesn't sound all that appealing to me, but this idea is our best bet, so I nod. "See you later."

Ben rises and steps to the open door of the lab. "I'll tell Gabrielle the plan before I head to bed."

"Sounds good."

I tidy the lab, throwing out a few food bar wrappers Ben must have forgotten and then walk to my room. From the hall, Meyer's deep voice echoes from a room on the left where Aron has been working on drones. I peer through the opening.

"You know," Aron swings toward Meyer, "I didn't have a *choice* in the matter."

Still unaware of me, Meyer straightens up, and two lines form between his dark eyebrows. "You had a choice back in Elore when you went into that building after Avlyn. You had no training in warfare. What were you thinking?"

Aron scowls. "I was thinking the girl who was my future spouse pairing was in danger."

"You two knock it off," I cut in, entering the room. "We are a team. Not this."

Aron takes a step back toward the wall, holding a golden micro drone in his hand.

"You have no frame of reference how the world functions out here," Meyer growls, ignoring my words. "And how am I supposed to know if you're trustworthy? Sure, you're doing this drone work for us that could protect us from Manning, but this was a guy who, up until a week ago, you agreed with."

"Meyer, stop," I plead.

"You're holding that against me?" Aron snaps back. "I had no *idea* what was happening in Elore. *Nobody* there does. We're bombarded with propaganda daily, and if you question the system, they'll cart you off for 're-education', if that even exists. When you experience something your entire life, you come to accept it, and you feel like a lunatic if you start to ask questions." Aron turns my way. "You trust Avlyn, and she was in the same place as me."

"Guards didn't have to arrest Avlyn and detain her in New Philadelphia," Meyer says.

"It's not as if I was doing anything wrong." Aron straightens and opens his hand to release the drone. The tiny piece of tech comes to life and whirs about the room. "None of this is about my loyalty." Before I can say another word, Aron casts his eyes on me. "You know Avlyn and I are friends. It digs at you, and maybe it should."

Meyer stands near the door, silent. The heat of

embarrassment climbs up my face. I like Aron's new-found confidence, but I'm also mad at him for his attempt to goad Meyer because of a girl. *Me.* This sort of problem was nonexistent in Elore. Competing candidates for a spouse pairing contract would never even meet, so jealousy or competition was rare.

Maybe some aspects of the system in Elore weren't so bad after all. That and the printed blueberry muffins.

Aron's drone zips around the room and buzzes no more than a foot from Meyer. Without warning, Meyer grabs it. "You're not coming with us."

"Where?" Aron hurtles back.

"If we aren't able to stop Manning and have to search for a safer place, Gabrielle will find somewhere else for you to go."

Aron steps toward Meyer. "No way. It's not your choice anyway."

"I'm not risking Avlyn to take a chance on you." Meyer squeezes the drone and smacks the thing onto the table next him. A piece of it breaks and flies off, skittering over the floor.

Aron stands there, stunned.

"Meyer," I warn him, "you should go cool off. We're not making this decision right now."

Meyer whips his gaze to me. "I'm not risking you," he growls, then spins and heads out the door.

The tension he and Aron created hangs in the air like a cloud. I move to retrieve the broken piece of the drone. "Here," I say, handing it to Aron. "You deserved some of that."

He takes it without acknowledging my statement.

"Can you fix it?" I ask.

Aron nods. "I can fix anything."

The cloud in the room lifts slightly and I chuckle. "I'll bet you can."

Aron places the broken tech on the table beside him. "You're leaving me here?"

My mind circles with what to say to him. I never pled the case that Aron shouldn't be left behind with Gabrielle.

"I don't know. Plans have changed. Who knows what will happen."

Aron crosses his arms over his lean chest. "I get Meyer's problem with me. Inexperience brings liability. If we have to get out of here quickly I don't intend to be responsible for risking you and the others."

Aron's acting himself still. Logical, but with enough humanity to make himself endearing. On the other hand, Meyer is acting as himself, too. Impulsive, but loyal. He protects the people he cares about, and he cares about me.

Aron interrupts me from my thoughts. "Avlyn? If things do go to plan, and there's peace again, what are you going to do with your life?"

"You have no idea *if* that is going to happen. What we're doing is a longshot." I counter.

"I'd rather think more positively than that." Aron grins and leans his hip to the side of the table. "I've seen your skills."

To be honest, I haven't thought much about it. "What I want is to rest. Maybe in a town like Thornton. No tech, no one worrying what I can do except for the fact I have little other skills. I'm a computer programmer."

"Well, you're a reasonably decent shot, so you might enjoy taking up hunting."

I giggle, almost forgetting Meyer stormed off just a few minutes ago. "That's a terrible idea. Lately, I've longed for a food printer."

Aron smiles, melting my heart a fraction. No, *greater* than a fraction.

"I've always liked your sense of humor," he says, looking at the floor. "Would you have gone through with it?"

"Gone through with what?" I ask.

"The spouse pairing contract. If we were still in Elore. Even though … you know. Meyer."

Heat burns in my chest. Aron was my Affinity mission, but he was more than that. Or at least he could have been.

"Yes," I whisper.

Aron's gaze lifts my way and he stands straighter. "And now?"

My eyes grow wide as he moves toward me. I should tell him to stop, but beyond reason, I don't. Part of me wants to find out what he's planning to do, but even if I tried to prevent him I have no time before he gently slips his hands around my waist, sending a thrill through my body. His lips, soft and warm, touch mine. Really, I should stop him now. Instead, my arms wind over his shoulders and my lips return as many kisses as he gives.

A sound in the hall snaps me back to the reality beyond kissing and I pull from him.

"Aron, this is wrong."

He takes a step back, dropping his hands from my waist and crossing his arms over his chest. Hurt and disappointment washes over his face.

I reach up and stroke his cheek, grazing my finger over the spot where his dimple would be if he smiled. I ache to kiss him again, just to experience it, but it's not right. Not now.

"I don't know much about love yet, but I do know I might

love Meyer, and I don't want to hurt him. I don't want to hurt you either," I say.

He shifts from me, but I inch forward to look him in the eyes.

"Here's what I think: I'm all you know out here, and this is your attempt to cling to the known, the comfortable. You're amazing. I've thought so since the day I met you. It would have been an honor to be your pairing, and you're right, we *would* have known happiness. But I need to explore what I have with Meyer, and I can't unless we're just friends."

Aron nods his head sadly. "I'm sorry. It was unfair of me to put you in a position you didn't intend to be in. I'm not thinking clearly."

A wave of exhaustion and guilt sweeps over me, and I know I'm not thinking clearly either. What I need is to go to bed and forget any of this happened, but instead I have to talk with Meyer.

"Go to bed, Aron," I say. "Everything will be better in the morning."

But I know it won't be. There's too much at stake beyond stolen kisses.

CHAPTER TWENTY

Meyer's voice echoes from the eating area, and the brick in my stomach drops again. To get to my room, I must go that way. I straighten my shoulders and begin to walk, carefully placing one foot ahead of the other so as to not make my footsteps heard. Instead of speeding up as I should, I slow near the open doorway.

"Meyer, there are times in everyone's life where they have to let go of control," Gabrielle whispers, but despite that I can hear. "This is one of those times in yours. You don't make choices for others, only yourself."

I close my eyes and listen to the conversation, knowing I should move on. But how do I sneak past without them seeing me?

I gather myself up and make a break past the opening.

"Avlyn," Gabrielle says.

My heart drops at her beckon. *Can't we sleep on this tonight?*

I pause and turn toward them. Meyer and Gabrielle sit at the table, steaming drinks in front of them. Meyer's face is still slightly pinched into an annoyed expression. From the looks of it, he didn't expect Gabrielle to call me in here either.

"Hon, would you like to join us for tea?" she asks, her eyes gleaming enough for me to know she did this purposely.

"Um—"

"You should. Tea always seems to help." Gabrielle stands and pulls out the chair beside her at the table, its legs scratching over the concrete flooring. Not waiting for an answer, she steps to the counter and grabs a navy-blue cup and saucer from the cabinet, filling it with hot water from the tap at the sink. She reaches into a box, retrieves a packet and tosses it into the cup, saying, "Come, have a seat."

I ask Meyer if it's okay with my eyes and he motions for me to sit. Hesitating, I shuffle my way into the room and slide into the chair next to Gabrielle but across from Meyer.

Meyer stares into his own cup and lifts it to his lips, gulping the remainder of his tea. "I need sleep," he says after he's drained it.

"You sure?" Gabrielle asks, placing my cup and saucer down.

"Yep." Meyer looks at me while rising and nudges his cup and saucer into the center of the table. "Night, Avlyn. Gabrielle."

The anger and frustration from earlier is gone, replaced by a flat, distant expression. Honestly, I don't know what to make of it. He turns back to me and lightly touches my shoulder.

"Sorry about what happened. I'm just tired. I'll apologize to Aron tomorrow."

His words only make me feel worse for the kiss. "Night," is all I get out before he exits the room, leaving Gabrielle and me alone. I sigh. "I should do the same."

"What should you do? Get upset and overreact when life doesn't go the way you expect?" she asks in a completely matter-of-fact way. "The world is full of the unexpected. It's not worth getting worked up over. Believe me, I spent enough time in my life trying."

I chuckle lightly. "Gabrielle? Why did you settle out here? Without Jayson?"

"Oooh ..." A crooked smile falls over her lips. "Getting right to business?"

"Well, you brought me in here for a reason. I figure maybe we should understand each other a little better."

"Touché." She glances up at the clock on the wall. "You have some time?"

I ignore the tiredness of my mind and body, giving Gabrielle my full attention. "All the time you need."

Gabrielle takes a sip of her tea and then motions to mine. "How about I start before all that? Probably nineteen years ago. I didn't want to be a member of Affinity anymore. Jayson and I were together for several years, and I was pregnant with Sanda. We existed as nomads and I *hated* it. With the prospect of having a family, I needed to settle down."

"So you left him?" I ask as I lift the soaked packet of tea from the cup and place it on the side of the saucer.

She shrugs. "Jayson and I were on and off for years. I thought if I left with our daughter, he'd come. For a while he did, but more often than not, he was away on some mission. He was too drawn to the cause. While I fell away from it and focused on Sanda, Jayson stayed connected to Affinity. He always came back to us because, in the end, we loved each other, but Sanda and I were on our own a lot. Then, one day, Jayson came home with

Meyer. He was little and his parents had just been killed. We lived happily for many years. I think raising Meyer was a way for Jayson to bridge his desire to support Affinity and have a family life. But he hung onto the cause, and since Sanda idolized him, she got the bug. Then Meyer followed her directly into Affinity. He worried about them and it was a good excuse to work his way back into the rebellion—to keep an eye on them."

"What did you do?" I ask.

"Eventually, I decided to settle here. It's a safe place, and I knew he wouldn't worry too much. Over the years, I always welcomed Jayson when he returned home. I loved Jayson, but I didn't intend to control him, and he didn't want to push me into an existence I didn't long for either."

"So you simply let him go?"

What if Meyer and I end up wanting different lives? Will I have to let him go?

"Oh, it feels that simple now," she says. "There were plenty of fights, but none matter anymore. Jayson did what he believed he was meant to do."

"I don't get it. You supported Jayson's choices. Why didn't you want to be a member of Affinity?"

Gabrielle drifts back and takes a sip of tea. "Oh, what Ruiz is doing is noble, but I'm not an adventurer. Never have been. One of the requirements of Affinity is you must be willing to be in the field, on the front lines. I'm kind of a 'behind the scenes' person. I couldn't commit myself to it, but Jayson did." She places her tea on the table and leans into me. "But don't get me wrong, I occasionally do what I can from here. It's why Meyer brought you to me. He knew I'd be willing. For him and Sanda. And Jayson."

Sadness sweeps her face, and it's the first time I've seen her show any emotion over the loss of Jayson. I think in her arrangement with him she must have grown used to hiding her emotions, tucking them away. She loved him, but they desired incompatible lives.

Gabrielle leans back in her chair, face contorted in an effort to hold back tears. I reach for her, gently patting her arm.

"I want everything to turn out ok."

"I know you do, dear." Gabrielle rises, wiping at her eyes. "Everyone does, and this is our one shot. Despite my personal want to stay out of politics, even I know you're on the right path."

I rub my eyes. *Am I?* "It would be safer for me to mind my own business."

"You should get to bed," she says. "*I* should get to bed."

Sleep won't come with the weight of the world on my shoulders, but I don't tell Gabrielle. She obviously needs her privacy. Instead, I nod and thank her for the tea as she makes her way from the eating area, no doubt to her room, leaving me in silence.

Finally, my body droops from the effects of an exhausting day. I take a drink of my now-lukewarm tea. The minty liquid fills my mouth.

After I wash and put away the used tea cups, I shuffle through the silent hall, the lone sound coming from my feet. On the way, I pass the shut door to the guys' sleeping quarters. *Wonder how that went, Aron and Meyer sharing a room?* I guess if secrets were shared, I'd probably already know about it, even at this late hour. It would be stupid for Aron to brag to Meyer he kissed me—and that I happened to kiss him back—but out-of-control emotions make us do dumb things we don't want to, and Aron's getting his feet wet with his emotional self.

If only I could understand people the same way I understand computer systems. Life would be considerably easier.

Once in my room, I flop onto my cot, not bothering to change my clothes. Lying here alone, the smell of sweat and dirt meets my nose, making me regret not changing sooner. How Aron kissed me, I'm unsure anymore, but there's nobody around to smell me but myself, and while taking a shower sounds great in theory, I'd have to get up for that to happen.

If there ever was a time when a dose of sleep MedTech would be useful, it's now. But since I have none I toss and turn with the thoughts of Father stuck in New Philly haunts me. I've been too busy and wrapped up in other problems, but who knows what he's experiencing. He probably thinks I've abandoned him. Then there's Kyra's vid, publicly announcing me as a traitor. To them I am, but it's not as if the words are comforting.

Tightness creeps through my center at the thought. A month ago, I was nobody. Regular. Invisible. I liked it.

How did I get here?

I suck in a deep breath to try to loosen the tension building in my core, but fail. I flick on my EP and reach for my Flexx to look for a distraction, since I won't be sleeping, bringing up information concerning Thornton and other similar towns. While most of it is fascinating and different from everything I know, something I saw especially piques my interest. That horse I saw tied up in Thornton.

In Elore, we barely knew of any animals. Direction found them purposeless. There was no want for meat if we all had food printers, and no requirement for companionship if we weren't supposed to need it, but horses? I hadn't seen anything like one in real life until today. Majestic and beautiful, I still can't believe they let people sit on them.

I visualize myself on the horse, how it might feel to be so tall and have to trust an animal to take me where I wanted to travel. It's a little silly. Flying used to terrify me, but the idea of riding a horse somehow calls to my soul. Maybe it's a means of escape, but I think it's more.

"Wonder how you ride a horse?" I mumble.

Unexpectedly, the EP transports me to a virtual dirt road. I squint at the bright sun and raise my hands to my eyes to search the simulation. It feels real. More than real. A relief.

Warm rays of light settle on my bare shoulders, and I look down to a white top with no sleeves and a pair of tan pants. A snort comes from behind me, and I swing around to see a tall golden horse, its flowing mane a slightly darker shade. On its back rests a type of covering, and straps wrap surround its head and mouth. The beast bobs its head at me and makes a snorting sound once more, as if to beckon me over. If animals could speak, it might invite me anyway. I suppose in here horses *could* talk if I programmed them to, but instructions fly across the bottom of my vision instead.

Instructions to mount the horse:
Hold the reins in your left hand.

Overlaying the straps affixed to the horse's head and mouth is an illumination indicating that they are named the bridle and reins. To me, it seems close to impossible for me to maneuver myself to the animal's back and saddle, according to the EP. It's so tall. But life is about impossibility these days, so I suck in a

206

breath to calm my nervous stomach and try not to overthink the process. Directions scroll in my vision, and I follow them.

Somehow, it works. Soon enough, I find myself on top of the horse, the animal walking us along the dirt road, me holding the reins. The warm sun and the breeze flowing between the trees is a sharp contrast to the actual crisp autumn weather outside, and I want to take the time to enjoy it.

Will I see an actual summer again?

"Horse, run," I say without hesitation.

The beast accelerates into a trot, as shown in my vision. Then it builds, increasing speed until the scenery around us is little more than a blur. I lean forward and draw in the rush as the wind blows the hair off my face.

This is what freedom is.

All I can think about is how I need to share my new favorite place with Meyer.

CHAPTER TWENTY-ONE

My EP wakes me at 4:45 am, and, strangely, the heaviness in my body has lifted. I take in a breath and slowly let it escape. To be honest, I don't know where the sim of the horse-riding lesson ended and sleep began. I must have dozed off at some point, but I can't remember exiting the program.

But anyway, the new day is more hopeful. Even at this early hour.

After peeling my clothes from myself and quickly showering, I head to the lab to find Ben. He's already seated on a chair when I get there, eyes closed, as if lost in thought. Maybe he's asleep. Five *is* too early to be awake.

As I step toward him, he slowly opens his eyes.

"Morning, Avlyn." He gives me a strange half smile that's mixed with curiosity. "What did *you* do last night?"

My mind muddles with what to tell him. I hadn't considered he'd pick up my emotional state from the argument with Meyer, and then Aron's kiss.

"I taught myself to ride a horse?" I say quickly. I'm sure he knows it's a partial truth. Should be plenty to distract him, though.

Ben's half smile morphs into disbelief. "You did what?"

"In town, I saw a horse. Meyer told me people ride them. It sounded amazing, so I used a training sim to teach me how to do it. I think I learned a lot, but I fell asleep, so who knows." I jitter with excitement from the memory of the wind in my hair and the illusion of freedom. "Have you ridden before?"

Ben shoots me a wry smile. He definitely knows I'm avoiding a conversation. Heat crawls up my back and neck, but he doesn't pry.

"A few times as a kid. I was never great at it. Guess I didn't like it enough to make a training sim. Once I moved to New Philly, it wasn't as if I *needed* to learn to ride one anymore."

"Well, you should try it with me sometime. It seriously is one of the best things I've done."

"You obviously enjoyed it, so I will." He spins on his chair to face the blank screen. "You ready to work?"

I nod. Thankfully, Ben doesn't press for extra information about last night. "That's why I'm here. What do you want to do? Work on taking out the grid?"

"Not yet. But I was up late thinking, too. I believe if we strengthen our connection, the ability will increase. You know how I reached out to you through visions in Elore?"

"Of course. Telepathy or something."

"Yeah. It seems like your ability's growth has blocked that from happening like it was. All I get now is emotions when we're at a distance, which is amazing, but we can do better. I've theorized that a reciprocal connection will allow us to function more effectively within the system."

"It would be beneficial for keeping in contact, too."

"Exactly." Ben rises and gestures for me to sit in the unoccupied chair beside his. "I constructed a visual program that I think will help us get past the blockage."

Excitement wells in me to see what he's done. "Let's get going."

He activates Gabrielle's system with a touch. The screen comes awake with stats and information related to prior testing sessions. He taps on the keyboard to set up today's data.

"Go ahead and attach the monitor to your temple."

I pick up the disc on the arm of my chair and affix it to my head, the identical way Gabrielle has done in the past. Ben does the same and stretches out the wiring coming from the system, pressing it to his temple.

"What do I do when I get in?"

"That's up to you. I created the program, but it customizes to you."

I give him a quizzical look, unsure what that means, but decide not to worry about it. "Ready when you are."

Ben returns to his seat and reaches for my hand. I accept it and clear my thoughts. A cool, icy feeling deluges me. *Blue.* It's the only way to describe it. I concentrate on the strange sensation of experiencing a color and try to interpret what it represents emotionally, what Ben is trying to communicate. Once more, Meyer's advice comes back to me.

Don't overthink.

I let my mind go blank and the feeling washes over me. The cold vanishes, leaving a sense of trust, security. Warmth. I slowly crack my eyelids to strange space filled with memories that zip and twirl around me as if each one is a separate entity. Alive.

One of them hurtles toward me, slamming into my body and through it. Ben and I are in the experimentation room. He's crying. Despair floods over me, dropping me to my knees, and then the sensation is gone. Another slams into my back, forcing me to my feet another time. The vision is of me hiding the heart-shaped necklace Ben gave me from Mother and Father beneath my mattress, the place where it stayed for years. The next passes through me like a breeze. Meeting Ben again, the relief he still lives, an embrace. This is the connection Ben and I share, one formed by horrible experiments, nanos, or maybe just our DNA. I don't know, but somehow the connection exists.

"Ben?" I call, but no answer comes back.

The memories move from me into a cluster and the entity teams with random patterns, forever creating a dance of new designs while retaining the appearance of a cluster.

I take several steps forward and place my hand onto the memories. In a way, they are solid, but, strangely, it also gives beneath my palms. I harness my thoughts and energy into the cluster and press into it. My hands fill with warmth, which quickly travels into my arms, back, and out to the rest of my body. The good memories.

As fast as they come, something replaces them. Darkness flows into my hands and slowly spider-webs up my arms, growing and growing until it fills me. It's not only the fears of my past, but Ben's, too. He had fears of being discovered for his ability, and I had fears of being overly emotional, that I'm not enough, too weak and incapable.

This is not my identity anymore.

My instinct is to pull away, but instead I lean into the

memory cluster with greater force. The cluster vibrates under my hands. At first, it's barely noticeable. The vibration speeds up and shudders through my whole self. Sharp pain screams from my nerves, but intuition tells me to press harder, to let it consume me.

And consume me it does. Every inch of me.

I let it. I invite it to mold me and make me stronger. The memories release and whirlwind around me, the sound of wind roaring in my ears. I plant my feet, aware of what is coming, and I wait as the sound grows louder, then *louder*. I fight to keep from covering my ears to block the sound. I need to experience this fully.

The force pounds against my body and face, but I embrace it, experience it, let it forge and shape me as everything in my life up to this point already has, good and bad.

In an instant, the visual of the memories is gone and a figure appears. Ben.

"Whoa," he says with awe.

I smile and hurry to him. "Maybe I made a breakthrough."

"I'd say so." A wide smile forms on his lips. "Let's test it."

Ben frees us to the real world of Gabrielle's lab. I sit up and look to him.

You did it, he says in my mind. *We can both communicate telepathically at will. This is big.*

Butterflies skitter in my stomach. I return a thought to him. *We should tell Gabrielle.*

Ben nods and moves to stand, but he falls back into his chair instead, rubbing his temples with a pained grimace. The sight of it makes my stomach turn, and any excitement I felt is instantly turned sour. Springing from my seat, I rip the monitor from my head and toss it aside.

"I'm okay," he says, studying the monitor. "My brain activity is within normal function."

He's right. Everything appears normal on the screen. And it would capture if something was off. Wouldn't it?

"It's only a headache," he insists. "Your development was new, and I think overwhelming to my system. Who knows, you might develop one later, too."

But I don't have a headache. My head feels clearer than ever. I narrow my eyes at him. "Gabrielle should know that, too. To keep an eye on potential problems."

"I said I'm fine. There's no requirement to tell her every time I get a headache. People get them." Ben lifts his Flexx and messages Gabrielle.

"She might not be up yet," I reason, but as the words escape my mouth, a response arrives.

"She'll be here soon," Ben says, looking at the screen.

Gabrielle studies the data as Ben and I wait. "I told you not to do this without me in the lab. Avlyn, the activity in your brain is off the charts. To be honest, I didn't know a brain could function that way. It's incredible. Beyond incredible, really."

Ben's beaming. "Of course she's special. She's my sister."

I laugh and the warmest yellow, like sunshine, floods me.

You know, you're pretty special, too, I think.

Thanks, I hear in my head, plain as day.

"Your abilities are really progressing, and we're close to a breakthrough on the Direction grid structure," Gabrielle says, pulling me from my connection with Ben. "I believe it's time to contact Ruiz. She needs to know what we're planning."

I rub at the back of my neck. "So soon?"

Gabrielle chuckles. "Yes, Avlyn. What we're doing is only going to delay Manning. If Affinity can move in when the system goes down, we have a chance for long-term peace."

"As much as I hate to involve others," Ben says, "I think Gabrielle is right. If we're doing this success is much more likely with help."

I open my mouth to speak.

"Mom?" Sanda's voice calls from the hall.

Oh, nice. A distraction.

"In here," Gabrielle says, not diverting from her screen.

Sanda pokes her head into the lab. "Oh, good, you guys are around, too," she says, slightly too chipper for first thing in the morning.

"What do you need, Sanda?" Gabrielle asks.

Sanda waves a folded piece of paper in her hands. "A messenger arrived from Thornton."

Gabrielle spins her chair toward the door. "What is it? They asking for more food bars?"

Sanda chuckles. "No, they're having a get-together tonight. A dance. They invited us."

What's a dance?

I look at Ben, but his eyes are trained on Sanda, ignoring me.

"Sanda, you told them no, right?" Gabrielle asks.

"Um, no. You always say to extend goodwill to the town whenever you can. Refusing would be rude."

Gabrielle sighs. "You're right."

"What's a dance?" I ask, this time out loud.

Gabrielle chuckles. "Oh, yeah. You'd have no frame of

reference."

"It's a ... gathering," Ben explains. "Where people listen to music and ..." He stops and considers for a moment. He closes his eyes, and instantly I'm transported from the lab into a group of strangers swaying and twirling to the most beautiful sounds. The men and women swish around Ben and me as if we're invisible. The corners of my lips turn up into a gigantic smile.

"*This* is dancing," Ben says. "It may not be the type of dancing that the invitation means, but it's one kind."

The dancers are lost in another world, one I want to be a part of. As fast as it came, the vision is gone, and I'm back in the lab.

"Can I go?" I ask.

Gabrielle glares at Sanda. "Why'd they have to do this now?"

"It will be fun, Mom."

Gabrielle pinches her lips together, then sighs. "I knew I shouldn't have let you go in the first place. But you can go since they already saw you. I don't want them to think anything was out of the ordinary about your visit. People are nosey, and I don't intend to give them any further reasons to be."

Gabrielle stares at Ben, then me. Ben throws his hands into the air. "I'll stay."

"Avlyn, if we finish enough testing in here today, I need to take the time to evaluate the data with Ben," Gabrielle says. "It will provide you a rest."

I leap up, clasping my hands together. "Today will go well. I can tell. It's already off to a great start!"

She shakes her head at my childishness. "All right. Let's get down to business."

"I'll let the others know." Sanda squeals.

❊❊❊

Ben and I are both exhausted from our work today. His body shows it as well as his face. Gray emotion emits from him. He looks at me, and a meager smile crosses his lips. My mind clouds as well. I'm as tired as he seems to be.

"It's time to be done, Gabrielle," he says. "Avlyn needs to prepare to go into town."

The words perk me up slightly. We've been so engrossed in the digital world I'd nearly forgotten the real one.

Gabrielle checks the time. "You're, right," she says, and helps unhook us from the system.

I already know the answer, but ask anyway. "You coming with us, Ben?"

He shrugs and shakes his head. "Naw. You go and have fun. I told you, I'm sticking around here to assist Gabrielle."

The idea makes me feel guilty that I won't be staying behind to help too, and it must show on my face.

"Take a breather, Avlyn. Thornton would bring back too many memories of my life after Dad died. I'm happier here. It's only a couple hours, and I'll be working."

I stand and walk to Ben. "You feel okay, right?"

"Just tired."

I don't receive any indication that he's lying to me, so I accept him at his word.

Ben turns and waves me toward the door. "Now hurry. It's nearly time for you to leave."

I focus to activate my EP, and sure enough, according to the time glowing in the corner of my vision, it's time to go.

"See you soon," I say to Ben. "And thanks, Gabrielle."

"Anytime," she says. "But you should know I'm contacting Ruiz tonight." She lifts a hand into the air to stay my protest. "I'll encrypt the message so she won't know who it's from, but she needs to know."

I know she's right, but I must go. "Fine."

"And if we call, you return from Thornton right away," she says as I fly out the door into the hall to locate Meyer.

"Yes, yes," I yell back.

I message Meyer to find out where he is, but no answer comes. Finally, after searching every room, I locate him above ground. An icy breeze kicks up and I pull the jacket I grabbed near the bunker entrance in tighter to ward away the near-winter chill.

"You're coming?" I call to Meyer, who's standing 64.2 feet from me, according to the EP, looking off into the tan scrub and trees.

He rotates to face me and the EP zooms in. Meyer's jaw is clenched slightly, and his arms are crossed over his chest. Not a positive sign, but I continue forward toward him.

"I want you to come," I say as I reach his side, sliding my hand into the crook of his arm.

"Why?" he asks.

"Well, for one, everyone was invited. It might look bad if the four of us don't show up."

"Tell them I felt sick," he says.

I scoff. "You're not sick, and I won't say that. Please come."

"Why?"

"Because I want to dance with you. It will be my first dance, maybe my last, and sharing it with you is important to me."

Meyer takes in a deep breath, shaking his head. "There's so

much to do. I should stay here and get prepared to leave." He touches my cheek. "Have fun." And with that, he jogs back to the bunker.

I follow after him, but he's already halfway there, leaving me to walk myself in.

Inside, I rush to ready myself, getting dressed in my room. I'm disappointed neither Ben nor Meyer are joining us, but I can make the best of it.

"Time to go," Sanda's voice wafts from down the hall.

"Coming!" I call.

I steal one final glance at myself in a mirror hung by the door and smirk as my short bob alters from brunette to blonde. I raise my hand and drag my fingers through the pale strands.

In the hall, Sanda and Aron ready to go. Guilt whirlpools in my stomach at the sight of him. Despite the discomfort, I tap Aron on the shoulder and his hair color shifts, darkening.

"Okay," Sanda says. "Let's go cut a rug."

"What's that mean?" I cast my gaze to Aron, his brow raised in a confused way.

Sanda chuckles. "Never mind. You two look great. Now come on."

CHAPTER TWENTY-TWO

I take the back seat of the pod so Aron can be in the front with Sanda. The air is thick inside the small space, making me ready to arrive in town sooner rather than later. Aron hasn't said more than two words to me since we left.

Finally, Sanda lowers the pod to the ground on the outskirts of Thornton. She decided, and I agreed, that we don't want to hike back from town once the sun sets, but she parks far enough from town that the pod won't alarm the residents. In the distance, I can hear similar types of sounds I heard in the sim Ben showed me with the dancers.

"What is that?" Aron asks.

Sanda tips her head quizzically and then chuckles. "Oh ... the music?"

Aron shrugs. "Is that what it's called?"

"Mm-hmm," she hums as she takes Aron's arm and hauls him in the direction of the city center. I hang behind them, watching the sun setting over the mountains beyond the town.

As we move closer, the music grows louder, lifting my mood. It also manages to increase the flurry of butterflies filling my stomach. Ahead, a sizable crowd gathers in the street, milling and talking in clusters. Surprisingly, even lacking electricity, they have lamp poles I didn't notice lining the street yesterday. A small panel sits below each light source, and I can only guess it must have the same sort of solar function the café uses because that power source seems to be acceptable here. Makes sense, it still keeps them off the grid and self-sufficient.

"You came. Couldn't stay away, huh?" a familiar low voice sounds from behind us.

We turn to Vincent, dressed in a freshly pressed, tan suit under a puffy, warm coat, left unzipped.

Without hesitation, Sanda reaches her hand for him to grasp. "Of course we did. My mom expresses her regret that she couldn't come, she's terribly busy, but we couldn't resist the opportunity."

Vincent chuckles and vigorously shakes Sanda's hand, finally releasing it. He gestures in the air. "Got the grid problem fixed. Some team from New Philly came out this morning."

My breathing stops at his statement.

"But you missed them. We invited them to the dance, but they had to go."

The tension he created melts and I force a smile as he looks to Aron and me.

"Please, enjoy the town's hospitality. I believe Katherine has organized some food if you're hungry." Vincent nods to me and gestures for us to continue. "Have fun, kids. Oh, and if you want to hear any more stories, I'll be around. Find me later."

Sanda thanks Vincent and eyes me after he leaves. No way she's finding that guy later. She smiles and grabs Aron, pulling him forward. I follow. The music grows louder and the crowd thicker as we weave around small groups. At first, we go mostly unnoticed, but the attention falling on us soon grows, sending a shiver up my spine. Aron must notice it, too, because his body has stiffened.

These people are just curious, I remind myself several times.

A tug pulls at the back of my shirt and I twist to the same shaggy-haired boy who watched us when we left town. His hand is behind his back.

"Hi," I say, glancing up at Aron and Sanda, still walking ahead. "What's your name?"

The young boy gives me a shy grin, one of his front teeth nowhere to be seen. "Ash."

"How old are you, Ash?"

"Five." He brings his hand from his back and presents me with a red flower. It's fake, identical to the ones from the tables at the café.

I accept it from him and lean in, whispering in his ear. "Thank you. It's lovely. I won't let Katherine see."

His lips form a broad smile and he turns and darts away. I chuckle and stand. Not quite knowing what to do with the flower, I shove it in my pocket and search for Aron and Sanda. I push through the crowd into an open space lit by strands of tiny lights above the dancing area. The two of them are dancing already. Beyond that, there's a group of two men, one of them Alen, the man who escorted us to Thornton the first time and three women, each with different devices producing the music. One of the devices is wooden with strings. The EP provides me no information on this. I stare as they make the beautiful sounds. The magical scene makes me forget any uncertainty about coming.

The sounds from the music makers are like nothing I ever heard in Elore. I guess I've heard people make music with their voices before. Maybe Bess did, but I can't be certain. This is all so new.

Despite the music, I feel awkward standing here. Everyone has someone to dance with but me. It's not as if I'm going to ask Aron. Sanda is already dancing with him anyway. I scan the scene and something else catches my eye. Someone. Behind the dancing group is an unexpected figure I know.

Tall and handsome, Meyer's dressed in the same clothes I saw him in earlier, except he's bundled in a heavier coat with a stripe decorating the length of each sleeve. His eyes lock onto mine until finally he breaks away and stares at the ground, his lips forming a wide smile. My pulse surges. Avoiding the dancing couples takes a bit of skill, but I make it past them to the opposite side.

"You came?" I ask, my heart skipping to the beat of the music. "How'd you get here so fast?"

"Gabrielle said I needed a break and she and Ben could handle the preparations. So, I decided to take a run. Funny how fast you can move when you're motivated to." He rakes his hands through his messy hair. "And ... I ended up here."

"Because there was nowhere else to go?" I ask with a smile.

"No, there were plenty of places to go. But none of them were where you'd be." He lifts his eyes toward me, sending heat up my neck. "I heard a rumor that you wanted to dance with someone."

The electricity I feel for him burns in my chest. "I want to dance with *you*."

I grab his hand and direct him to the area where the townspeople are dancing, as well as Sanda and Aron. Inside, I chuckle at them. Sanda seems like she knows what moves to make to the fast-paced music, but Aron is clueless. He looks a little ridiculous, but it doesn't seem to matter since they're both laughing and having a fun time. I'm tempted to activate my EP and download a program to boost my own lacking skills, but instead decide to learn without it, watching the other dancers and copying them.

I lean into Meyer, raising my voice above the music. "Have you done this before?"

"A couple of times." An amused expression overtakes his face. "I see you have not."

I smack him on the shoulder and roll my eyes. "Be nice."

"I'm nice." He laughs.

Thankfully the music slows. Most of the dancing couples move in closer, kind of swaying in place.

"I can do *this*," I say, pulling Meyer in. In front of us, Sanda's attempting to instruct Aron, placing her arms around his shoulders. Inexplicably, a wave of jealousy consumes me as the memory of last night's kiss comes to the front of my mind. Quickly, I push the thought away and avert my eyes to Meyer, but when I do, the guilt of not telling him eats at my stomach. Telling would only hurt him, and it would drive a wedge further between them. They still must be able to work together.

I clear my throat. "You look good tonight."

Meyer grins. "You always look good." He reaches for my hand and interlaces his fingers with mine, bringing me tighter. His strong arms wrap my body, building an illusion of safety I wish would last forever.

We sway to the music below the twinkling stars of the night sky. My mind wanders to the first time Meyer and I really talked, before I joined Affinity.

"How old were you again when you came to live with Jayson and Gabrielle?"

"Hmm, about two. My parents had just died on a mission into Elore. Jayson brought me home and the four of us became a family. Me, Sanda, Gabrielle, and Jayson. We led a pretty quiet life for a long time, far from civilization."

"So, why'd you join Affinity?"

"Jayson stopped working directly for them, but he stayed connected. I can't count the number of times he had some Affinity member over. Sanda and I were always around the movement, hearing the plans, the excitement. It rubbed off. I believe in their cause."

"And you came with me out here anyway? Gave them up?"

Meyer stops dancing and makes space between us. "You aren't getting it. I believe in freedom. If you thought yours was threatened, I needed to support you. If that meant coming out here and getting some breathing room, great. If it meant I'd need to help you disappear, then I'd do that too." He inhales deeply. "I've seen too many people I care about die, and I don't intend to waste time wondering how life could have been. Avlyn, I love you. I don't want to be without you."

My eyes widen and nervousness wells in my chest. Meyer doesn't just care about me ... he *loves* me.

Come back, Ben says in my head as clearly as if he were standing in front of me, snapping me from Meyer.

Why? I think.

I found something, and it's big. It's the answer to our

problems.

I hold my breath, excited for his news. *Tell me.*

Not until you get back.

Fine, I think, frustrated.

I shake my head, continually in awe that Ben and I can communicate in our minds.

"It's time to go back to Gabrielle's," I tell Meyer.

"Now?" he asks, frowning in disappointment.

"I know, but Ben contacted me. Gabrielle said if they called, we needed to go."

"When?"

"Right now. We had an advance in our communication this morning." Meyer shakes his head in amazement as I step closer to him and rise up on my toes to whisper in his ear. "I'm pretty sure I love you, too."

The smile I see on Meyer's lips as I pull back is wider than I've ever seen it, and he leans in and gives me a gentle kiss. If only time would freeze right now. He twirls me around to Sanda and Aron, laughing and smiling as if they're having the best time in their lives. Maybe they are.

"They won't be happy to go either," Meyer says.

I chuckle. "Nope."

"You think they'd give me a lift?"

I reach for Meyer's hand and weave us between the dancers to Sanda and Aron. "They want me back at Gabrielle's."

Sanda rotates toward me and scowls. "Not so soon. We've barely had any time."

"I know, but Ben says it's urgent."

Sanda sighs at Aron and he shrugs. "Let's go." She sighs. Sanda notices Meyer, a sparkle forming in her eyes. "Couldn't resist?"

Meyer's lips curl into one of his signature smiles that makes me slightly rubbery in the knees. I also wish we could stay.

"Can I get a ride?" Meyer asks over the music and conversations.

Sanda nods. "Back to the real world."

We're on our way, I think to Ben.

CHAPTER TWENTY-THREE

"So, let's have it," I say, barging through the lab door and willing my hair to return to brunette. Gabrielle is seated, the screen in front of her displaying a mass of data. Ben's in one of the testing chairs, hooked into the system, almost as if he's sleeping sitting up. He's immersed.

Gabrielle stops scrolling the data and addresses the rest of us.

"I only want Avlyn in here. You three go find something else to do."

I turn to Sanda, Aron, and Meyer, their faces each displaying disappointment.

"I'll call you if I need you." Gabrielle raises her hand to shoo them from the room.

I lock eyes with Meyer. "Good luck," he says, exiting the room.

"We could help," Sanda protests.

"You are helping," Gabrielle replies. "By leaving."

Aron steps toward the open door. "I need to fix a drone

someone broke last night. We should go."

Sanda reluctantly follows Aron from the lab. I shift my attention to Gabrielle. "So, what's happening?"

"First, I heard back from Ruiz. She's on board. Tentative, but on board. And Ben may have found a safe way into Elore's mainframe and grid structure. I've run the data and am pretty sure he's correct."

"*Pretty* sure?" I echo.

"As of now, it's the best we have. We're losing time. The latest intel is informing me Manning is preparing for another invasion in the next few days. It's time to move and figure out specifics."

"What is it we're doing?" I ask, looking to Ben in the chair. A strange wave of nervous emotion radiates from him.

"Ben will fill you in," Gabrielle says, drawing my attention back to her. "Just get started."

I throw my attention back to Ben, still immersed. The nervousness is gone, but I'm not getting anything else either, no emotional readings. I focus in on him, but can sense nothing.

"You'll guide us, right?" I ask Gabrielle.

She nods and returns to her system to recheck the data. Reaching out for a headset, she places it over her head and eyes. "I'm syncing the system to your EP, so I'll see everything you do."

"See you inside," I say, pulling up a seat and placing my hand onto the system information port. As usual, the world disappears and goes blank for a second, then Ben appears.

He stands at what appears to be a gigantic screen of transparent code, bringing up data and swiping it to the right or left. A few to save, a few to toss.

"Ben?" I say, but he doesn't respond.

I walk to him and gently tap his shoulder. A red emotion smothers me, buckling my knees. I fling back my hand as Ben whips around.

"Are you okay?" I ask.

He stares at me, as if in a sudden trance.

"You're not." I grasp his shoulder, bracing myself for whatever the touch might bring. This time there's no effect.

Ben comes out of it, wiping his brow and returning to the code. "I'm fine. Help me and I'll get you up to speed."

"Everything all right in there?" Gabrielle's voice says over my comm.

"That's what I'm trying to find out. How is Ben's brain function?"

"Normal range," she says.

I watch Ben as he manipulates the code. Suspicion waves over me. I tap off the comm and disable my EP.

"You're manipulating the brain scans so Gabrielle believes you're all right, but you're sick or something." I say. Darkness instantly clouds my thoughts and I shrug away the sensation. "And you're trying to manipulate me, but it won't work."

"Why would I do that?" Ben keeps tapping, but his agitation is contagious. The sensation of it vibrates through my body.

"I don't know, but it's what you're doing."

Ben turns and straightens his back. "I'm just tired."

Like a flipped switch, the vibration pauses. He gives me a strained smile and holds my stare until I go back to the code, placing both hands on it. A deluge of information floods me, and it's my intention to transfer the bulk of it to me, away from Ben. I reactivate my EP.

"I lost you for a second," Gabrielle's voice says.

"Yeah, sorry," Ben mutters before I have the chance. "Glitch."

I look toward him, knowing he lied a second time, but remain silent. Inside the system, we carefully approach the Elore mainframe. We're not making it our goal to trigger alarms or anything.

"What exactly are we doing?" I ask Ben.

"I think I found a way we can temporarily take out the grid, but I need to go in with you and confirm it."

"Temporarily?"

"Yeah. Probably for a few days or a week, but it should make them scramble. None of the communications or drones will function and food supply will be disrupted. Control on the DPF will be released."

"Ok," I sigh. "If it looks like it will work, Ruiz will be able to move in and assume control." I'll have to trust her if I want to help and avoid a life on the run.

"Exactly. I'm analyzing the data on the back-up generator, you take the grid system."

"And we're only downloading the files for us to study with the group right now?"

"Yes," Ben confirms.

In my head, I start the scan of Ben's isolated data locations, narrowing my search to the most likely areas for the information we require to cripple the grid.

"What's next?" I ask as we arrive at the data.

"Okay, so the whole scenario seems easier than it is," Ben explains. "Direction was smart. There's no central grid location. It's a series of networks through multiple companies including;

GenTech, SimCorp, and their sister companies in Level Three. So, in order to do this right, we must find each one and set up an exploit for both the main grid and the back-up. If we miss one, the effect will not be the same. Then we have to launch them at the exact time, otherwise it won't work."

"But there's got to be some sort of failsafe, right? A function to stop a widespread grid outage?" I reason.

"Yep. As I said, Direction is smart. Every company has its own unique hardware and software, and since some of the tech is kept secret between the organizations, we won't be able to assume once we've mastered one we've deciphered the next. Luckily, Elore is only so big."

I shake my head. "This is going to take a while, then."

"We're quick. I have the list of companies and we can sort through them one at a time. Just be careful not to leave a trail."

I chuckle. "You don't know me at all, do you?"

Ben eyes me. "I know you're skilled, but don't get overly confident. I've been doing this kind of hacking for years when I needed to. I've never been caught, but I've made sure to be careful. For now, all we're doing is taking notes on memory corruption vulnerabilities. Access the data, download, and get out of there. We can analyze later."

Some of my ego deflates and I turn from him.

"I mapped the data. Everything to get you started is in there."

"Sounds good." I close my eyes and allow myself to merge with the data, letting Ben's plan lead me to what I need. A sense of calm flows over me and my mind clears. I open my eyelids and Ben is gone, but somehow I know where he is the mainframe. He takes SimCorp; I'm at GenTech. The thought fills me with dread, but I cram it away. This *must* be done.

I inhale and visualize the GenTech mainframe.

"GenTech grid access."

The data whirlwinds around me and, with a flick of my hand, I command it to a stop. Quickly, I arrange the code and evaluate.

I need to inject some new data into their program ... overflow their buffer. That's what will take this out.

I download the data and location within the GenTech mainframe so we can map it later and note the overflow attack option. The download completes and some of me craves to stay and search for anything odd, like infant experimentation. I could know more about what Ben and I experienced and why, but now is not the time. We can do that later, maybe together.

"What now?" I ask, realizing I don't know. Ben's the one with the list of companies we must infiltrate. "Take me to Ben," I say when I receive no answer.

In a tumble of code, I open my eyes to Ben's location and join him in his task.

"Ben? Have you got what you need here?"

"Not quite," he says as he manipulates and swipes at the code he's working on.

"I downloaded GenTech. Do you have my next destination?"

Ben selects a file to his right and turns to me to speak, but instead immediately freezes. My heart leaps in my chest as a rush of black-and-red emotion overruns my entire body. Every inch of me is frozen except my brain.

"No, no, no! What's happening?" I scream. Or, at least, that's what I *want* to scream, but no words come out.

In my mind, I reach for Ben, but it's an inky nothing.

Can you hear me? Ben? I call to him.

Ben struggles to make our connection. *Avlyn, you must get out.*

What's doing this? I have to know how to fix it!

You might still have enough strength to break free. Get out! he thinks to me.

No way. What happened?

When I opened the last file ... it must have been a Trojan.

If Manning ordered Trojans concealed in the files, he must know that people are attempting to hack in. He also knows the files are compromised. Our plan is not going to work.

My mind races and I struggle to focus and understand exactly what's happening to us. He's trying to upload a virus to whatever computer is hacking his system, in this case, *us*. I have no clue what a computer virus might do to Ben and me, but I do know it can't be good.

I must disconnect from him. Mustering all my strength, I fixate on my link with Ben. When nothing happens, I grit down further.

"Release me!" I finally scream, ordering the virus. The space reverberates, first slowly, then the sound speeds up, rattling me to the core.

Crack. Bam. An explosion of light hurls me forward into Ben's weak self. I push up to my knees with a groan, closing my eyes to settle on freeing myself from the system. If I can get out, I can manually sever his connection, but when I open my eyes again, it's the same. I'm still in.

"Gabrielle!" I yell. "Get us out of here!"

No response comes. The virus must have infected her entire system, too, including the comm.

"Go," Ben whispers, the blood draining from his tearstained

face and lips.

"No way. It's not going to happen." I place my hands on his arm, gritting my teeth in opposition to whatever comes next. A cold jolt rips over me, forcing me to suck in air from the pain, but I don't let go. The sensation makes me grip harder. I focus on Ben until I find the problem.

"Die," I command the virus.

The cold morphs into intense heat.

Well, at least I know it heard me.

"Die!" I yell and direct everything into making it do that. I force the heat from myself and hone in on the bug that's filling Ben and attempting to overrun me. My thoughts surround it and I snatch it from Ben's body. I reach for the small snippet of code, grabbing and smashing it to the ground. The virus code explodes into a burst of light.

"Avlyn, Ben?" Gabrielle's voice fills the space. "Are you okay? I lost you. Ben's vitals are weak."

"Help us now!" I cry, lunging for Ben's lifeless frame, my frame slumping over his.

CHAPTER TWENTY-FOUR

I suck in a gasp of oxygen. Adrenaline surges through me, and I rip off the monitor tethering me to Gabrielle's system. I race from my seat to Ben's side. He's still unconscious.

"Is he okay?"

Gabrielle is already motioning a scanner over him. The computer screen displaying his stats blinks like crazy.

"Something caused his nanos to attack his body. They've stopped, but are performing at 5%. They're barely repairing the damage at all."

"Tell me his health status?" I demand, angling to the screen and touching it. Immediately, the data downloads. I call up my EP to translate it to my brain—

"He's *dying*?" I thrust myself Gabrielle's way, but she blocks me with her arm. "Gabrielle! Let me help him!"

Gabrielle plunges an apparatus with a needle into Ben's neck.

"I'm stabilizing him," she growls, pushing me back. "Let me do it."

Tears erupt from my eyes and my knees buckle. I land in a heap on the lab floor, eyes trained on the screen. The flashing slows.

"It was a virus," I say, panting.

"A virus?"

The thumping of running feet sounds from outside the door. Seconds later, Meyer, Sanda, and Aron burst into the room.

"What's happening?" Sanda demands, barreling toward her mother.

Gabrielle whips her head up with a stern expression that halts the three of them. "I need you to *leave* the lab."

"But Gabrielle—" Meyer protests.

"Get out!" she growls, waving them off.

Meyer gives me a concerned look, but no matter how much I want him to stay, I agree that Gabrielle is probably right. Too many people in here might make the situation more dangerous than it already is. I motion to them that I'm fine, even though the reality is I'm not.

Sanda plants her feet beside Gabrielle. "I've been trained as a field medic, Mom."

"Go, Sanda. This is beyond that," Gabrielle instructs.

Sanda's stiff shoulders lower slightly and she does an about face, exiting the room. Meyer grabs Aron's arm. "Come on," he mutters before giving me one last glance and pulling Aron into the hall.

"They're gone. Now tell me what you're doing," I say to Gabrielle.

"I was forced to put him into a coma to figure out how to heal him."

"What do you mean?" I palm Ben's forehead and get

236

nothing from him. No emotion ... nothing.

"I noticed a small vascular abnormality in his brain the other day. At first, I didn't know what it was, but I called up a bunch of old research. It didn't seem like much. You don't see conditions like that much anymore. When everything went haywire, though, it increased."

"Shouldn't his nanobots have repaired it? Even before today?" I ask, my palms growing sweaty. Brain damage was not a possibility I had considered, or that immersion could ever harm Ben or me. "There's no way this is happening."

"I reviewed all that, and his nanos appeared fine, performing optimally. But it was insignificant, possibly a hereditary predisposition."

My mind reels. *Was that what Devan died from? Is our ability making it worse?*

"Did you tell him?"

Guilt washes her face. "I did. We talked about it when you went into town. He said not to say anything to you. That he'd let you know about it."

Anger burns in my chest. "Gabrielle, you had no idea he'd be okay, but you let him go in anyway?"

"I was monitoring the problem and it seemed stable. I was certain we'd be able to avoid a situation like a cloaked virus. You two have such good instincts ..." She frowns. "I didn't even consider one with the ability to be uploaded to a human."

I ache to scream at her, tell her she should have known better, but how could she when Ben was hiding the severity of his sickness from her? His instincts were dampened by hiding his problem from me, but of course Manning would install a virus in the system. He probably used a coder in information security to do it. Security has probably been upgraded immensely as of now with the impending war.

"Do you think the Trojan took our information? Our location?" I ask. Normally, that would have been something I would have checked for, but my one goal was to get Ben out alive.

"From what I can tell, that particular Trojan's function was to destroy, not to download data."

"Destroy? How are Ben and I supposed to take out the grid, then?"

Gabrielle's face falls, and I know the answer before she says it.

"Avlyn, you may be doing this on your own. If you can't, we'll have to come up with another strategy."

I pinch at the bridge of my nose as I rack my brain for a solution. None comes. Gabrielle is completely right, and without Ben, this whole thing is impossible.

"I can go in and repair his nanos like Sanda's."

Gabrielle sighs. "That was different. This is an actual upgrade, not simply a repair. If you don't code the upgrade just right, it's likely to kill him."

"My nanos are upgraded," I say remembering the last VachTech upgrade. "What if you could take mine and implant them?"

"Avlyn," she says. "Your upgrade was specifically designed for your DNA. It might take me days or even weeks to pull it apart and re-sequence it. It's possible, but not now."

I approach him as Gabrielle sits distracted at her viewer, scrolling through code. Gently, I place my hand to his shoulder and shut my eyes. No emotions, only emptiness.

Honing my energy into him, I slow my breathing. I will the

real world to fall away into nothing but haze, and it's gone. The space I transport to is dark. Viscous. My heart speeds up, and I fixate on the beats to slow them.

"Ben?" I call.

No answer.

Fear wells in my chest, but I call again.

"Ben, can you hear me?"

Silence reverberates through the thick air. He doesn't seem to hear me, and I'm getting emptiness back from him.

"Take me to Ben's nanobots."

The space around me shimmers slightly.

"Ben's nanos. *Immediately*," I say, more forcefully this time.

Out of nowhere, the tech appears. Several of the spider-like units float. I step toward the nearest one and place my hand on it. The strong urge to repair the system and try to heal Ben takes over me, but Gabrielle said it was too dangerous. Instead, I prompt it for information. The units themselves are functioning properly, as Gabrielle said, but because of the modifications in Ben's brain from using his ability so much, it's not syncing. I scan the code and analyze the reporting file to see where it's falling short. The problem lies within a few lines of code. I think the nanos are causing the short circuit in Ben's brain. When they try to connect and heal, they're doing the opposite and damaging him further.

I can fix this. I can help him.

I place my hands on the nano to bring up the code structure, one by one changing the symbols and moving them to new destinations. As I complete each sequence, heat moves from my fingers and up my arms. Through gritted teeth, I ignore the sensation. I've felt something similar in the past when modifying code while immersed, but I know this is different. The heat grows, stinging and engulfing me like fire.

My mind spins and I fight to remain conscious.

I must complete this ... for Ben.

As I stretch for the last line of code, I wince at the pain. Quickly, I lower my finger to tap the symbol set, but before my hand reaches it, a burst of light slams me backward into the air. My body crashes into the earth. Someone seizes my shoulders and rips me back further. The immersed world is gone and the lab appears.

"What are you doing?" Gabrielle yells.

In my vision, my EP flickers on and off until static takes over the view. The static bursts into a white light and then the EP is dead. Gabrielle continues speaking, but her voice now sounds no stronger than a muffled murmur in the distance.

"Avlyn?" I barely hear her say.

With a snap, my hearing returns to full volume.

"Avlyn!"

I throw my hands to my ears, overwhelmed. A sharp prick digs into my neck and everything goes black.

I suck in a huge gasp of air and shoot up from lying flat on my back. A pair of strong hands grabs my shoulders, holding me in place. I whip my head to the side to find Meyer inches from my face, terror filling his coal eyes.

"She's up!" he yells.

I swivel my gaze around the room. I'm in the lab, but this time Ben's not here.

"Where's Ben?" I swing my legs off—I turn to see what I'm

on—one of the tables made into a makeshift bed.

Meyer clutches my arm, stopping me.

"Let me go," I growl.

"Ben's fine. For now."

I swivel my head back to Meyer. "For now? What's going on?"

"Gabrielle knows more than I do." Meyer narrows his eyes in worry. "She believes if his nanos were fully operational, he could have handled it. But when you connected with him, it made his bots go berserk. He was headed toward a cardiac arrest."

"What? I ... I tried to *patch* his nanos." My body stiffens with guilt. "Is he okay? You said he was okay."

Meyer exhales a lengthy breath. "For now. The patch worked, but he's weak. Gabrielle did a scan and he's stable."

I sink into a slouch, relieved. "Can I see him?"

Meyer shakes his head. "He's sleeping in our room. Gabrielle says it's speeding up the healing process."

"What happened to me?"

"Gabrielle's theory is you basically crashed and rebooted," Meyer explains.

I try to activate my EP, but nothing happens. "I think my EP crashed, too."

"I guess you'll be relying on your instincts until we get it fixed, because there are no extras around here."

A soft beeping sound comes from Gabrielle's still-active screen. Meyer approaches it and taps the surface. Up pops a link.

Urgent Message for Avlyn Lark.

My heart nearly vaults into my throat at the words. *Who else knows I'm here? Did Gabrielle tell Ruiz already?*

I hop from the table, any dizziness I had before clearing instantly. I reach for the link, then stop, asking, "Should we get Gabrielle?"

"It says the message is for you, not her."

I click my tongue and hesitate a moment longer, then activate the message.

Place your hand to the screen for identity check.

I look to Meyer, confused.

"Well, do it," he says.

"Is it safe?"

Meyer laughs. "Gabrielle is basically you in twenty-five years without the crazy abilities. She's a systems *genius*. No one is hacking her unless she invited them to do so."

I do as Meyer and the message say and press my hand to the cold screen. A scan slowly runs the length of my hand.

DNA Scan complete.

The words disappear and an older woman with straight dark hair peppered with gray strands comes onto the screen. My breath hitches. Something in me tells me I know her, but I'm unsure from where.

"Avlyn?" the woman says.

I straighten in my seat. "Yes?"

"I apologize for this being a recorded message."

I relax, knowing it's not a live vid.

"My intention was to speak with you in person, but that is no longer an option. My name is Cynthia Fisher—"

That's where I know her from. The vid I watched last month showing her and Ruiz resigning as Elorian directors over thirty years ago.

"I'm in contact with Ruiz. She's stuck in New Philadelphia and feels contacting you is too dangerous. Somehow, Manning has learned what you're fully capable of. You must *not* let him locate you. I would advise relocation, but I cannot provide you with any options in case of compromise. Manning may have released scouts to find you. There is no time for different plans." Cynthia pauses and looks away from the screen. She turns back to face me, and pleading lingers in her eyes. "You must evacuate from your current location with Ben *immediately.*"

The mention of Ben forms a lump in my throat. Cynthia regains her composure and signs off. The screen goes blank.

"How does she know about Ben?" I ask Meyer.

"I don't know, Avlyn. But we have to wake everyone and decide what to do."

❖❖❖

"I made no mention of Ben in any of my messages," Gabrielle says.

"Then how does she *know?*" I demand.

Gabrielle paces in the hall as everyone in the group, except an absent Ben, stares at her. "Your guess is as good as mine. But despite all that, Fisher's advice was sound. You're not safe here anymore."

Suspicion battles the trust I have for Gabrielle, but I don't have time for it. Trust is going to have to win out.

Meyer looks to me and I nod that I'm fine to move on. "Okay, so what are our orders?" he asks Gabrielle.

Gabrielle pinches the bridge of her nose. "Nothing was finalized, but I was able to set you up in a remote location. The fuel cells in the pod should get you there before you'll require a recharge."

"It's not the best time to travel, but I'm still headed to outside Elore," Sanda says. "I'll go tonight, too."

Gabrielle nods. "Then that leaves the three of you to get packed. I'll prepare everything for Ben."

"Already on it." Aron swings around and sprints down the hall toward his room.

Meyer touches my arm. "See you in a few minutes."

I give him a thin, nervous smile and he follows Aron. Guess Aron's coming with us after all.

"Thank you for what you've done for us," I say to Gabrielle.

"No thanks are needed."

From the lab door behind us, Gabrielle's system beeps with another incoming message. I turn to the noise and she hurries for the door.

"Maybe it was a false alarm," I suggest, clinging to the hope of it as I follow her. Gabrielle taps her computer screen and writing scrolls across the surface. It's a message from her Underground communication system.

Warning to outlying community projects: Elore has launched a full-fledged attack on New Philadelphia. Outlying communities are likely to be targeted. New Philadelphia will be unable to assist. Evacuation Procedure 2.

"What's evacuation procedure two?" I ask, a numbing chill creeping over my scalp.

"Everyone for themselves," Gabrielle says.

CHAPTER TWENTY-FIVE

My hands suddenly have no place to go and I shove them in my pockets. My fingers catch on something and I pull it out. The crushed red flower Ash gave me at the dance sits on my palm.

Sickness roils in my stomach. *Everyone for themselves? What about the families, children? How are the communities supposed to know what's coming when they aren't on the grid? They won't get this message before it's too late.*

If I went there, I can warn them and activate the community grid again so the message would be spread.

"How can we let Thornton know?" I ask.

Gabrielle stands and grabs for my shoulders, rotating me toward the door, the flower dropping from my hand to the floor. "I don't know, Avlyn."

"We could help them. *I* could help them, activate their grid system—"

"No, you can't. They're completely offline and the system is inaccessible from here. The one way to do that is for you to physically *be* in Thornton. It's too risky and you need to be out of here in a couple hours." She hustles me into the hall. "Go fetch your brother."

I turn to her and intend to protest more, but the expression on her face quiets me. I let out a frustrated sigh and sprint the way of Ben's room.

I activate the door and it slides back. Ben stands, slowly pulling on the top of his camo suit. His face showing the signs of exhaustion, but he's up.

"You lied to me about being sick."

"I never lied to you," he replied. "I didn't tell you."

"That's the same thing." Anger mixed with relief that at least he's *alive* burns in my chest.

"Avlyn," he drops heavily back into a chair, blinking blearily, as though dizzy, "you're the one who convinced me we needed to stop Manning when you got back from Thornton. I was doing what you wanted."

The anger in my chest morphs into guilt. "You seem better," I choke out.

Ben tips his head, his expression softening. "I'm sorry. A job needed to be done, and I didn't want to worry you."

"Well, you did."

"I know, but I feel better, thanks to you. Gabrielle says I have to take it easy. The abnormality in my brain is still there."

"I was able to patch your nanos, but the sudden reboot almost caused a cardiac arrest—" Tears sting in the corners of my eyes. I quickly blink them away. He's okay for now. I simply must construct a way to upgrade his tech, and he will be healed. If mine hadn't been upgraded in Philly, I might be having this problem, too.

"You shouldn't feel guilty," he says. "It was my choice to hide it."

I nod, inhaling deeply.

Ben scans over the clothes I'm wearing. "You should get your camo suit, too. Meyer said they would be best for the journey. Bring whatever else you have."

"How long until we leave?"

"Gabrielle said we must be out of here in about two hours, max."

I rush to Ben and throw my arms around his neck, the corners of my eyes burning with tears again. "I'll figure out how to fix you."

Ben sighs. "I'm fine."

I pull back from him. "I know you are. It's not just that." My mind lurches with the thought of the impending assault on Thornton. They need to know it's coming. If I ran, I could make it in less than thirty minutes. Meyer made it in that time.

Ben frowns up at me. "What's the matter?"

I look away to avoid Ben's stare, trying to block my emotions from him. "Nothing. I'm nervous about leaving."

"No, this is different." He reaches and gently moves my face toward him, staring deep into my eyes.

I yank from him. "Don't read me."

"You're headed into town. Why?"

I clap my hand over his mouth. "Elore may attack Thornton. Their grid is totally down again, so Gabrielle can't get a hold of anyone. Someone has to warn them. Maybe I can reactivate the grid network to alert any other communities."

The blood drains from Ben's face and he shakes his head, pulling my hand away. "That's not going to work. There's not time."

"I have to try. It will take me half an hour to get there."

"It's too dark, and if we lose you—" he says.

"Just in case, I'll bring my Flexx for you to track. I'll contact you to pick me up in the pod."

"This is a dumb idea, Avlyn."

"I won't have those people's deaths on my head if I can stop it."

Ben shakes his head and an overwhelming sense of confusion and sorrow reaches me. "Go now."

I hug him one last time. "I'll put my stuff on my bed. Keep the others off my tracks."

In my room, I throw my limited belongings into a bag and squeeze into my camo suit and coat. I check the time on my Flexx and grab the stunner I brought with me from New Philly, holstering it to the side of my suit. After, I hurry above ground, luckily avoiding anyone else.

The frigid air nips at my face, but my suit provides surprisingly good insulation from the cold. Even with the full moon lighting the path, I stumble a few times. Soon the muted glow of the town's solar lights gives me hope, and I race toward them.

28 minutes

That's how much time my Flexx tells me it took to get here. As soon as I'm done, I'll contact Ben and let him know I'm headed back.

This late at night, the streets are empty. I hadn't considered I might not be able to find the sheriff. I hustle to his office and am met with a locked, old-fashioned door. No fancy automatic slider, of course, which makes it that much harder for me to break in without waking anyone else before I want to. The sheriff should be first to hear the news so he can decide what to do.

Standing at the door, I rap on the wooden surface. Hopefully the sheriff's inside.

Nothing.

"Sheriff?" I call, knocking louder this time, about ready to kick in the door.

Footsteps sound from indoors, probably from the back room. I comb my fingers back through my hair, waiting impatiently for him to come, then my racing heart nearly jumps into my throat.

I didn't change my hair color.

I close my eyes and will the nanos in my hair to shift and bring the end of a short lock forward. Blonde. As I do, the handle rattles and the door flies toward me. The sheriff stands there, ruffled hair and rumpled clothes, holding a bluish, glowing cylinder. He extends it to my face and squints. "What is— You? Why are you here?" The sheriff peers past me into the mostly darkened street, lit by the stars and the moon and a few dim solar lights. "Where are the others?"

"There's not time. I need to speak with you."

With narrowed eyes, confusion crosses his face, but he allows me to enter. I step in and shut the door behind me. The room's sole illumination comes from the glowing item the sheriff holds.

"They're coming," I say, looking to the weapon holstered on his hip, just peeking out from his untucked shirt.

He blinks owlishly. "Who's coming?"

"Elore is en route to attack New Philly, and might be taking out the communities on the way."

The sheriff's eyes grow wide. "Why would they do that? We're not a threat."

"Gabrielle received a warning—Evacuation Code Two."

All the blood drains from the sheriff's face. "Philly won't assist?"

"Sheriff, bring up the grid again and warn the other communities. They won't know."

He shakes his head. "I can't bring it up. A representative from New Philly came in and took the entire operating system off to repair it."

"But the grid is still there. You can't access it?"

"Yes, but it does us no use. The one thing to do now is get this place evacuated. There's little we can do about the rest of the communities. Please excuse me." He turns and scrambles behind the counter into the back room, returning with a coat and a pair of shoes. "Unless you want to help, you should get back to your people and evacuate."

I gulp. He's going to find the next statement I have to say ridiculous, but I won't let the outlying communities be destroyed.

"Did they take the connection to the information port?"

"For what?" he asks, pulling on his shoes.

"For the computer system."

"They took everything." He reaches for the door to exit. "I need to go."

"Let me look."

The sheriff pulls his hand back from the doorknob. "What do you mean?"

I swallow thickly. "I'll access it."

"There's nothing *to* access," he insists, confused.

"There might be." I scan the room where the system was. The table is empty.

The sheriff narrows his eyes at me, realization rising. "*You* did it. You and your friends activated the grid. Why?"

It's as if his words punch me in the stomach. "Let me help you assist the other communities."

"You did something to the system, and because of it we're stuck out here with no emergency communications!"

He kicks at the leg of the table, revealing the capped-off information port on the wall. "They put that on. Said it was a safety precaution and they'd have the system back in a day or two." He clenches his jaw and waves his hand, motioning for me to move.

"I'm sorry," I whisper. "It was an accident. But I can fix it now."

"Accident? Something like that is *not* an accident. Now leave before you make this situation worse than it already is." The sheriff latches onto my upper arm and forces me into the door he opens, pushing me into the street. "I have a town to save. Go save yourself."

With that, he reaches to his hip and produces a gun. Not a stunner, an old-fashioned model. Without my EP, I'm unable to identify what kind.

In shock, I throw my hands into the air. "But the communities—"

"You're talking crazy. Now let me do my job."

My mind spins, trying to find an alternative, but he's right. If there's nothing for me to access, I'm locked out of the system.

Ben's voice enters my brain. *Get out of there now.*

Why? I ask.

Gabrielle has detected incoming ships on the scanner.

Can you get me?

Not yet. They're still making preparations, but Meyer's worried sick and Gabrielle won't let him leave the bunker. Hurry.

I shake my head from the conversation with Ben and return to the present. I give the sheriff one final look, but he motions with his gun a second time.

"Yes, I'm gone." I raise my hands in surrender. "But I just got word Elorian ships are coming right now. Get your people far from here."

The sheriff tips his head skeptically and turns, bolting down the road, shouting for people to wake up. I can't do anything else for them now, so I sprint from Thornton.

With the dark world lit only by the night sky, I come to a halt as something thunders over the dirt in back of me. I swing around at the sound. A shadowy horse and rider grow larger as the sound increases.

"Who's there?" the rider calls, slowing his horse to a walk.

I recognize the voice. Vincent. Instinct tells me to bolt, but he might follow.

"I'm leaving," I shout. "But you should go help the sheriff. Elore is on the way."

"Whoa," he says, pulling at the reins. The horse stops and Vincent stays seated on its back, never taking his eyes from me. "Evacuate?"

"Elore is coming, destroying everything in its path."

He directs the horse toward me. "How do you know?"

"Gabrielle heard it on the Underground Comm. You said

you have connections. You haven't heard?"

"I've been out. What's your name again?" he asks.

I grit my teeth at the unexpected question. *Why does he care?*

"Um—Kyra," I spit out. I don't know why I said her name, but I couldn't reveal my real one.

He pinches his lips together for a second. "You sure?"

My heart tells me to go, but I know I won't be able to outrun him. I must play this carefully.

"You really need to get to town," I insist. "The ships are arriving soon."

"Kyra, huh?" Vincent leans forward on the horse. "I believe you're the girl Philly's searching for. A representative who came in to investigate on the grid activation was chatty. I like that type. Always get lots of information."

Philly's looking for me?

Of course they are. Both Manning and Waters need my ability.

An uneasy laugh escapes me and my breathing picks up. "I don't know what you're talking about."

Vincent sits wordlessly, a deep shadow cast on his face from the moonlight behind him.

"You have me confused," I insist. "I'm here to visit Gabrielle. That's it—"

Overhead movement catches my eyes. I gasp. *That's an Elorian pod, and it's headed Gabrielle's way.*

"See, they're coming!"

Without warning, the pod pitches and makes a slight descent. The horse whinnies and kicks at the ground with its front foot at the movement. The ship gathers speed, and I expect it will pull up at any moment, but it doesn't. Instead, it plummets to the earth.

Fire lights up the sky as the pod collides with the earth, a crashing *boom* shaking the ground beneath my feet. I should leave. *Now.*

"Something big is happening, and you're at the center of it, girl," he says.

"Mister, that may or may not be true, but as of now, I have to go to Gabrielle's. Please let me."

A second explosion blasts from up the hill and the sky lights red. The horse lets out a whinny and steps backward.

"Whoa, girl!" Vincent calls. He yanks on the reins, but it's too late. The agitated beast rears up and I scurry from its kicking legs.

Vincent flies from the saddle, landing in a heap on the ground. The horse gallops a few yards and pauses. It bobs its head, agitated. Fear swells in my chest as I stare at Vincent, lying on the ground unconscious. He knows who I am and that Philly is looking for me.

My eyes flit to the horse, swishing its tail. I know I shouldn't leave him like this, but I can't risk helping him.

I beeline to the horse and grab for the saddle, pulling myself onto its back. I click my tongue and lightly squeeze my legs around the horse's side, compelling it to advance. The two of us trot overtop the terrain, closer to the bunker and toward the burning wreckage of the ship. Its flames kick up into the dark sky, painting it orange and red. I send a message to Ben.

I'm on the way.

CHAPTER TWENTY-SIX

Ben's response flows through my thoughts.
A ship crashed halfway here. Be careful.
I know. I'm nearly there.

The horse struggles up the hill to Gabrielle's, but with my continued encouragement and leaning forward over the animal's neck, we make it faster than I could have on foot. As I ride, the smoking wreck grows closer, as does the acrid smell of burning foliage and metal. The horse becomes increasingly agitated, tossing its head. To avoid it throwing me off, I slow the beast and dismount, tying the reins to a low branch on a tree.

"Shh, you're ok," I whisper to the animal, but it fails to soothe it much as it sidesteps and pulls against the tether.

I leave it be, covering my mouth with the top part of my zipped-up coat to block any smoke and gasses. The poor horse can't do that, but I need him. As I get nearer, a strong caustic odor burns my nose, making my eyes sting. I scan the area for any survivors, but the state of the wreckage makes that scenario unlikely. The once-teardrop-shaped silver pod is smashed in on the front and sides, and flames lick skyward from the body of the pod. So far, I don't detect any life except the horse, who surprisingly remains patiently behind me despite the destruction ahead. What a time for my EP to be dead. I grab for the hidden stunner under my jacket and ready the cold metal weapon.

What are you doing?

I suck in a breath, but it's just Ben.

I'm at the wreck.

Circling the burning pod, I spot the globe and arrow symbol of Direction. Confirmed Elorian ship.

Avlyn, don't worry about that, Ben urges. *Meyer's already gone to check it out.*

I might be able to get some information we can use.

As I continue to circle, I spot a shadow, pushing away the thought of Ben's request—order—and blocking him from my brain.

There's someone about thirty feet ahead of the ship on the ground. They're not moving.

If I only had my EP to tell me if they're alive or not.

I keep my stunner extended and lock onto the injured person. I creep forward as the heat of the fire licks at my cheek. The injured male—maybe in his mid-twenties—is sprawled out on the ground. Brightness from the full moon highlights the dark blood dripping from the side of his head. His uniform, smeared with dirt and what must be more blood, displays the letters DPF— Direction Preservation Force—across his chest.

This citizen is most likely a Level One citizen under Manning's control. Who knows what he's been programmed to do out here? The rising and falling of his chest is so infrequent and shallow I'm surprised I can even see it. Despite that, I continue with my weapon trained in his direction.

From behind, an explosion rocks the ship. I whip around as the horse pulls loose from where I tied it and bolts back toward the town. Nothing I can do about that, but I can get this guy further away in case the pod completely destroys itself.

I hustle to the fallen soldier's side, bracing myself. I grab his arms and drag him from the flaming pod with all my might. When I get him a safe enough distance, I drop him, bending to his side and studying his blood-smeared face in the moonlight. Something about him seems familiar, but I shrug off the feeling and place my hand on his shoulder to access his nanos.

Instantly, the night disappears, replaced by silvery haze. Code swirls around me, but unlike the times before when the symbols felt warm and welcoming, this time it's cold. Stiffness racks my body. I'm not wanted here. I ignore the cold and make the tech obey.

"Take me to his nanobots."

The code vibrates and tightly whirlwinds. When it pauses, the representation of his nanos floats ahead of me. The teardrop-shaped tech hovers in the air, its tentacles released and hanging. The energy emitting from the tech is hot; red. If this were Ben and I read his emotions, I'd say he was angry—furious, in fact.

Despite that, I need to figure out what Manning is doing to the DPF, and how to stop him.

I thrust my hands out and grasp for the frame of the nano. A shock travels through my fingers and courses my entire self. Heat follows. A scream sticks in my throat and I focus the energy of it forward.

"Display tracking program," I gasp.

The code spirals in front of me and I manually sort the data strings, making sure to disable the program.

"Download data," I say through gritted teeth when satisfied the tracking is no longer operational.

A shot of electricity grips me, but I don't let go. Instead, I harness the power and direct it into the bot. Sparks fly around us and then freezes. In the tech's moment of weakness, I force into the surface of the nano. This time, heat spiders out from my hands, overtaking the tech. A deluge of information engulfs my body and brain, some of which is how Manning upgraded the nanobots to control the DPF and how he's using them.

I pull my hands back and the calm of the floating code returns. The nano disappears and leaves me alone in the room.

New knowledge spirals in my brain. These nanos are supercharged. Everything about them is upgraded. For some reason, they're not healing this soldier.

I analyze the nano structure and they appear fully operational. They are designed as a general upgrade and not specific to the DNA of the host.

What if these upgraded nanos might help Ben? Heal him? *I have to get this back to the bunker.*

I release to the current reality, which is much colder and darker than the one in the immersed world. In front of me is the still-dying soldier. *DPF-UNIT682* flashes in my mind. I must have downloaded that, too.

I pat his body for anything he might be carrying and dig into his pants pocket, withdrawing a tightly folded piece of paper. Slowly, I peel open the folds, revealing a childish drawing—stick figures of a family. The largest is labeled Father, the second Mother, and a child with the word 'Me' scrawled over the head.

Encircling the family unit is a heart.

I fold the paper up and return it to the soldier's pocket, touching the place where the golden pendant Ben gave me sits buried under my jacket and suit. Manning stole this person from his family, and he won't see them again. Maybe he slipped the contraband paper into his pocket before Manning's upgrades took full hold, who knows, but it's there. Guilt grips me. I want to assist him, but at this point, it's likely impossible.

His eyes start to flutter. There's no way for me to carry him, and even awake he'll be too weak to manage without assistance. I won't just leave him either. His nanos should be operational and could heal him, and I can't have him reporting Gabrielle's whereabouts to Manning.

Not thinking, I stroke the metal of my stunner.

It would be quick. He wouldn't even know it was happening.

My head dizzies with the thought.

No, I refuse to kill him in cold blood.

I lean in, studying his face in the light of the moon. I *know* this man. I rack my brain to place him and then it hits me. I only saw him briefly, on the street of Level One, but he's the spouse of the woman who was experimented on in GenTech. The one who died in the explosion.

DPF-UNIT682 … no, no … his name is Jensen.

How do I know that? I fumble for the drawing from his pocket and unfold it again. Sure enough, the woman in it has long blonde hair.

What was her name? Naomi … Naomi Jensen. I can't kill this man. If I do, their child will be left an orphan. Not only his mother, dead at my hands, but his father, too.

I fold up the paper and shove it into my pocket, then shift back to him. Without warning, his hands are squeezing my neck. I gasp as he forces me to the ground and pulls the stunner from my grasp, turning it my way. It's set to stun, but at this range—

The burst of the stunner explodes, but instead of me, the soldier flies back. I whip around, grabbing at my stinging neck. A moonlit figure races out of the darkness—*Meyer,* I think with relief—and slides up to my side, demanding, "Are you okay?"

I glance over to the soldier. "Is he dead?"

"I stunned him. You've got to get back. It's time to leave." A crease forms between Meyer's eyes. "What were you *doing* out here, anyway?"

"Warning the town Elore is on the way. I was hoping to start up the grid again." I motion to the stunned soldier on the ground. "It's my fault they're going to attack the communities. They needed a chance to get out."

"Did it work?" Meyer asks.

I shake my head. "No. The sheriff wouldn't listen."

Meyer lets out a frustrated sigh. "Did you tell him about your ability?"

"It was the one way to contact the other communities."

"But now the sheriff knows who you are." Meyer latches onto my arm and drags me with him. "We should go. I brought the pod."

"We're going to abandon the soldier?"

Still gripping my arm, Meyer stops and looks me straight in the eyes. "We don't have time to deal with that guy."

"He has a family."

"Avlyn, *you're* my family, and I need to keep *you* alive."

His confession sends a shock down my spine, filling me with

emotions I'm lost at how to express.

"Meyer ... I can't leave him," I protest weakly. "I know who he is, and he might be useful. He's pumped with supernanos, the ones Manning is using to control the DPF. I downloaded data, but I think the actual tech might solve Ben's problem. We won't know for certain unless we take the soldier with us."

Meyer releases his grip and furrows his brow in thought. "Fine," he finally says.

He holsters his stunner and bends to gather the soldier. The stiffness in his body from the stun has dissipated, but he should stay unconscious for at least another twenty minutes. Lucky for Meyer, most Elorian males tend to be lean, and this one is no exception. Even so, Meyer grunts as he maneuvers the soldier over his shoulder and lugs him to the pod. I jump in the front passenger spot as Meyer dumps the soldier into a heap onto the seat in back of the captain's chair and secures the door. He then opens his door and slides into the front, activating the pod.

"You should be more careful with him," I murmur.

"I couldn't care less about this guy," he says gruffly. "I'm doing this because *you* think it's important. Sorry if I don't provide him with the preferred treatment."

It's no use arguing with him. He's doing what I asked, and we're wasting time.

The pod lifts off the ground, the engine humming lightly. Meyer flies it forward and over the wreck, rotating it toward Gabrielle's bunker.

CHAPTER TWENTY-SEVEN

Meyer lowers the pod, and as soon as it powers off, I'm out. Quickly, I search the sky. There's a chance of a rescue ship coming to retrieve the missing soldier. His tracking is disengaged, but I'm sure they have his last known location. If I'm to do this, I have to hurry.

I help Meyer pull him from the back of the pod, and after he hoists the soldier over his shoulder, I sprint ahead to Gabrielle's bunker.

We're here, I think to Ben.

A sense of relief from him rushes over me.

At the door, I'm met by Aron and Sanda. Aron's jaw is tense, his brow furrowed. "Where have you been? Ben knows, but he wouldn't tell anyone."

"My mom is going nuts," Sanda adds. "You took a huge risk, Avlyn."

I cross my arms over my body and stare her straight in the eye. "Sorry, but I'm not the only one to do that recently."

Sanda pinches her lips together. She's one to talk of risky behavior. The whole reason she was captured in Elore was because of a choice to graffiti a wall with an Affinity rebellion message.

"I'm aware my choices got good people killed," Sanda says. "I have to live with that every day. You and I both know it's no fun."

She and I lock eyes while Aron watches on. The statement stabs me in the gut with the reminder of Lena's capture, which resulted in her death.

Aron steps outside and attempts to help Meyer bring in the injured soldier. "Who's this?" he asks.

Meyer answers in a low tone. I'm unable to make out what he says, though I'm confident it involved a few choice words.

"Let's hope nobody dies this time," I say to Sanda.

She lowers her eyes.

"Have your mom get the lab ready. We have to get this guy hooked into her system."

Sanda gives me a tentative look, but nods and sprints down the corridor toward the lab. Into the open door, Meyer heaves in the dead weight of the soldier. Aron follows.

"Where do you want him?" Meyer asks me.

"Lab." I flatten to the wall and let Meyer pass, then tail him down. On the way, I spot Ben seated at the table in the eating area. His face is still white and dark circles paint the area below his eyes.

I hang on the door frame, my heart aching to see him well. "Come with me."

He shakes his head, letting out a sigh. "Avlyn, we need to go. This is important to you, but you're not thinking clearly. You're putting everyone at risk. You're making decisions with your emotions, not your head."

"But I have thought this through logically. *Not* healing you puts everyone at risk." I check the time on my handheld. "We have about thirty minutes. I can do this. *We* can do this. Now come on."

Reluctantly, Ben stands and tails me.

In the lab, we're greeted with a sour-faced Gabrielle. "The four of you should be gone. I've secured a place for you to lay low, but if you leave too late, I can't guarantee your safety."

I square my shoulders and plant my feet. "Gabrielle, you can't guarantee anyone's safety."

Instead of lecturing me further, she twists Meyer's way as he dumps the soldier onto the table.

"Get him paired with your system," I say. "I accessed his nanobots in the field. Although it's tainted with Manning's control mechanism, I believe the upgraded system will heal the abnormality in Ben's brain."

"Avlyn—" Gabrielle starts.

"We need to take a physical sample, and then transplant a small amount of the upgraded tech into Ben after we strip them of Manning's control. I can guide the fusion." I turn to Aron. "The nanos are not much different from microscopic drones. I'd like you to monitor their health and the progress on screen."

Aron looks to Gabrielle for approval, his eyes wide.

"Avlyn," Gabrielle says, "this is all well and good and sounds plausible, but it's too risky. This is the kind of thing to do under much less stress. Where I'm sending you, there will be resources. I'll get the sample and send it with you. Otherwise, you might convert Ben into some sort of killing machine like the DPF."

Her last words stop me in my tracks. All my energy and

excitement drains away. My original plan and Gabrielle's change snake in my brain, my hands balling at my sides in frustration. *Ben needs to be healed now*, my mind insists, but I know she's also right. We can't afford to make a mistake.

"Agreed." My eyes move to the soldier on the table, still immobilized from Meyer's stun. Blood is flowing from his wounds. I have no need for my EP to tell me his life signs are continuing to fail, despite his upgraded tech. It doesn't make sense. "Either way, I can go in and fully disable Manning's control, then get you the sample."

Gabrielle locks her eyes onto mine and I can almost see the thoughts running through her head. "I think we have time for that." She retrieves the wiring to patch the soldier into her system and attaches it to his head. As she does, he struggle for a breath.

Gabrielle turns to our group, scanning each one of us. "Meyer, go ready the pods up top. Sanda, if you have nothing left to prepare, go help him."

Meyer glances my way and wordlessly holds my gaze for a second. "Good luck," he finally says. He gestures Sanda toward the door and they both leave.

"Aron," Gabrielle says, "Avlyn was right. I could use your assistance monitoring the nanobots to get this done faster."

Aron grabs a rolling chair from behind him and sits at the viewer.

"Initiate the program," Gabrielle says to him as she finishes adjusting the disks affixed to the soldier's head. She then hands one to me, and I stick the disk to my temple. "Are you ready, Avlyn?"

I move closer to the table and scan the man's face. *Why is the tech failing even though it shouldn't be?* I hover my hands above the soldier's chest until Gabrielle tells me to touch him. I look at Ben, standing to the side, drawing in the whole scene. The unease coming from him shivers down my spine.

"Ready," I say.

Gabrielle zips to her chair. Her fingers fly over the touch screen, activating the same program she used to test Ben and me.

"Three ... Two ..."

When she hits one, I thrust my hands onto the soldier's chest and command the data to surface. Immersing, everything goes blank, but I'm immediately hit with a wave of pain, resistance.

"*Get out of my head!*" a voice screeches.

I scream and throw my hands to my ears, but it's no use.

CHAPTER TWENTY-EIGHT

The voice tells me to leave over and over. Instead, I plant myself. Overwhelming fear consumes me, but it's not mine. It's the soldier's, and for some reason, I'm experiencing this person's emotions the same way I feel Ben's. Because of it, I know he's not telling *me* to go. It's the tech he's fighting.

"I'm not here to harm you. I can help."

Silence.

I command his nanos to return while I still have the chance. Three of them shimmer into view and hover in the space, as they did the last time I immersed. I call for the tech, and one of them floats to my side.

"I want to heal you," I repeat to the soldier, focusing on the nano. Slowly, I lower my hands to the pearly body.

"You—can't help me—too late," the soldier's disembodied voice finally struggles to say, making me flinch.

I look from the nano, keeping my hands on its frame. "I think I can, but I need full access to your tech. Then I'll monitor for a malfunction."

The voice groans. "There is—a mal—function."

"Where is it?"

Vibration worms its way into my fingers and up my arms.

"Who are you?" he asks, avoiding the question.

A shock of nervousness speeds into my gut. I can't tell the soldier who I am. What if it triggers a reaction?

"A friend. Someone who believes what they did to you is unacceptable."

"They made—me—into a machine," he says after a stretch of silence. "I don't want to be a machine—and that's why I'm broken."

"Yes, I know your nanos are malfunctioning. They're not healing you. I can fix it if you let me."

The vibration grows stronger, and the burning heat of frustration comes with it. The emotions are mixed: anger, sadness, loss.

I lift my hands from the nano. "I understand you're frustrated, but we don't have much time for me to explain. Please stop fighting and give me access."

"It's *you* who doesn't understand," the voice booms. "It's not my tech that's faulty—it's *me*. I'm preventing it from healing my body. It's the only way to retain part of my humanity."

"I'm confused."

The voice groans. "After I was drafted, they installed this new tech. I could sense it taking hold, snaking its way through my body and brain. They intended for us to forget everything. For a while, it worked. I couldn't remember who I was. But—but I knew I was somebody—had something, *someone* to live for. I found what I had hidden in my shoe. I guess they didn't find it when they brought me in because they couldn't detect it. It was so simple, so childish. It should have been nothing, but it wasn't."

My chest tightens as the memory of the paper with the stick people family. The heart comes to mind. "The drawing."

"Yes." The voice raises in pitch and becomes more excited. "How did you know?"

"I found it in your pocket ... before you tried to choke me."

"I'm sorry for that. Are you injured?" he asks.

I touch my neck. "I guess not."

The voice sighs. "I'm glad you weren't hurt. I don't want to hurt anyone. It's why I crashed my ship."

"*You* crashed the ship?" I say.

"I—" The voice pauses and struggles to get out the next words.

"Why did you crash your pod?"

"I refuse to do what they designed me to do."

I remove my hands and step away from the floating nano. "And what did they program you to do?"

The voice goes quiet for a disturbing moment. "I can't say."

"Why not?" I ask. "To stop Manning, we have to know."

"If I reveal information deemed sensitive in my mission, it will begin the self-destruct sequence." The voice becomes agitated, as if he's fighting some of his programming. "With you inside my head, I'm unsure what will happen."

A wave of pain washes over me and I can feel his brain waves waffling between what's true and the lies fed to him his entire life in Elore. His emotions struggle to suppress the tech. At this point, I don't know what it would do to me either, and we don't have the time to risk it.

"Where did the drawing come from?" I ask to distract him.

"I can't ... remember." The voice softens, no longer agitated. "That part was taken from me."

Suddenly, I grasp the problem. This soldier has a glitch, one caused by seeing his child's drawing. It didn't fully return his memory, but it made him question his new program. Because Manning truly doesn't appreciate the importance of love, he didn't factor it into the equation when he created it.

If I heal this man, repair the glitch, the patch will overwrite the emotions he still has, and if it doesn't work, he'll probably manually self-destruct anyway. Either way, he's going to die, and to get what I need, I have to destroy the single thing left that's keeping him human.

"I don't know if I can do anything for you."

The voice releases a paltry laugh. "That's what I've been trying to say—but there is part of you I trust. I'm not sure what it is—I know you want to help. I also know you're here for personal reasons. A human you're close to requires the tech running through my body."

His word takes me aback. It's not only me that can sense this soldier's emotions. He senses mine.

Guilt swirls in my middle. This man is no more or less important than Ben. He has a life, a son that is still alive, and I'm here to take from him.

"You're right," I admit. "There are several reasons, one of which is to understand this new tech. My brother's nanos are not compatible with his brain anymore. It's a complicated story, but it's killing him."

"And you—l-love him?"

The voice says the word love as if it's foreign, and for this man, it is. Love is rarely spoken of in Elore. Any love he felt was hidden, covered up. If guardians would have found the drawing of the heart, he, as well as his son, would have been disposed of immediately. Naomi was already dead. There are plenty more Level Ones to replace them.

"Yes, he's my twin. For thirteen years, I thought he was dead."

The soldier relaxes, and the space around me turns a pale green. Calm bathes me like the waves of the ocean lapping over a sandy beach.

"Take what you lack. I will allow the nanos to continue, but doing that means my body will again become a weapon. Without a doubt, I will attempt to harm you or anyone else who gets in my way. I will hold it off as long as I can, but once you get what you need, destroying the tech inside me will be necessary."

My stomach clenches. "But that will kill you. The damage is too great."

The voice is silent for what seems like an eternity. I know it's not.

"In the end, I'm going to die anyway. I won't survive. At least this way you might have information to assist your brother, and maybe more."

How can I be party to this man sacrificing himself for someone he doesn't know? To give up the possibility of returning to the family drawn on the paper folded in his pocket?

But this is so much bigger. With the capability to heal Ben, we might be able to use our ability to free the people of Elore, to free his son.

"Okay," I whisper, dampening my own emotions because that's not what's important right now.

"I know your struggle," the soldier's voice says. "Please, do what is necessary."

Hot tears sting my eyes, but they hold fast. Slowly, I re-approach the nano and hover my hands over it. "Are you ready?"

"Not really," the voice says, "but yes. Please, do good."

"I plan to."

As if repelled, my hands refuse to touch the tech, but I shut my eyes and relax, lowering my hands until they reach the surface. Electricity buzzes through me and memories that are not my own swarm my brain.

The face of a newborn. A son. The immediate test of his Intelligence Potential. Level One. Relief. The child stays. A private embrace of his spouse. Naomi Jensen. White-blonde hair. Her smile. Her *smile*.

The images swirl and meld into one another and become a part of me, then they're gone. Ripped away. Dark sadness swallows me whole. I drown the feeling and focus.

"Download DPF program."

A surge flows through me as if I were hit by a streak of lightning, but instead of releasing, I lean into it, forcing the download. Now that he's not resisting the update, I'm fighting the soldier's programming.

The soldier's emotions deplete as he grows weaker and the tech fights to consume him. The energy traveling my veins saps away as the upgrade fights me, but I push harder to take what might save my brother, the Citizens of Elore, maybe even this man's family. A scream exits my throat as the integrity of the space begins to collapse in a flurry of sparks.

Download complete flashes in my consciousness.

"Get the sample now, Gabrielle!" I shout.

"Got it," Gabrielle's voice says in my comm.

"Abort program," I command the nanos, configuring a virus in my mind to destroy it. I drive forward to release the bug into the nano, but it lurches and pulls. Slowly, it inches backward, and then without warning its tentacles thrust out toward me.

I throw my hands into the air, willing it to stop. The tech struggles, but I wave my hand to the side and the tech crashes to the earth and explodes. The other two are en route, and I whip around with a flick of my hand, commanding them to smash into each other.

A wave of dizziness overwhelms me, making my thoughts weak, hazy. Something compels me to stay. The sensation creeps from my feet up the rest of my body as if it demands me to freeze.

Remembering why I'm here, I shake the fog from my head and free from the nano's deadly influence. Again, I form the virus, and this time visualize it taking over. The world cracks apart. Code flings through the space like white-hot shrapnel.

"End!" I shriek as everything goes dark.

I throw open my eyes and suck in a gasp. In front of me is the body of the soldier. He's motionless. Gabrielle and Ben seize me from behind and rip my hands from the man.

"He's gone!" Gabrielle yells. "Did you get it?"

My knees give way and I nearly collapse to the lab floor, but Gabrielle catches me. Ben helps me to my feet.

"Got it," I whisper, looking at Ben, unable to speak any louder. "He gave his life so I could have the DPF program. I know its weakness. It's love.

Ben stares at me. "What do you mean?"

"This man's love for his family severed the connection between him and the nanos controlling his brain. Flooding the programming with emotions shuts it down. I know how to fix the problem. Patch me into Elore's mainframe."

Gabrielle shakes her head. "No way, Avlyn. Your body is weak. Your vitals nearly stopped at one point. Dealing with one soldier was difficult enough for you, and on top of that there is no *time*. I got the sample. Take it and make a plan. Meyer's ready, and you *have* to go."

"If I do this now, I can end the invasion," I insist.

Ben grabs my shoulders. "The DPF is only a portion of the problem. Doing this now is jumping the gun. Accept the data and let's go."

"At least let me upgrade your nanos," I say to Ben.

He shakes his head. "That will need to wait, too."

CHAPTER TWENTY-NINE

Ben grabs my arm. "Let's go."

Gabrielle thrusts a tiny data drive and the blood sample, containing the upgraded nanos from the now-dead soldier, into my hands. "I downloaded the information we gathered concerning you and Ben onto this. It also includes the instructions for how to enter the Underground, where to go online and who to trust in there if, for some reason, you're unable to contact me."

"Wait." I pull from Ben, shoving the sample and drive into a hidden pocket at my waist. "You're not coming?"

She laughs. "There's no room in your pod for me, and I belong here. You'll be secure where I'm sending you. A contact from Affinity will be in touch."

"Affinity? You said they wouldn't know where we were." I glance at Ben, but he doesn't respond.

"Avlyn, I went over your head and made the decision. You *need* to trust Ruiz." She gestures for us to go and Ben and I hustle into the hall. On the way to the surface, I retrieve a few articles of clothing from my room and stuff them into a bag. We burst from the bunker and spot Meyer, Aron, and Sanda loading the pod.

"They're here!" Aron shouts, one of his drones buzzing over his shoulder. He waves the rest toward the back of the pod hull. They settle on the outer surface as if magnetized.

I turn to Ben, whose face suddenly is too tired and pale. Sweat dots his brow. I'd been so consumed with the download I'd forgotten how weak he's become.

A lump gathers in my throat. "I can't lose you this time," I choke out.

"We might have to make sacrifices."

Stunned, I try to read him but I get nothing back. "You mean yourself?"

Ben is silent.

"Don't make me choose between the mission and you," I whisper.

"Life *is* making choices you'd rather not," Ben growls. "Get used to it."

That's the problem. I *am* used to it.

"Are you two ready or what?" Meyer calls, waving us to the pod.

Ben gives me a last look and motions for Meyer. I clutch my bag and hurry forward, Ben moving slowly behind.

"Have we got what we need?" I ask, swinging my attention back and forth between Aron and Meyer.

"Probably not," Meyer says. "But it's good enough."

"I double checked your fuel and operating system," Sanda adds as she steps up next to me. "Everything looks like a go."

"Are you coming?" I ask her, my thoughts whirling with confusion from the chaos.

She smiles and combs a hand through her short curls. "I have an assignment I need to get to, remember? I'll help my mom finish securing the bunker, and then I'm gone."

"What about the soldier?" I ask.

The smile disappears. "You worry about you now."

There's no way my mind or heart has the ability to discard these problems, but I push the worries aside and stuff them down. I wrap my arms around Sanda's neck and squeeze, which she returns with an equal amount of vigor.

"Be safe," I whisper.

"Same to you." She releases me and hustles to the bunker.

Gabrielle's voice comes over the comm inside the pod. "You haven't left yet?"

Meyer swings into the captain's seat and taps the front console. "Give us a second." He spins toward me and tosses a gun to Ben, who weakly catches it. "You have yours, Avlyn?"

I nod and pat the stunner on my hip.

"Good," he says. "Now we all have them. Everyone get in."

I fling my bag into the open hatch onto my spot in back of Meyer.

"I have incoming," Gabrielle's voice says.

Meyer leans into the comm. "Incoming what?"

"On the radar, five miles out. Multiple ships, and these aren't all tiny pods."

My heart aches for the residents in Thornton. These are families, mothers and children, people who want a peaceful life, and Manning could be coming for them as we speak. Maybe he'll pass them up.

I throw myself into the seat alongside Ben and reach to lower the hatch. Aron taps the Flexx on his wrist and waves a drone into the front with him. It settles to his side. All the hatch doors click to lock in place and the pod lifts from the ground as Meyer's hands fly over the controls. No one speaks, but the air in the pod is thick with tension. There's no need for words. Meyer sets the course and the nose of the vehicle rises slightly as we make our way above the trees flanking and concealing the bunker.

My mouth drops at the sight several miles away.

I stretch my neck to see the pod's viewing screen. It indicates one large warship as well as a few smaller vessels hovering atop Thornton. Through the front window, a bright pulse emits from the main ship and at least a quarter of the city center erupts into bright yellow and orange flames.

CHAPTER THIRTY

Horrified, I watch the night sky light up with embers and fire.

"Why are they doing that?" I yell, working to get a better view out the front window of the pod. "The townspeople have no defense system."

Wordlessly, Ben clutches my arm, guiding me back.

"Stop it!" I yank from his grasp, adrenaline racing my veins. All I can think of is that nice woman, Katherine, and the little boy, Ash, who gave me that flower. "We can't leave those families to die!"

"Avlyn!" Meyer snaps. "I don't know what you believe *we* can do for them. We're four people in one pod with our own limited defense system. The fact that Manning is attacking them is the very reason we need to get you two away. You must see the bigger picture. If we go in there and all get killed, you can't help *anyone*."

He's right, Ben's voice says in my mind, and it brings an overwhelming sense of calm. *I know you want to fix this, but getting us out of here is what needs to be done.*

I tear from the horrible view of Thornton and stare at my lap, my eyes stinging with hot tears. "Fine."

The pod responds to Meyer's touch on the console and turns slightly right to follow the coordinates Gabrielle gave us.

"I'm headed out," Sanda's nervous voice sounds over the pod comm. "After this, we're all on radio silence."

Meyer lets out a long, steady breath. "I'll miss you, sis. Good luck."

"You too," she says. The comm goes silent, as does everyone else in the pod.

It's going to be okay, Ben thinks to me.

I stare at him. *You have no idea if that's true.*

You're right. Ben looks from me and exits my thoughts. He leans back in his seat and closes his eye, his body slumping in exhaustion. Loneliness buries me as I twist toward the view behind us. Thornton becomes a small, bright dot, slowly swallowed up by the night and distance.

A pinging sound comes from the console.

"What's that?" Aron asks, his mini-drone humming to life and lifting a few inches in the air, agitated.

Meyer is silent as his hands fly over the controls, nervous energy radiating off him. "We have visitors. I'm unable to identify them, but it must be the DPF. Probably caught a whiff of our pod outside Gabrielle's scrambler. I'm changing course for now."

I lean forward to study the screen. Three glowing green dots are set on an interception course for us.

"These are definitely not friendly. Aron, it's time to release your drones," Meyer says. "How many are there?"

"Twelve, not including the one in here. Aron grabs his Flexx from his wrist and unfolds it into a tablet. The golden drone inside with us buzzes excitedly. His fingers tap over the screen and the popping of the drones affixed to the pod hull release sounds from behind. The drone purrs at the window as if it's ready to join its clan. Aron reaches out and pulls it down.

"Kill or disable?" Aron asks Meyer.

Meyer pauses and rechecks the screen, jaw tightening. "Kill."

The word sends a shock down my frame and I fight the urge to protest. It's what has to be done.

Without hesitation, Aron taps the screen. I watch as the drones flying alongside the pod go from green to red, and they zip away in sets of two in the direction of our pursuers. The screen on the console matches with the tops of each piece of tech lit red.

Meyer redirects our pod and increases the speed, throwing all of us to the side. Aron nearly drops his Flexx, but recovers and studies the screen that also displays a visual of the drones. Ben and I remain silent in the back, allowing the two of them to do what they need to. My shoulders tense, and I rack my brain for additional solutions, but there's nothing either of us can do. I look to Ben, realizing I've lost our emotional connection again. A painful emptiness rests in my mind. He glances back, and by the expression on his face, I can see he knows, too.

"We'll make it through this," he whispers.

"How can you know that?"

"I just do. It's the same feeling I had all those years when I knew I'd come back to you."

For the briefest of seconds, yellow and blue emotion surges over me, filling the void like a strange mix of happiness and sorrow synchronized. Then it's gone.

A crack of thunder sounds from outside the pod.

"Got one!" Aron shouts triumphantly.

I stretch up to see the tracking on the console, and sure enough one of the chasing ships has disappeared from the screen. Two of the red dots loop toward the other enemy ships, but the ships take evasive action and a streak of light flies past our craft. Extra bursts illuminate the sky in back of us as a battle between the drones and the enemy ensues, and two of the drone dots disappear.

Meyer curses under his breath. "They're in firing range. Get those guys on them."

"That's what I'm doing." Aron swipes at his Flexx screen frantically, and the micro drone with us buzzes about. Explosions sound and two more drone lights disappear from the screen.

I gasp as Meyer dodges another streak of light. Ben reaches out and grabs the little drone from alongside Aron. The thing calms instantly in his hand. He immersed with it. I throw him a look to tell him not to do that, but he ignores me and angles his face away. I grip my armrest to hold my body in place, trying to anchor myself from Meyer's ever-changing maneuvers.

"They're pushing us back to Thornton," Meyer growls.

I strain to see the console again. We're several miles out from the town.

"It's why they haven't shot us out of the sky yet," I say. "They want us back there."

"Manning must know where you are," Ben mumbles.

As he says it, a pulse jolts the pod. The humming of the flight mechanism slows.

"What happened?" I yell, swinging around as two added bursts light up the sky behind us. The two green lights on the display go dark, and then the screen goes black.

"We're hit and losing power." Meyer's hands fly over the controls and he switches to manual. "I need to land. It's going to be bumpy."

The pod pitches as Meyer shifts into a different flight capability. The craft lifts slightly and then lurches forward, gliding toward the earth. My stomach contracts at the sudden altitude drop and the four of us brace for impact.

Bam.

The underside of the pod hits the ground, throwing our bodies ahead, only to be held back by the safety belts securing our waists. A shuddering *screech* from the metal hull dragging over vegetation and rocks fills the inside of the cab. My lip trembles as I attempt to form logical thoughts. Ben blinks beside me.

"Are you okay?" I ask him, my eyes flitting to the front seat to visually assess Aron and Meyer. They appear unhurt.

"I'm fine," Ben gasps, letting loose the drone still in his hand. The golden orb floats up and buzzes to Aron.

"What did they do to the pod?" I ask Meyer. "Can I can fix it?"

"They took out the operating system and overheated the engine, so unless your ability can cool it off, no," he says.

"Should I try?"

"There's not time." Meyer hits the activation for the hatch door, but nothing happens. He curses in frustration.

"I think there might be a manual release." Aron fumbles his hand over the bottom of his door. I turn and do the same to mine, catching on a hidden handle. I pull and the hatch slides up. The other doors slide up immediately after mine. They found the latches too.

I scurry out, ignoring the pain charging down my neck and back and run around toward Ben. He's bent over, hands on knees, and his face is pale, as if all the blood has drained. Eight remaining drones join the one hovering over Aron. As I reach for Ben, he collapses into my arms. Aron lunges forward to help me catch him.

Meyer rounds the pod. "Stop wasting—" He pauses when he sees the state Ben is in.

"You need to leave me," Ben whispers in my ear. Aron and I lower him to the ground. Memories of my mother dying in the tunnel overwhelm me and my knees give way.

"No, way," I protest. "I'm not doing that again."

Meyer grips my arm and draws me up. "Avlyn, we don't have any other choice. It's miles back to Gabrielle's. Even if he makes it, he's going to slow us down and put you at risk."

I jerk from him. "You won't make me do this."

Avlyn, Ben's struggling voice enters my conscience. *Be logical and go. Do it for me. I need you to live.*

I detach from his connection.

Ben looks at Meyer as he stands on wobbly legs, using the side of the pod to help him up. "Take her, now."

Meyer grips my arm a second time and readies his stunner with his free hand. He addresses Ben. "You have a gun. We'll come back for you if we can."

"I've programmed the drones to stay with you," Aron says to Ben. "Hide. If anyone moves to attack, they'll protect you." Six of the orbs zip into place over us, following Ben's every move. The other three whir to Meyer, Aron, and my sides.

I throw my arms around Ben's neck and squeeze. "I'll make him come back for you."

Ben doesn't reply. I release him, tears streaming my face. Aron, Meyer, and I spin and pound over the terrain to safety, wherever that is.

"Where are we headed?" I ask, pulling my stunner off my hip.

"Back to Gabrielle's for her hover," Meyer says.

My mind reels. There's no way this will be successful, and going back puts Gabrielle in more danger.

"What if they're already there?"

"We'll have to risk it."

When we've gotten maybe a mile away from Ben, another unmarked ship flies overhead. The three of us bolt for cover, but it's too late. The vessel shifts and descends in our direction.

"We have to split," Aron says.

I go light-headed and all I can do is think about Ben. I reach out to him with my thoughts.

They've found us. Are you hidden?

No voice comes back. Panic rips through me and a voice jolts me back to reality.

"That way," Meyer says, pointing north and giving me a shove. "Try to make it to Gabrielle's."

Gripped by my panic, I scramble to my feet and swivel my head, searching for Aron. His frame, shadowed by night, rushes in the opposite direction, but his drone is still with me.

"Go!" Meyer shouts over the roar of the descending ship.

I bolt, and a surge lights up the space above me. The drone shot at something. I turn to look and my body slams to the dirt. My hands rake over the gravelly surface, and fiery pain launches from my wrist up my arm. Ignoring it, I push up, but some force won't allow it. I try again, but some invisible energy surrounds me. I'm trapped.

"Meyer, help!" I scream.

No answer comes back.

Ben! My thoughts shriek as a figure comes toward me. The moon casts light on his shoulders, and down the sleeve I see familiar markings. Three red stripes.

These ships are not the DPF.

I gasp as the soldier lifts his weapon. A blast emits and racks my body.

Then the obsidian night consumes me.

CHAPTER THIRTY-ONE

A sharp jolt of electricity upshots me against something stiff and covering my body. *I can't move.* My lungs heave desperately for oxygen. Dark and pale shapes crowd my vision, and I blink to clear them. I try to lift from the lying down position I'm in, but it's no use.

"She's up," an unfamiliar female voice shouts as my memories rush in and my vision returns. The voice belongs to a woman not much older than me, but with reddish bobbed hair. The lantern street light confirms what I saw before I passed out; the woman wears the identical tan uniform with red stripes on the sleeves as Ben wore when I met him. These soldiers are from New Philly.

What happened to the Direction ships?

I turn my head, which is still somewhat free, and dart my eyes to locate Aron and Meyer, spotting them to my right about twenty feet or so, unconscious, a guard with a gun trained on each of them. At least they're alive. Ben is nowhere to be seen. Maybe he's still hidden.

I struggle again to sit and press into whatever it is that's constraining me. As I force myself against it, a shimmery grid appears in my vision, covering my body. It's some sort of netting, but it's also tech. I close my eyes and try to merge with it, but only resistance comes back.

"What do you think of it?" a deep voice from behind me says, severing my unsuccessful attempt to free myself. "There's no use trying to immerse with it. The data we collected from you allowed us to develop the restraint. Part nano, part organic. You can release her. We've proven our point."

In seconds the pressure dissipates, and I push up into a seated position. I twist to the voice. A man with a stocky build stands to my side, the overhead moon lighting his leathery skin. It's Waters. He's responsible for this. Another guard, with a weapon pointed my way, beside him.

"You are a difficult one to find. So many rumors to investigate. When one came in about a grid activation, it made me curious, yet we get out here and nobody says anything. Still, I had a feeling you were here. I just didn't know exactly *where* yet, so I had to give them a bit extra incentive. They were reluctant for some reason, so it's a good thing you emerged."

I realize that most of the townspeople seem to be rounded up beyond him. Overhead, a layer of smoke floats in the air, a remnant of the destroyed buildings.

"Where are the Direction ships?" I ask, ignoring his words.

"Direction? No, that was to stir the pot. I figured I'd start my own rumor."

"But there was an Elorian ship. It … it crashed," I say thoroughly confused and glancing up at the two smaller, unmarked ships hovering above Thornton and the larger metallic craft on the road cutting the middle of the town.

He shrugs. "Well, thankfully we were able to get to you so soon. Who knows what Manning would do to you."

Meyer groans. I whip my head toward him lying on the ground, then turn back to Waters. "So it was *you* who destroyed Thornton?"

"My intention was to play nice with you. If you'd stayed in Philly, none of this would've occurred."

"*Nice?*" I snap back, standing with my hands on my hips. "How were you *nice?* By planning to send me off somewhere to study my ability against my will for who knows what while planning to dispose of my friend?"

Waters shakes his head. "You don't see the big picture, do you? All you do is focus on the immediate. We could have gotten more data from you and used it to fight Direction without all this," he waves his hand in the air, "extra destruction. But, Manning had an overblown sense of superiority, and it's dangerous to everyone. His attempt to let a new virus loose on us was the final straw. I'll be making the first move this time, and you're my ticket to that."

Behind Waters, the sheriff moves from the group of townspeople. One of the guards trains a gun on him. "President Waters!" he yells.

Waters holds his hand up to the soldier, who lowers his weapon.

The sheriff jogs toward us, and as he comes beneath the lamplight, his stress becomes obvious. Brow furrowed, he halts alongside the president. "You need to let my town go. The children are frightened. You said if we cooperated, you'd leave us alone."

His words prompt me to scan over the group again. I find the little boy, Ash, in the group, huddled by a woman. His mother, I guess. Next to them stands Katherine from the café. Vincent is nowhere to be seen. Maybe he died in the woods.

For a few beats, Waters considers the sheriff's plea. "I don't know. I don't feel as if you're all completely loyal to Philly. You're still holding back."

Fright fills the sheriff's eyes. "No, no," he says, shaking his head.

"Then who was Ms. Lark staying with?" Waters says, raising his eyebrow.

The sheriff hangs his head, defeated. "A woman named Gabrielle. She lives several miles from here."

Waters smiles and places his hand on the sheriff's shoulder. "Now, wasn't that easy?"

The sheriff glances at me and casts his eyes down. Out of the corner of my eye, Waters' other hand makes a quick motion, drawing something from his side. A ray of light discharges from a stunner. The sheriff's body goes limp and falls to the ground in a horrible thump. Blood drips from his lips and dribbles from his chin.

That was not on stun.

I gasp, nausea lurching in my stomach. Waters doesn't respond, swinging around to address the townspeople. "Who wants to take me to Gabrielle's?"

The crowd momentarily shrinks back in horror, cries sounding from several men and women. Not waiting on their answer, Waters turns back to me, weapon continually readied.

"Get her on the ship and bring her friends. They'll keep her cooperative," he instructs the female guard beside me.

She clutches my upper arm and tugs me toward the ship. A flash lights up the night and the craft explodes into blazing yellow. My guard clutches me tighter and shoves her weapon into my back. I spin around and scan for Meyer and Aron again. Across the road they're both up, but still held by several guards. The people scream and scramble to escape from whatever is happening. Soldiers scatter to contain them, thankfully not shooting. Yet.

Another burst comes from above and makes impact with one of Water's ships on the ground.

"Stop them!" Waters' muffled voice shouts through the chaos, a soldier ushering him to safety. He waves someone from the crowd of townspeople to follow him, a tall man with dark hair.

Vincent.

My chest tightens at the sight of him. He's alive and I abandoned him outside the town thinking he might be dead.

My guard swings toward Waters, momentarily distracted by his words. Without another thought, I slam my elbow into her face. I meet her cheek with a satisfying crunch and grapple for the stunner in her hand. She screams and lunges for me. Out of the corner of my vision, three soldiers rush us. As her body collides with mine, the stunner slips from my hand. Everything goes white as I immerse with her nanos, and in the blink of an eye, all her data downloads to me. She has *CosmoNano* tech in her hair. I command her tech, and the reddish-blonde locks assume the same color as mine. I might be able to get myself out of this mess.

I open my lids and compel my hair and camo suit to change to mimic her appearance. With all my strength, I thrust the guard from me.

"She's getting away!" I shout to the oncoming soldiers. They lift their weapons and waffle between the two of us, settling on her in the dim light. The female guard stumbles backward, confused, and another ship roars above and releases a blast.

I grasp for the stunner on the ground and immerse with it, reversing the setting to nonlethal. I aim and hit the female soldier, then wheel around and strikes the next three in the chest. They fall limply to the ground, stunned, but not dead. The rest of the guards are busy rounding up townspeople for the moment, not paying attention to me.

A burst of wind and dust hits my face as one of the attacking ships descends, followed by a smaller pod. Whether they're friendly or not, is a mystery. I cover my eyes and mouth and search for someplace out of view to figure it out. Someone grabs my arm, and I wrench from the grasp, forcing myself around and pointing my stunner into the air at my attacker.

Aron tosses his hands up. "Not again," he chokes out.

Instantly, I lower the gun. "Sorry, but don't do that! Where's Meyer?"

"Here," Meyer's voice calls.

I dash for him and throw my body into his. After a beat I pull and drag him through the confusion toward Katherine's Café, waving for Aron to follow. We make it to the door with glass on the front and I reach for the handle. Locked. I raise my elbow to smash the glass.

"Meyer, Avlyn," a woman's voice sounds. I turn to see Gabrielle jogging our way, lowering my arm from breaking the window. Ruiz and a group of soldiers are exiting the craft that just landed.

Affinity.

Gabrielle jogs to our group. "I was able to get in contact with Ruiz, but Affinity figured out the attack and was already on the way," she says, out of breath.

"Where's Waters? Do they have him in custody?" Meyer peers around as if to search for him.

"I don't know," she says.

Adriana saved me. *Again.* I reel with guilt for not trusting her. "Who are all these people? It can't be only Affinity."

"When Ruiz realized what Waters had in store for you, that he didn't care who needed to die to get you back, she rounded up support. The ships are from Philly. There are factions who desire peace. She sought them out. Some guy named Sloan helped her organize the whole thing."

My mind moves to my strange experience in New Philly with Dr. Sloan; how I felt as if I trusted him when we spoke in Virtual Reality.

Ruiz's soldiers continue to round up the ones brought by Waters and contain them apart from the townspeople. On the opposite side of the road, Ruiz bends to comfort a group of small children and their worry-worn mothers. One of the kids is Ash. I look down at my tan camo suit with red stripes on the sleeves and compel it to return to black, then convert my hair to its original color.

I holster my weapon and step from the café door, away from Meyer, Aron, and Gabrielle. "I'm going to speak with Ruiz."

As my foot hits the street, the roar of a vessel above fills the air and shudders through my body. I duck as Ruiz's soldiers raise their guns toward it and shoot, but the shots are absorbed by the hull, doing nothing. A pulse emits from the front of the vessel, and as if the world moves in slow motion, the beam stretches over the sky. With a kick, time resumes and explodes into a burst of light.

My mouth opens to let out a scream, but I'm blown to the ground with heat, flying shrapnel, and pressure. Dazed, I force myself to stand as screaming residents run past me. The building across the way, and everyone in front of it—Ruiz, the mothers, Ash—are dead. There's little left but fire. They never had a chance.

I flinch as shots come from the side and up at the ship, but it's already flying away, unharmed. Terror and anger twist in my chest and I turn back to the café. Aron's on the ground, shaking his head, and Meyer is already on his feet. Gabrielle's not. Blood flows from her neck. Meyer stares at me wide eyed, then to Gabrielle, rushing to her side.

"No, no, no!" he yells as he lunges for her lifeless frame. "Not you, too!" He feels for her pulse. "We need to move her. She's hit."

Aron and I both rush to them as soldiers fire shots into the sky and toward any threats on the ground. I grasp for my stolen stunner and ready it to protect from potential attackers. Meyer grasps Gabrielle's shoulders and the jostling snaps her eyes open.

"You all need to get to my pod," she chokes out, blood seeping from her mouth.

"I'm not leaving you," Meyer argues.

"Sweetie," she says in a low voice, "I know enough to be certain this is not good. Now, take your friends, and get in my pod."

I look up to check if Gabrielle's vessel even still exists. The four-seater is sitting down the road, for now.

I touch my hand to Gabrielle's shoulder to confirm her nanos are working properly. Maybe she has a chance. I shut my eyes to immerse, but nothing happens.

She doesn't have *any.*

I open my eyes to watch her labored breath against her blood-saturated shirt. "She's right, Meyer. She doesn't have nanos, and where would we take her?"

"The coordinates are programmed," Gabrielle whispers. "They're encrypted, but Avlyn can decode them. Get Ben and Avlyn to safety."

The mention of Ben slams my heart into my throat. I reach out to him with my thoughts, but emptiness comes back.

Gabrielle struggles for breath and then she stops. Meyer leans into her and Aron grabs his shoulder. "Come on. She's gone."

Meyer shrugs him off and plucks the gun from Gabrielle's side. He motions a 'let's go' and follows the two of us as we book it for our one hope of escape.

Somehow, through the barrage and explosions, we make it to the craft. "I'm flying," I say to Meyer, sprinting ahead of him toward the pilot's door.

He opens his mouth to protest.

"Get in on the other side," I say firmly. No way I'm backing off.

Brokenness washes over his face and he obeys. Aron climbs in the back as I rip up the hatch and throw myself into the craft. My hands fly over the console and with barely a thought I decrypt and download our destination. The screen displays the hovercraft in the air and on the ground, but at this point I don't know which is friendly. Their call tags are all cloaked. I activate the pod and it hovers over the ground.

"Get us out of here," Meyer mumbles.

"I'm doing that." I merge with the pod's computer system another time and propel the craft forward using the on-ship sensors to avoid fire. I weave the pod through the lightshow and flames that are soon to engulf the town, staying trained on the data fed to me by the pod as we exit and scramble to the hill. Somehow, we aren't followed.

My mind carousels and I focus to settle it. *We have to locate Ben. We can't just abandon him.*

Ben, I think to him again. *You have to answer.*

But all I get back are my thoughts and the inky wasteland of my own emotional state.

"Where did we leave Ben?" I ask Meyer.

"After Water's ships went after us, they drove us off course. I've forgotten the coordinates where we crashed. It could be anywhere."

"If I had my controller, I could track the drones." Aron leans toward us from the back. "But it's gone. I lost it."

My stomach drops at his words. "That means they might find the drones and Ben."

Meyer runs his hands nervously into his hair. "There's no way to know if they haven't found him already. You can't connect with him?"

"Well, he wasn't in the city, so I'm not going to give up hope."

"Avlyn," Meyer says in a low tone. "He might be dead."

Anger and fear burn in my chest. "I'd know if he were dead!" I shout. The emotions overwhelm and consume me. My head goes light.

Avlyn.

Ben's voice weakly cuts through the viscous state of my emotional being. He tells me his coordinates.

My eyelids fly open. "I know where he is." I download his location to the pod's computer and check the vicinity for enemy vessels.

"What?" Meyer says, confused.

"I know where he is. It's not far."

"Then we pick him up. But we won't have long." Meyer twists to Aron. "I might need your help getting him inside. We have no way of knowing what kind of shape he's in."

Aron nods. "No problem."

"You have to stay here, keep the engine on," he says to me.

I swing the ship around, hope building in my chest as we fly over the terrain.

I'm coming for you, I think back to Ben.

In the distance, I spot something shiny in the night light. Our crashed pod. I propel us toward it and start my descent, ever alert for new vessels. Below us are two additional wrecked enemy crafts, still smoking, and at least ten dead bodies.

What happened here?

Gabrielle's vessel brushes the ground and I look to Meyer, who pulls his stunner out. In an instant, he and Aron have the doors open and surge out.

"Ben!" Meyer calls.

A glowing green orb hurls toward Aron across the sky and halts in front of him. Aron waves to Meyer and the two of them sprint in the direction of the abandoned pod. Five more orbs follow close behind. Ben's shadowy figure inches out from the pod and everything in me wants to go and help, but I need to keep put.

I study the scanner on the operating console and my breath skips. Two unknown green vessels blink on the screen. I jerk up my head to face my friends and watch as the once-green orbs switch to red.

CHAPTER THIRTY-TWO

I shove open the door and hurtle from my seat. "Attack imminent!" I shout.

Meyer's shadowy figure rounds his head my way and grips Aron by the arm, pushing him back to the pod. Aron shakes his head and continues to Ben, who's now dragging toward them. Aron's drones zip over my head with a *whoosh* and fly in the direction of the oncoming ships. Lit by the moon, Aron slips his arm under Ben's and moves him in my direction. Meyer stays on guard, weapon ready.

"Hurry!" I scream as the roar of a ship sounds from behind me. The drones circle above, shooting at the opposition. The already-bright night lights up with energy, pulsing back and forth. I step from the pod and raise my stunner, compelling it to the kill setting.

The orbs assume an attack formation and descend on one of the hover pods, weaving in and around it, releasing a steady stream of energy pulses. The ship returns the charge, but the drones are too small and agile. Flames and smoke burst from the hull, and the craft pitches, crashing to the earth.

The six drones turn on the second ship, but it's faster and better at avoiding them. Smoke fills the air and my lungs, but I hurry through it to find my friends and brother, mouth covered.

"Meyer?" I shout over the rumble of an explosion inside the crashed ship. The hatch on the vessel groans open and a group of soldiers, five— no, *six*—emerges, their guns extended. A fusillade of light races our way.

I raise my stunner and shoot, a blast hitting a soldier straight in the chest. He falls and I move to strike the next, but an energy burst comes from Meyer and Aron's way, then another from the direction of the soldiers. A beam zips past me, just missing my shoulder, but the energy drives me to the ground. I pivot to right myself and fire again. One, two, three. The pulses enter the soldiers' bodies and they collapse.

The second ship lands just beyond the crashed one, despite Aron's drone attack, opens. Ten soldiers pour out of the now-released hatch, guns blaring. The drones zip in and destroy several. I get to my feet and dart in the direction I last saw Meyer. Through the smoke of the burning ship, Aron and Ben emerge, dragging to our pod. Gunfire surges in their direction, and I toss my arm out and start discharging to cover them. Some of the soldiers take shelter behind the wreck, but keep firing.

Still not locating Meyer, I throw myself down, hoping for camouflage in the brush. I twist Aron and Ben's way. They're nearly to the pod.

"Meyer!" I yell, my chest heaving for breath.

As if the call made him appear, he slides in alongside me. "Get to our ship," he pants. "I'll cover you and be right there. I think we have a chance with the drones. Most of Water's troops are down."

"I'm not leaving you."

Meyer looks back at me. "I'll be right behind. I promise."

I stare up to the battle between the drones and soldiers, quickly scanning for the fallen fighters. Meyer's right. I think there are only two left now.

I hesitate and give him one last plea, then rise and tear off for the pod. A shot lights up over my head, but I ignore it and keep running. I meet with Aron, whose loading a nearly unconscious Ben into the pod. I nab Ben by the opposite shoulder and shove him in.

I flash a look to Aron and he shuts the hatch, then rounds to the opposite side of the pod. I do the same and release the door to the pilot seat, flinging myself in and activating the controls. With a *beep* the screen comes to life, and I merge my mind with the ship computer.

"Meyer made it," Aron says.

Thump. Meyer slams his body into the other side of the pod, making me jump, and forces open his door.

"They're all down, but I don't know about the pilot. Let's go!" he yells.

Once he's in, I command the ship's system to secure the doors. As they do, the navigation screen fills with several new arriving ships. I gasp at the sight of them.

"There are more ships half a mile out!" I shout. My hands fly over the controls and the ship hovers slightly from the ground.

"You need something bigger to cover your escape," Meyer says. "And I can fly that ship. Put the pod back on the ground."

"Back *down?* No way."

Meyer's face grows stern. "If you want Ben and Aron to live, do it now!"

I hesitate, turning to peer back. Aron sits terrified, gripping his chair and Ben is passed out beside him.

"You're out of time!" Meyer yells. The pod lowers with a *thunk* to the earth and Meyer twists to Aron. "She doesn't need it, but take care of her."

Without waiting for an answer, he grabs his stunner and frees the door, throwing it shut in back of him, bolting for the enemy ship. He waves two of the circling drones our way and takes four with him.

My stomach drops when I realize what he's doing. "He's going to be the bait!" I yell, pushing open the pod door and leaping from the seat to the ground.

"Get back in!" Aron's muffled voice comes from inside. "Don't waste his sacrifice!"

The two drones Meyer commanded in our direction race toward us.

"Meyer!" I scream, tearing after him, but he's already entered the ship. One of the downed soldiers lying in front of the ship lifts and points his weapon my way. My reaction is too slow.

With a burst, the world goes white, and I fall limp. I fight the desire to let the world go and my eyes blink open to Aron's terrified face. My body hits the back seat inside of the pod and falls next to Ben.

"Avlyn?" Aron says in a voice that could be miles away.

The brightness returns, but dims as I acquiesce to the darkness chasing it.

My lungs gasp for air as my eyelids pop open. I squint, trying to take in my surroundings, but the brightness burns my eyes and I snap them shut again.

"She's coming to," a muffled female voice says.

A moan escapes my mouth, and I straighten to sit, but my body feels like it weighs a thousand pounds. I collapse backward. Something pinches my neck and I gasp once more.

"There," the voice soothes. "Is that better?"

My head clears and I roll in the direction of the voice. I make out a female shape with short dark hair sitting in a chair by me.

"You're safe. We have you," the familiar girl says in a sorrowful voice, stroking my cheek.

"Sanda? Where ... where am I?" My eyes flit around the space. It's some type of sparse room with green fabric walls

"Hi." Her eyes are filled with moisture she's somehow holding back. "You're at an Affinity camp. Mom—" Sanda's voice cracks and she pauses, taking in a deep breath. "Mom must have known what might happen, so she recalculated the coordinates to lead you here."

I replay all my memories from the night. "Ben?" I mumble.

"Ben's okay."

The words relax me. I try to sit up again, but my muscles refuse. "I need to see him."

Sanda gently touches her hand to my shoulder and guides me back to the bed. "You need to rest. Whatever they stunned you with did a number on you. I think they realized their mistake not totally knocking you out the first time."

"How do you know?"

"Oh, Aron told us what transpired. Meyer saved you all, you know."

A replay of the minutes before the world went black rockets through my head: the incoming ships on the screen; Meyer racing of Water's ship; I chased him, and a pulse hit me; Aron pulling me into the pod.

Everything else until now swirls together into an inky haze. My heart pounds in my chest and I force myself to sit up, brushing Sanda's hand off my shoulder.

"Where's Meyer?" I demand.

Sanda's jaw tightens and she glances from me. "We don't know yet."

"You don't *know*?"

"All we are sure of is he got that ship up and running and led an attack on the approaching ships. Aron flew you all out of there as fast as he could."

My body floods with emotion I have no idea where to place. Red and black pour over and through me, mixing and mingling, consuming me.

My eyes snap up to Sanda, anger and fear burning in my chest and throat. "How are you just sitting there? Your whole family is dead. Gone. Everyone. Jayson, Gabrielle, Meyer—Ruiz is dead, too. I *saw* her get blown to bits. I doubted her, and she died, too!" I scream.

Sanda sits stunned, the expression on her face collapsing. "I still have you," she whispers.

Her words overwhelm me, and I throw my arms toward her, pulling her into a tight hug. "I'm sorry—I'm *sorry*," I sob. For some reason, she accepts my offering and returns the embrace.

"Sanda?" a new, soft female voice I've heard asks.

Sanda unwraps her arms from me and shifts to face Cynthia Fisher, backlit in the opening of the fabric-walled room.

Just as before, when I see Cynthia, something about her tells me I know her. The way her slightly longer than shoulder-length hair skims her chest and her voice that fills me with both a sense of dread, and somehow home. Yet, other than seeing her on vids, I've never met the woman.

"Sanda, let me have some time to speak with Avlyn," Cynthia says, gesturing out the flap serving as the room's door. Beyond it is scrub brush and a grouping of trees. Several people walk past, ignoring anything that's said in here.

"Okay," Sanda says, turning back to me. "I'll look in on Ben for you."

I give her a slight smile. "Thank you."

Sanda nods and leaves. Cynthia steps forward, taking in a deep breath as she sits. "I heard some of your conversation, and yes, Ruiz is gone. Only a few escaped from Thornton."

The townspeople? Are they dead too?

I open my mouth to talk, but she raises her hand to me.

"Ruiz knew the risk. She knew the odds. But getting you out of there with Ben was her priority."

There she goes about Ben again.

"Now Meyer, we don't know yet. He's missing in action, but not presumed dead."

I lock onto her hazel eyes for a second, then my eyes move over the graying brown strands of hair. "So, he could still be out there?"

She bows her head slightly. "I don't want to give you false hope, but yes. Good soldiers have gotten out of worse situations, and we are looking."

I ignore the emptiness in my stomach and try to settle on her words. At least some hope may exist.

I have to fix this.

"So, what happens next?" I ask. "What do I need to do?"

"It's what we need both you *and* Ben to do. First, we'll work on getting him well with the help of the data you brought."

My heart surges at the reminder of the drive and blood sample from Gabrielle. At least Waters didn't find them. I touch the pocket that held them, but they're missing.

"What do you mean Ben and I?" My chest tightens at the thought that Ben's been exposed without intending to be.

She tips her head and places her hand on top of mine. "I know he's your twin, and that you both share a unique ability."

"Who told you? Gabrielle?"

A soft smile comes onto her lips. "No. I've known he was your twin since you were born, but only recently did I come to understand your immersion abilities."

My mind spirals. "I'm so confused. I don't understand."

"I know you don't. When Ben is well, I will explain it to you both." She rises and pats my shoulder once more. "For now, rest."

Cynthia turns to exit and then glances back, giving me a tight smile that makes the skin beside her eyes crinkle. Her skin is slightly tanned, weathered, making the freckles on her face more prominent.

The expression hits me like a wave. I *do* know this face. I'm unsure why I hadn't seen it before. It's Bess ... in thirty years. Me in fifty.

Cynthia Fisher is my grandmother.

And she needs Ben and me to put the world right again.

Book two of Avlyn's story is at an end, but you can find out what happens next in Actualized (Book 3 in the Configured Trilogy) when it releases.

Dear Book Lover,

Thank you SO much for your support. I am truly humbled. I would be incredibly grateful if you took the time to **leave a review on Amazon.** Short or long is JUST fine. Your review will make a big difference and help new readers discover The Configured Trilogy.

I would also love it if you joined my book club at **JenettaPenner.com.** When you do, you will receive a FREE printable Configured YA coloring book, as well as YA book news and information on upcoming releases. You can also follow me on **Facebook** and **Twitter.**

XXOO,
Jenetta Penner

FINAL THANKS

I'd like to thank my readers for first reading Configured and then moving on with Avlyn's story in Immersed. I am constantly in awe that so many people love the Configured Series.

Thanks to my husband and children for supporting me, as well as my parents. Big thanks and a million cat gifs to David R. Bernstein and Stacy Morgan. You guys keep writing fun and are a fantastic support. Thank you to Kathy Ziegler, who's been a friend since my wedding photography days for your expert advice on horses.

And lastly, thank you to Saint Louis Covenant School. You don't know how thrilled I was to have Configured featured for your Extreme Read in 2017.

Made in the USA
Columbia, SC
01 February 2018